Dear Reader,

Would you attempt a five-barred fence on horseback?
Were you "born for adventure"? Willing to try any
dare, reach for any star, challenge any rule?

If so, Nicole Daughtry is your sister. If not, then she's
what we all wish in our heart of hearts we could be,
even just once in our lives.

When Nicole runs into Lucas Paine – literally! – the
sophisticated marquess is for the first time in his life
totally at a loss for words.

He looks at her and thinks marriage (and a few other
things men tend to think about when presented with an
unimaginably beautiful woman!).

She unabashedly looks back at him and thinks
adventure!

And an adventure they will have: one fraught with
danger from an unscrupulous man's ambition to their
own desires – their all-consuming hunger for each
other that will defy convention, thanks to a mutual
passion that cannot be denied.

I hope you enjoy *How to Tame a Lady*. *How to Tempt
a Duke*, the story of Nicole's brother Rafe Daughtry,
came prior to this story.

Nicole has a twin, by the way, the much more
circumspect and careful Lydia. Stay tuned for her
story, coming soon. And don't forget to visit my
website at www.kaseymichaels.com for information
about all my books!

Enjoy!

Kasey Michaels

HOW TO TAME
A LADY

BY
KASEY MICHAELS

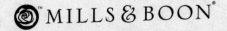

First published in Great Britain 2010
Harlequin Mills & Boon Limited,
Eton House, 18-24 Paradise Road, Richmond, Surrey TW9 1SR

© Kathryn Seidick 2009

ISBN: 978 0 263 88298 8

37-0110

Harlequin Mills & Boon policy is to use papers that are natural, renewable and recyclable products and made from wood grown in sustainable forests. The logging and manufacturing processes conform to the legal environmental regulations of the country of origin.

Printed and bound in Spain
by Litografia Rosés S.A., Barcelona

USA TODAY bestselling author **Kasey Michaels** is the author of more than ninety books. She has earned three starred reviews from *Publishers Weekly*, and has been awarded the RITA® Award from Romance Writers of America, the *Romantic Times* Career Achievement Award, the Waldenbooks and BookRak awards, and several other commendations for her writing excellence in both contemporary and historical novels. There are more than eight million copies of her books in print around the world. Kasey resides in Pennsylvania with her family, where she is always at work on her next book.

HOW TO TAME
A LADY

To Missy Augustine, who keeps it all together
so I can fall apart.
Thanks!

PROLOGUE

HORSE AND RIDER EMERGED from the trees in an explosion of unleashed energy that sent a pair of long-eared hares fighting to be the first to scoot head-first into their burrow. Birds fled the treetops, their dark underbodies shadowed against the high, uncharacteristically bright blue sky.

Shod hooves encountered the soft, just-turned earth of the field. The mare momentarily scrambled for footing, and then gathered itself for the gallop.

The rider, head low over the mare's neck, held the reins in both hands, elbows up and out, almost standing in the stirrups, knees tight to the horse's flanks, rump slightly above the saddle, in the way of jockeys once seen racing at a country fair.

Horse and rider both knew the route. The hedge-row first, followed by the low gate at the end of the second field. The stone wall, wide if not that high, which fronted a good three-foot drop-off and rather boggy landing.

Another long, liberating gallop would follow, and then the five-bar gate. That was the test, the five-bar gate. The undeniable challenge. The ultimate triumph once it was behind them.

The mare was strong, and fleet of foot, but it was the rider who held the control. Control was important; it might be everything. Control of your surroundings. Control over your own mind, heart and destiny.

And the *freedom* that control gave you.

The minor obstacles cleared, the five-bar gate was now visible in the distance. It was not a jump for the faint-hearted or those of only mediocre talent. Skill and confidence were needed. And perhaps a measure of luck.

But the rider had always been lucky.

The mare's head bobbed and stretched as its strides lengthened, the muscles in its neck straining, its hot breath sending puffs of white vapor into the cool morning air.

The rider melted into the mare, their movements meshing, feeling the precise snap of the mare's knees as it dug in one last time and then launched itself into the air.

Horse and rider became one in the jump. Soaring. Flying. Free of the earth and all its cares. The world waited below them, completely silent for one long, sweet moment in time.

And then the mare's front hooves touched the earth once more and the thunder of its hooves, the steady *thud, thud, thud,* matched the heartbeat of the rider who now stood up completely in the stirrups. One gloved hand went to the soft wool toque and lifted it high into the air, waving it like a victory banner.

Masses of coal-black hair, no longer confined by the toque, tumbled free and blew about in the breeze. A full-lipped, wide mouth fashioned for smiling, for flirting, for kissing, formed to deliver hopeful dreams and crushing disappointments opened, and a delighted *whoop* of triumph echoed across the field.

Dark-lashed eyes the color of drenched violets sparkled and danced above a pert nose and high-boned cheeks dusted with freckles that enticed, hinted of an innocence the sensual mouth denied.

The same breeze that danced in those midnight tresses caressed the high, pert breasts outlined beneath a man's white lawn shirt that was tucked into a pair of tan breeches even a hardened libertine might call licentious.

Eighteen-year-old Lady Nicole Daughtry knew many would call her beautiful. And different. She reveled in the facts that she was young and brave, heart-whole and achingly alive. Marvelously, gloriously free.

Today was for celebrating that youth, that joy, that freedom. Tomorrow was for saying goodbye to one world and hello to another as she set out on her first London Season, approaching it just as she would a five-barred fence.

Head-on, and certain of the outcome.

CHAPTER ONE

March 1816

Lucas Paine, Marquess of Basingstoke, was classically handsome, with his thick dark blond hair, clear blue eyes and leanly muscled body. He dressed impeccably, had excellent manners, cherished his widowed mother and was good to his dogs.

He tipped his hat to all when out on the strut, and he belonged to the best clubs. An accomplished horseman and premier whip, he was also no stranger to the boxing saloons, where he excelled, although he would say that he was better with the rapier than his fists. He did not take snuff, affected no airs, graciously danced with all the wallflowers, flattered the dowagers and never gambled above his considerable means.

If there was even a breath of scandal still attached to the memory of the marquess's late sire, that scandal did not touch the son.

In fact, as his friend Fletcher Sutton, Viscount Yalding, pointed out that mid-March day as the pair sauntered along Bond Street, one eye on the low, threatening sky, if the marquess could only manage to control the weather, he would be elevated to the status of near-god.

Both Lucas and Fletcher knew the reason for this pervasive unpleasant weather, the near constant rain and cold, the lack of sunshine. Although it boggled the mind to believe that a volcanic eruption nearly a year ago and halfway around the world in some be-nighted spot called Tambora could cause such pro-longed misery for most of England and Europe.

"You're quiet," Fletcher said as they paused to unfurl their large black umbrellas, for the mizzle had moved on to a drizzle that was sure to become a steady downpour in a few minutes. "Still chafing at what Lord Harper said yesterday at White's? That wasn't nice of him, Lucas, saying he'd heard cheerier speeches at funerals, and then he and his friends all but turning their backs on you. Although I will admit he had a point."

Viscount Yalding was referring to the incident that had taken place at one of London's premier clubs. Lord Harper, a buffoon even in the best of times, had made a comment about the "ruffians and other low creatures accosting him for coins each time he stepped outside."

Lucas—surprising even himself—had launched into an impassioned defense of the cold and hungry and frightened populace, and had even warned the gentlemen within earshot that if no steps were taken to assist their fellow countrymen the consequences could be serious.

It had been a very good argument, perhaps even bordering on the inspired. Not that anyone had listened.

Lucas looked at his friend, one eloquent eyebrow raised. "The day I am cast in the glooms by that buffoon's opinions I shall have to race home and slit my throat."

Fletcher acknowledged this with a tip of his head. "All right, what is it, then? The weather? No sense repining on that, according to you, as it's not going to change any time soon. Your new boots pinch? But they're Hoby's, correct? So that can't be it. Yet you look like you've just watched your very last friend walk away from you, which you haven't, because I'm still here. In fact, please feel free to make a cake of yourself again any time you wish, and I'll stand up on my chair and cry *hear, hear* as I lend you my support."

"Is that so? How gratifying, Fletcher, truly. Except I'm now left to wonder if you are pledging your support or hoping to goad me into making a cake of myself again, as you so tactfully put it."

Viscount Yalding, a handsome young man of five and twenty, a man with a sparkle in his light brown eyes and a pair of impish dimples in his cheeks, threw back his head and laughed aloud. "And that's the real beauty of the thing, because you'll never know which, now will you?"

"You know what it is, don't you, Fletcher? We don't learn. It wasn't that long ago that our dear Prince Regent was hatching escape plans, sure his loyal subjects were going to rise up the way the

French did against their king. Now, thanks to that damnable volcano, we face high prices and farmers losing their positions, our brave soldiers suffering, our children falling sick because there are no fresh vegetables for them to eat. We're not preparing for that eventuality, or its inevitable result. Civil unrest."

"Yes, yes, I remember what you said, but please stop now. Not the cheeriest thing I've ever heard, to quote Lord Harper. And you're not completely correct, Lucas. Our government is taking steps, although probably not in a direction you'd approve— Watch out!"

Lucas looked down the flagway to see a young woman running toward him, looking back over her shoulder at another young woman who had stopped beneath a canvas awning to wait for a female servant to raise an umbrella.

"Oh, don't be so missish, Lydia. The coach is just down here—you won't melt. It's only a little— *Oof!*"

Lucas caught the female by the upper arms and held her in front of him, saying, "Steady there, young lady. And far be it from me to stand in the role of teacher, but it is usually deemed equally important to see where you are going as where you have been."

The female, who stood only as high as his chest, lifted her head so that her face was visible beneath the wide brim of her bonnet, and looked him square in the eyes.

When had he seen eyes like these? Had there ever been eyes like these, so darkly blue as to be closer to sun-washed violet, so alive, so fearless and amused, daring him to—to what? The heart-shaped face in its frame of wonderfully dark hair, the perfectly centered nose, the slightly bee-stung lower lip, the single dimple that came and went in her right cheek. The skin that spoke of fresh peaches doused in cream, and sprinkled with a dusting of freckles that invited him to touch, to trace them with his fingertips, the tip of his tongue…

"Yes," she said, biting that bottom lip between her fine, small white teeth for a moment as she ran her gaze over his features, "I believe I can see the wisdom in that statement. Although, as I already know where I've been, I'm always much more interested in what lies ahead. You may let me go now."

Lucas, a man who could not remember the last time he'd been flustered, and knowing the answer was *never* if the other person involved was a female, was finding it difficult to think of anything to say.

"Lucas?" Fletcher gave his friend a gentle jab with his elbow. "She says you can let her go now."

He brought himself under control, but not without conscious effort. "Yes, of course. Forgive me, young lady. I merely wanted to be certain you hadn't been injured by our…collision."

"I believe I shall survive, sir, thank you. Ah, and here is my sister, frowning, and with a good scolding eager to escape her lips as she points out, for at least the tenth time, that we are not at Ashurst Hall anymore, and I cannot just behave as if London is our familiar village. Although I don't see why not, do you? It's not as if a person is likely to encounter anyone too dastardly right here on Bond Street."

"I wouldn't say that, miss. We could be quite dastardly, I'm sure, if we just put our minds to the thing," Fletcher said, winking at Lucas, who believed his friend was enjoying himself entirely too much.

"Ashurst Hall, you said?" Lucas pursued, turning back to the young beauty, whose luscious skin was now lustrous with the misting rain. She was fresh as a strawberry just plucked from the fields, yet the intelligence evident in her eyes told him she might be young, but she was neither shallow nor silly. "Then I may assume that the Duke of Ashurst is known to you?"

"You might assume that, yes. Rafael is our brother. And now that you have the advantage of me…?"

"A thousand pardons," Lucas said as the beautiful young blond woman who'd been addressed as Lydia joined them beneath their now trio of umbrellas. Sisters? Yes, he could see the resemblance, but at first blush this one seemed to lack the dangerous fire of her sibling. "Lady Lydia, if I heard the name correctly? Please allow me to introduce myself and my friend here."

"My lords," Lydia said moments later, dropping into a graceful curtsy while motioning for her sister to do the same. "And in return may I present my sister, Lady Nicole Daughtry."

Nicole. From the Greek, Lucas was fairly certain, and meaning "victorious people." Yes, it suited her. He could see her riding at the front of her own army, rather like Eleanor of Aquitaine. The queen, to inspire her troops, was rumored to have ridden bare-breasted.

Lucas shook off that disquieting thought and bowed to the young woman.

"A distinct pleasure, Lady Nicole."

"Yes…" she said, smiling at him as if she totally agreed that the pleasure was his, the minx. It was difficult to believe that the duke let this one out without a leash. She looked down the length of his body and back up again. "Did you happen to notice, my lord, that you're standing in a puddle?"

Fletcher gave a bark of laughter as Lucas looked down to see that a drainpipe aimed toward the gutter had been emptying rainwater the entire time they'd been standing here, and a dip in the flagway had served to collect quite a bit of that rainwater around his new boots.

"Why, yes, Lady Nicole, I did know that. I've made it a point to always stand in puddles. They're rarely crowded, you understand."

The dimple appeared, and that small, quick bite at her lower lip came and went almost before Lucas could see it. Almost.

"But I'm standing in it, too, my lord."

All right. If she wanted to play, he would not disappoint her. "Which now makes it *our* puddle, doesn't it, Lady Nicole?"

"I'm not sure. As my twin here could tell you, I have never been all that comfortable with sharing. You might wish to step back, my lord."

She was giving him a warning? *Him?* He was the Marquess of Basingstoke, and she was a young miss fresh from the country. He should be warning her, although of what, he couldn't be sure.

Fletcher nervously cleared his throat. "Yes…ah, um, yes indeed. Well, stap me if I haven't just remembered something. We have that appointment, Lucas, as I recall. Going to be late, and you know how his lordship frowns when we're late. And the ladies will take a chill, there's that, as well. We shouldn't keep them."

"Indeed, no, we shouldn't," Lucas said, agreeing with his friend's fib, as he already had a plan in mind to see Lady Nicole again. He turned to Lady Lydia, who might not have much influence over her sister, but who probably could be relied upon not to scramble his brains and tie his tongue into knots. "It would be our distinct pleasure to wait on you ladies tomorrow, if your brother will give his permission for the four of us to drive out to Richmond. Would you be amenable to such an arrangement, Lady Lydia?"

"If she knows what's good for her, she will," Lucas heard Lady Nicole whisper under her breath as she covered her mouth with one gloved hand, and once again Fletcher cleared his throat, this time to cover a laugh, no doubt.

"I should imagine you will have to apply directly to our brother, my lord," Lady Lydia said, earning herself a weary shake of the head from her sister. "We dine at home in Grosvenor Square this evening, and if you and Lord Yalding are free, we would be honored if you'd join us. You can ask him then."

Lucas glanced toward Lady Nicole, who was now looking at her sister in some astonishment. He quickly agreed, thanked Lady Lydia and then escorted the ladies to their waiting coach, the one with the ducal crest on it.

"What a mischievous piece of work that one is," Fletcher said as they watched the coach pull off into the light afternoon traffic. "And what was all that ridiculousness about puddles? Not that it wasn't all innocent, I suppose, but I was beginning to feel like a voyeur, listening to the pair of you. She's nearly a child, Lucas. Not your usual sort at all."

"A child, Fletch?" Lucas turned to head to his own coach, for he needed to go back to Park Lane, spend some time alone to consider all that had just happened to him. "That one has never been a child."

"No, I suppose some females are like that. But they aren't usually sister to a duke, if you take my meaning and no offense intended. And I'm supposed to be keeping the other one occupied so that the two of you can keep on speaking whatever private language you were spouting back there?"

They both handed their umbrellas to the waiting groom, who would return them to the nearest umbrella shop to be dried and refolded and be supplied with replacements. Umbrella shops were probably the most prosperous enterprises in the city this year.

"If you wouldn't consider it a hardship, yes."

"Absolutely not," Fletcher said. "Lady Lydia is a beautiful young woman. Such a contrast to her sister, though, don't you think? It would take a special eye to see her quiet beauty when matched up against the fire and flash of Lady Nicole."

"And you have a special eye?"

"Hardly," Fletcher said as they settled into the coach. "As you well know, I can't afford one. Although I have observed that your mood has improved by more than half since our encounter with Lady Nicole. I thought you said you weren't chafing about that business at White's."

"I'm sorry. Although I will admit that I am rather disappointed in my fellow man at the moment. Nobody wants to hear anything but good news. We'd rather close our ears and eyes and go on repeating the same mistakes over and over again."

"Well, I agree with you there, I suppose, at least with that business about making the same mistakes. For instance, m'father might have thought to learn that a Faro bank in a gaming hell is a harlot's tease. We all could have benefited if he'd taken that particular lesson to heart. But that's not what you mean, is it? You're angry with the way we're treating the populace."

"More than I thought I could be, yes. An iron fist is never a good ruler, Fletcher, when a helping hand benefits us all in the end. Why can't our fellows in the House of Lords see that?"

Fletcher shrugged. "Perhaps because they're in the House of Lords, and not scratching out a meager existence on the fringes of Society? Still, perhaps you should drop the subject now? You've said what you felt needed saying, and nobody seems to care."

Lucas considered this for a moment, and then shook his head, deciding not to tell his friend about his early morning visit from Lord Nigel Frayne, a contemporary of his late father, and what that encounter might mean if Lucas chose to throw in his lot with the man.

"You're probably right. But I wish I could do more," was all he said.

Fletcher was silent for some moments, until the coach slowed and finally stopped outside his rented rooms in Upper Brook Street. He had his hand on the inside latch of the door before he turned to his friend and said, "If you're set on finding ways to help the downtrodden, and much as I'm certain I shouldn't tell you, you probably want to hear this."

Lucas, suddenly lost in thoughts of his dead father, merely lifted an eyebrow. "That sounds ominous."

Fletcher sank back against the squabs. "I didn't think so, to tell you the truth, not when I heard it. Perhaps you've softened my heart? At any rate, I happened to overhear something about our dear friend Lord Sidmouth at my club last week."

"Our illustrious Home Secretary is no one's dear friend, Fletcher. I doubt his own mother enjoyed him."

"True enough. Do you want to know what I heard, or not? Because after you surprised me with that passionate defense of the common man yesterday, I haven't been all that hot to tell you. After all, it was only rumor, and I overheard no more than snatches, at that."

Lucas gave a small wave of his hand. "Go on. I promise not to launch into another hot-blooded speech anytime soon."

"And thank God for that. What I heard was that, between them, lords Liverpool and Sidmouth are determined to introduce new punitive laws and sanctions against those unhappy with the government. You know, those persons you were so staunchly defending in your magnificent but probably ill-timed comments."

"I see. And did you happen to hear *how* they plan to get the whole of Parliament to agree to these new laws, considering that we've been introducing reforms this term, not new sanctions?"

Fletcher shook his head. "No, sadly, I did not, but I suppose they know. I'm sorry I can't be of more help." He took hold of the latch once more. "Should I be ready by six, do you think? Or is that too early?"

Lucas was once again deep in thought, lightly tapping the side of his fist against his mouth. "Excuse me? Oh, yes. Too early by half. I doubt the duke sits down much before eight."

"Then seven it is. Perhaps the lovely Lady Nicole can serve to take your mind off what I've just told you?"

"Fletcher, that young woman could take a man's mind, period."

Fletcher laughed and exited the coach, at which

time Lucas's smile disappeared as he thought about his strange encounter with Lady Nicole.

She had knocked him off balance, not physically, as a result of their small collision, but mentally, muddling his brain in a way that had never happened to him before that moment.

She was astonishingly beautiful. She was astoundingly forward and impertinent.

She possessed the most kissable mouth he'd ever seen. And clearly she knew that, or else why would she have affected that quick, enticing bite of her full bottom lip, if not to drive a man insane?

She was also a distraction. With what Lord Frayne had just asked of him, with the information the man had just that morning dangled in front of him so unexpectedly, did he need a distraction at this moment in his life?

No. No, he did not.

CHAPTER TWO

NICOLE TOOK HER TIME combing through her thick black hair, carefully working out a few tangles caused by having it all anchored up and off her neck. She could allow her new maid, the estimable Renée, the chore. But, since Renée seemed to be of the opinion that a woman should suffer for her beauty, Nicole had set her to pressing the hem of her peach gown instead.

Looking into the mirror of her dressing table, she studied her sister as Lydia sat in a slipper chair, her head buried in a book. There was nothing unusual about that. Depressing, certainly, as they were in the middle of the most exciting city on earth, but most definitely not unusual.

Nicole loved her twin more than she did anyone else in the world, but this past year had been very difficult. And so terribly sad.

When their brother, Rafe, had returned from the war to take over the reins of the dukedom, he had brought with him his good friend Captain Swain Fitzgerald.

And Lydia, quiet, levelheaded, studious Lydia,

had tumbled head over heels into love with the man, only to lose him when Bonaparte escaped his prison and forced one last battle on the Allies.

Even now, Nicole could see occasional hints of sadness in her sister's huge blue eyes during quiet moments.

Some might argue that Lydia, at seventeen, had been too young to really know her own mind, and that Captain Fitzgerald had been years too old for her. But Nicole would never say any such thing. Not when she'd held her sister in her grief, fearful that Lydia's very heart would break inside her and she'd lose her best friend, the other half of herself.

That terrible day, when the Duke of Malvern had come to this very house to inform them all of the captain's death, Nicole had promised herself that she would never open herself to such devastating heartbreak. Life was to be enjoyed, gloried in, celebrated. Allowing one's happiness to depend on someone else was to invite not only a chaotic mind but a vulnerability to pain that Nicole refused to consider.

No, Nicole would never allow anyone else, any man, to have so much power over her, and had stated that fact quite firmly to both her sister and her sister-in-law, Charlotte.

And they had only smiled indulgently. After all, what was a young lady of Nicole's station to do but marry? As a sister to a duke, her options were limited, if, to many, all quite wonderful. A husband. Children. She would be mistress of a grand estate, an arbiter of fashion, become a successful and sought-after hostess. It wasn't as if she could take to the high seas, or fight in wars or sit in Parliament...not that Nicole wished to do any of those things, either.

In truth, she didn't know what she wanted to do with her life or what she wanted out of that life.

She only knew what she *didn't* want.

Mostly, she didn't want to be desperate, like her mother. Mostly, she didn't want to be heartbroken, like her sister.

Mostly, she wanted to be left to her own devices so that she *could* someday answer that question as to what she wanted out of life. And in the meantime, if she thought the idea of some harmless flirtation and exercising of her charms to be a delicious entertainment, surely that wasn't so terrible?

She loved her family, desperately. She needed no one else. Although not the prodigious student her sister was, Nicole had not been above quoting Francis Bacon to Lydia. "He that hath wife and children hath given hostages to fortune; for they are impediments to great enterprises, either of virtue or mischief."

Yes, Lydia had reasonably pointed out that Nicole was not a man (which often chafed Nicole, as she believed men enjoyed much more freedom than women), and that she, Lydia, had never suspected that Nicole had aspirations to great virtuous enterprises. To her sister's already known propensity for mischievous enterprises, Lydia's response was only to roll her eyes and sigh in affectionate resignation.

They were so different, she and Lydia. Her sister obeyed the rules, accepted her place in the world, caused not a smidgeon of trouble to anyone, while Nicole strained against every leash, saw every rule as a challenge and, although never purposely, had occasionally caused more than her sister to breathe resigned sighs.

Nicole and Lydia had settled into their very different roles early in life, and Nicole realized now that she had allowed herself to become comfortable with always knowing her sister was dependable if sometimes boring, clearheaded if perhaps too intense, and always a model of propriety.

Which did not explain what had happened earlier that day.

"Lydia?"

"In a moment, please, Nicole," her sister said as she turned a page in her book and continued to read for several moments before closing the book over her finger. "I'm just reading the most interesting and rather bizarre argument."

"That's nice, Lydia. Then I take it you are not still reading Miss Austen's latest inspired bit of silliness?"

Lydia shook her head. "I finished that yesterday. Today is for something Captain Fitzgerald recommended to me, written by one Thomas Paine. This volume is called *The Rights of Man* and—well, listen to this."

It was Nicole's turn to sigh in resignation. "If it sounds anything like a sermon, please don't bother."

"No, no, I just want to read you this one thing Mr. Paine wrote. Here it is. He states quite firmly how necessary it is at all times to watch against the attempted encroachment of power, and to prevent its running to excess. Shall I read you his exact words?"

Nicole bit back a smile. "No, I think I understand his point. Lydia, far be it from me to declare myself a scholar, but you do realize that your Mr. Paine could be thought by some to be fomenting revolution and the overthrowing of governments, don't you?"

"I choose to think he is only warning us to always remain vigilant," her sister said, closing the book once more. "But I suppose you could be right. That's what America did to us, and France did to its king."

Nicole put down her comb. "Nobody is going to do that here, if that's what this is all about. We have a good king."

"Do we, Nicole? Then why did I find this in my maid's apron pocket when I went searching for the button she promised to sew back onto my blue pelisse? Which is why I'm reading Mr. Paine's warnings."

So saying, Lydia took a much-folded broadsheet from her own pocket and handed it to Nicole, who first looked to her sister, and then to the poorly printed call for everyone to join the "Citizens for Justice" and to "take up arms against an oppressive government determin'd to starve our children and screw honest men into the ground."

She quickly read the rest, and could see why Lydia might be alarmed. "And you found this in your maid's apron?"

Lydia nodded. "I'm going to show it to Rafe

tomorrow. He may know what it all means. Revolution is terrible, Nicole, even when it is necessary. And it isn't all that far-fetched, you know. It happened here."

"I remember from our lessons, yes," Nicole said, more concerned by the broadsheet than she'd allow Lydia to see. "But do you really think that—"

"Oh. Oh, no, I suppose not. Not when I say it all out loud. And I know you're not interested, in any event. I…I wish Captain Fitzgerald could be here. He'd know just what to say to me."

Nicole winced inwardly. "I didn't say I wasn't interested, Lydia. Or do you think I'm selfish, and care only for myself? That I couldn't be concerned about oppressed classes or whoever it is who raise these revolutions? Because that's not fair, Lydia, it really isn't."

Her sister was quick to agree, perhaps too quick to agree, and Nicole wondered if everyone saw her as shallow and more concerned with enjoying herself than she was with anything or anyone else. Was that the price a person had to pay for preferring a life without complications? Besides, was selfishness really a crime, if you were only selfish about protecting yourself?

Yes, she supposed many would see it that way. The conclusion didn't sit well with her.

"Nicole? Don't pout. I didn't mean to say you aren't the best of sisters, humoring me when I turn bluestocking, as Mama calls it each time she sees me with a book. If it were up to her, neither of us would have any conversation above commenting on the weather, as if anyone could say more than that they wished the rain would go away and the sun come back."

Delighted to have any awkwardness passed over so easily, Nicole changed the subject—to the one she'd attempted to broach a full ten minutes earlier. "What made you invite the marquess and the viscount to dinner tonight, Lydia? Not that I wasn't delighted down to my toes, but it was so unlike you."

Lydia got to her feet after glancing at the mantel clock and seeing the hour. "Yes, it was, wasn't it? I have no idea why I did that. Except that I believed I could sense that you wished to see the marquess again. It was no secret that he wishes to see *you* again. There's never been a man who has seen you and not longed for more."

"More what, Lydia?" Nicole teased, although inwardly, her stomach was doing a series of small flips. "So you saw it, too? The marquess's interest, that is?"

"I did, the poor flustered Viscount Yalding did. *You* did, and then purposely set out to torment the man."

Had she done that? Nicole didn't wish to admit it, but she could barely recall a word she'd said to the marquess. She'd been much too busy simply *looking* at him.

"Do you plan his to be the first heart you break while we're here?"

Nicole slipped her hands beneath her hair and lifted it up from her nape, piling it all on top of her head for a moment before allowing the heavy mass of waves to fall once more, shaking her head so that it tumbled free all around her face and shoulders. With any luck, Lydia would watch the gesture, and not pay attention to the flash of uncertainty her words had undoubtedly sent into her sister's eyes. She had been doing her best all afternoon to *not* think about the Marquess of Basingstoke and his unexpected effect on her.

"Truth, Lydia? I had selected the Duke of Malvern for my initial conquest. After all, Rafe is friends with him, and the man has already met us, knows us. And there's no denying how handsome the duke is. He seemed perfect for me to practice on."

Lydia fairly leaped to her feet, her cheeks suddenly ashen. "The Duke of Malvern? Nicole, no! He's the most loathsome creature alive. How could you even consider such a thing? I don't think I want to talk about your silly plans anymore. I'm going to take a nap."

Nicole wanted to kick herself for forgetting, even for a moment, the duke's effect on her sister, that to Lydia he was a living reminder of everything she had lost. She could lay the blame for that lapse on the Marquess of Basingstoke, who seemed to muddle her brains every time she thought about him and their short but singular exchange that afternoon.

"Lydia, wait—" she said, but her sister had already run toward the connecting door between their bedchambers.

"How can I be so stupid!" Nicole berated herself,

sinking back onto the low dressing table bench and dropping her chin into her hands as she contemplated her reflection. "I'll have to apologize later. Perhaps offer to accompany her to Hatchard's Book Repository again, and stand about for hours while she *oohs* and *aahs* over every other volume. Heaven knows that's penance enough."

That decided, she tipped her head to one side, wondering what it was that the Marquess of Basingstoke had seen when he'd looked at her that had seemingly upset him so much. Her eyes? Even she thought they were a pretty color, as well as unusual. Nicole liked to think of herself as unusual, singular.

She didn't think he'd necessarily been put off by her freckles, the bane of her existence, especially since her mama, when she deigned to notice her daughters at all, had begun insisting Nicole spread crushed strawberries and clotted cream on them twice a week.

Yet if she had to choose between skin as creamy and blemish-free as Lydia's and the freedom of riding Juliet across the fields of Ashurst Hall sans a hat, with the wind blowing her hair, well, she'd learn to live with the spots, and so would everyone else.

Although if she could rid herself of the childish habit of biting her bottom lip whenever she felt unsure of herself she would be happier, as it didn't exactly seem the sort of thing polished London debutantes did.

In any case, the marquess had thought her attractive, she wasn't such a ninny that she didn't know that. And he was handsome, and sophisticated, very much a London gentleman, which was quite exciting. He'd make a delicious first conquest.

Unless he thought her vain, and stupid. Frivolous.

"Stop that!" she told herself. "It doesn't matter what he thinks of you. You're here to enjoy yourself, not to end up like Lydia."

Still, before she rang for Renée to have a bath prepared for her, Nicole picked up the slim volume her sister had left behind and sat down on the slipper chair, hoping to improve her mind.

LUCAS STOPPED JUST INSIDE the doors of the drawing room in Grosvenor Square and said quietly, "Well, damn me for a fool. She said Rafael, didn't she? Captain Rafe Daughtry. Of course."

Rafael Daughtry, Duke of Ashurst this past year, a man who only recently had been a poor relation who, with no other prospects, had served with Wellington for half a dozen years, favored the marquess with a lazy salute. "Major. Good evening, sir," he said, smiling.

"What's this?" Viscount Yalding said, confused. "You two know each other? Why didn't you tell me?"

"That should be obvious, Fletcher. I didn't realize." Lucas moved forward, holding out his right hand. "Rafe Daughtry. My God, how long has it been? The last time I saw you, you and your Irish friend were marching away from Paris just as I was marching in. What was his name again? Ah, I remember. Fitzgerald. One of the fiercest soldiers I'd ever seen. Completely fearless. He's well?"

Rafe shook his head slowly, looking past Lucas to the ladies just entering the drawing room. "We lost Fitz at Quatre Bras. He was about to be betrothed to my sister Lydia."

Lucas felt the too-familiar punch to the midsection that overtook him whenever he heard of the loss of another brave soldier. Even now, with nearly a year gone by, those blows remained too frequent. "My most sincere condolences, Rafe. I'll not say another word." He then quickly introduced Fletcher, and, together, they all turned to bow to the ladies.

There were three of them. Lady Lydia, along with Rafe's clearly pregnant young wife, Charlotte, and Lady Nicole. Lucas bowed over Her Grace's hand, begging her not to bother to curtsy to a gentleman who should be leading her to a chair and not allowing her to stand about, and then smiled to the younger ladies.

At least he hoped he'd smiled to both, as it was only Lady Nicole that he really saw.

If she'd been appealing that afternoon, this evening she was positively bewitching. He'd wanted to see her hair sans her bonnet, but he hadn't been prepared for the impact of those thick black tresses, arranged with artless simplicity in the latest French mode, wondrously framing that perfect heart-shaped face and accenting the deep violet of her eyes.

Her pale peach gown was simple, as befitted a debutante, but there was nothing simple about the body beneath that gown. Her breasts were lush above the thin silken sash tied just below the bodice, and the sprinkling of freckles across the expanse of skin visible above that bodice made it impossible for him to think anything else save how he needed to know—had to know, *would* know—if the freckles extended everywhere, even to where the sun did not reach her.

Over drinks—wine for the gentlemen, lemonade for the ladies—Rafe told them all how he and Lucas had met many times on the Peninsula. He kept the telling light, relating an amusing incident involving a captured pack of supply mules and a shared meal fit for a king—but meant for the enemy.

"And you, of course, husband, only observed during this grand adventure in thievery," Charlotte said, her eyes sparkling.

Rafe took his wife's hand, raising it to his lips in a way that told Lucas the man was comfortable in allowing the world to see he was besotted with his lovely wife. "Oh, yes, certainly. I was always a pattern card of respectability, even while cold, half-starved and in mud up to my knees."

"No, you weren't," Charlotte corrected. "And I think we should applaud your ingenuity, all of you who had to deal with such extraordinary hardships."

"Why, thank you, darling. But it was Lucas here who masterminded the raid on the supply train, and it was brilliant. He even kidnapped the man's cook while he was about it. The cook spoke no English, we spoke no Spanish, but we managed. We hadn't eaten so well in months."

"I kept him for most of that summer, as I recall,"

Lucas told them. "Until we understood each other sufficiently for him to inform me that he had a wife and, as I remember it, a dozen children in a village just over the hill. At which point we said our farewells. I still miss his way with a chicken. At the time, I mostly missed the chickens he stole when he left."

By the time the majordomo announced that dinner was served, the small party had agreed to dispense with the formality of titles, and it was a fairly merry group that sat down to bowls of hot, clear consommé.

"Chicken," Nicole pointed out as Lucas lifted his spoon. "Feel free to wax nostalgic once more about your Spanish cook."

Lucas looked at her inquiringly. "You didn't enjoy our small story?"

"I did, yes," she told him quietly, her attention seemingly on her dish. "But I could not help but wonder, for all the stories you and Rafe told, that Captain Fitzgerald played no part in them. You know, don't you?"

"Your brother was kind enough to warn me off," Lucas said, chancing a look across the table to where Lady Lydia appeared to be listening with rapt attention as Fletcher spoke just as quietly, gesturing with his hands in that way his friend had about him. "He becomes excited enough about his subject," he said, indicating Fletcher, "and someone might be prudent to move those wineglasses. Once, when he was describing a boxing match he'd been to in Epsom, he knocked a candlestick into Lady Hertford's lap. She was not amused."

"I'd have been highly amused, and it will do no good to attempt to change the subject. I think my brother is entirely too protective of my sister. How will she heal if everyone continues to coddle her, to hide their memories of Captain Fitzgerald from her? To elevate him to sainthood, put his memory on a pedestal where he is no longer human, no longer real, is a disservice to the captain as well as to Lydia. He was a flesh-and-blood man, very much so. She will always love him, always remember him, but it's time she smiled when she said his name. It's time she makes him more than the dream he was to her."

Lucas looked at her in some astonishment. Clearly polite dinner conversation, safe and innocuous, was not going to be the rule of the evening. "You may be right, Lady Nicole. But do you want to chance upsetting your sister?"

"No, I suppose not. Not right now. But I would think we need not tiptoe around the subject when we all meet again. To constantly avoid the captain's name is cheating Lydia, and difficult for those around her."

"When we meet again? Ah, a glimmer of hope invades my being. Then you have permission to drive out to Richmond tomorrow?"

The dimple appeared in her cheek as she smiled at him. "Rafe considers you harmless, yes. How does it feel, my lord, to be considered harmless? I'm only curious because no one has ever applied that description to me."

"I can't imagine why not," Lucas said tongue in cheek as the soup plates were removed and the second course served. He had no appetite, unless it was for the woman sitting beside him, deliberately goading him, testing the boundaries to see how far she could go before she shocked him.

He'd like to know that, too.

"Lucas," Fletcher said, leaning his elbows on the table. "You won't believe this. Lady Lydia here has read Thomas Paine. Isn't that beyond anything you've ever heard?"

"Is that so, Lady Lydia," he said, truly interested, if mildly surprised. "His most famous *Common Sense* is thought by some to be the major goad for the then American colonies to rise up against us in the last century, did you know that?"

Lydia's cheeks had gone quite pink, but she looked directly at Lucas. "But there are things that must be said, don't you agree, wrongs that must be righted? As Mr. Paine wrote, we cannot allow ourselves to be complacent, and to never question authority."

"Yes, I remember. 'A long habit of not thinking a thing *wrong* gives it a superficial appearance of being *right*.'"

"You've committed him to memory, Lucas?" Rafe remarked from the head of the table. "Don't tell me you claim the man as family."

"Not at all, although sharing a surname has caused my family to feel forced to defend his memory from time to time. I admire some of his writings, but I wish he'd stopped before he vented his spleen with *The Rights of Man.* For a time, it was a crime for an Englishman to possess a copy, did you know that?"

"Lydia possesses a copy," Nicole said quietly. "I read some of it just this afternoon."

Lucas raised an eyebrow. He'd known it would only be a matter of time before she'd shocked him, but he hadn't expected that shock to come this soon. "Is that so? And have you read enough to form an opinion?"

Nicole bit her bottom lip for a moment and then nodded. "Truthfully? My sister may not agree with me, but for as much as I have so far read, I believe the man makes an incendiary argument consisting of a mixture of unpalatable truths and dangerous nonsense."

Lucas threw back his head and laughed out loud. "Rafe! Did you hear that? I couldn't have said it better myself."

"You *have* said it yourself," Fletcher pointed out, looking at Nicole curiously. "It's almost eerie."

Lucas caught out Rafe and his lovely wife exchanging rather confused looks, as if they'd never expected to hear Nicole say anything like what she'd just said. Yet they hadn't seemed shocked to hear that her sister had read Paine's works. Or was there more to it than that?

He decided to find out.

"As you read Thomas Paine," he asked Nicole as they ate, "I would imagine you've also read some of the works of Wieland, Gibbon, Burke?"

"You most certainly can imagine that. You can imagine that all you wish," she answered brightly, and he knew he had just been put very firmly in his place. By a young girl clearly not easily put out of countenance by clumsy buffoons like himself.

"I'm sorry. I shouldn't have done that," he said, only to have her place her hand on his forearm and lean closer to him.

"And I should not have pretended to be someone I am not. Lydia stole all the brains, I believe, leaving me nothing but an only ordinary intelligence. But I did sound convincing, didn't I? The use of *incendiary* was very nearly inspired, I think."

And that was that. Beauty such as Nicole's was not to be sneezed at and certainly he enjoyed looking at her, would like to possess her because of that beauty. But as he looked into those remarkable eyes, and saw what could only be a small imp of the devil looking back at him, Lucas was in serious danger of becoming completely and utterly lost. And he knew it.

CHAPTER THREE

As if to punish Nicole for what she knew to be her outrageous behavior the night of the dinner party, there was such a downpour for the next two days that no sane person in London ventured outdoors, let alone took drives to Richmond or anywhere else.

In desperation, she had picked up Lydia's copy of Jane Austen's *Emma,* and hidden herself away in her room until all of the characters were nicely settled with their soul mates and Emma had finally opened her eyes to the charms of Mr. Knightley.

She hadn't enjoyed the story very much. All this upset about matching this one to that one and keeping another one from making a mistake by bracketing herself to a clearly unsuitable person seemed silly.

Was there really nothing else for women to do but concern themselves with such mundane matters? Clearly her own decision never to marry would save her from a life of such nonsense, for which she'd be eternally grateful.

Although, considering herself more talented in the area than the fictional Emma, Nicole did think it might be fun to find a suitable husband for Lydia. For, although she saw no need to dip her own toe in matrimonial waters, clearly her sister needed to be loved, needed to love in return.

Nicole thought about the Viscount Yalding, who seemed a nice enough man, if rather nervous. Would he be a good match for Lydia? She hadn't mentioned him, not even once, since the dinner party.

Lydia had, however, spoken often about the Marquess of Basingstoke. He'd been a soldier, like Captain Fitzgerald. He read Thomas Paine, like Captain Fitzgerald. He treated her kindly and obviously admired her intelligence. Like Captain Fitzgerald. But what did that mean, other than that Lydia still thought and spoke often of poor dead Fitz?

By the morning of the third day, marked by a thin, watery sun and with their escorts just arriving in Grosvenor Square in a pair of lovely curricles, Nicole had convinced herself that Lucas Paine was a man just like any other man, and that her intense reaction to him had been merely an aberration. She had more worlds to conquer than just this one man, and he could not be allowed to invade her mind to the degree that he had thus far, in only two brief meetings.

Nicole prided herself on being in charge of her own life, her own mind—and most definitely her own heart. So why did just the thought of seeing the man again turn her insides into jelly?

Well, enough of that sort of missish silliness! Today she would make certain that *she* was the one in charge.

So thinking, as she watched Lydia tie the strings of her bonnet beneath her chin—the blue ribbon picked out for her most expressly by Captain Fitzgerald the previous year—Nicole tried to imagine her sister married to the Marquess of Basingstoke.

She bit her bottom lip between her teeth for a moment as she felt a slight, unidentifiable pang, but then pushed on with the idea.

"Lydia?" she asked her as they walked toward the staircase, for they'd been warned by Rafe and Charlotte both that it was not polite to allow their lordships' horses to stand waiting too long. "What do you think of the marquess?"

Lydia stopped with her hand just on the railing of the staircase. "What do I *think* of him? I'm sorry, Nicole, but I don't believe I think of him at all, not in any way that matters. What do *you* think of him?"

Nicole avoided the question by asking another of her own. "You don't find him handsome?"

Lydia took hold of Nicole's arm and steered her away from the stairs. "Nicole, what's wrong? I thought you liked the man. You seemed to the day we met him, and he certainly was a delightful dinner companion. Rafe likes him. Charlotte likes him. Are you going to be contrary and decide to dislike him now, because everyone else likes him?"

"I don't do things like that," Nicole protested. "Do I?"

"No, I suppose not, except maybe for needlepoint. And turnips. But you do worry me sometimes. You don't have to conquer every man you meet, you know. If you've decided that his lordship isn't going to be your first…conquest, as you call it, then please, don't feel you need to continue seeing him. Not that I approved of the idea in any case."

"I don't feel as if I have to conquer every— Do you know something, Lydia? Sometimes I don't like me very much. This Season was supposed to be fun. London, the parties, the gaiety. I've lived for this moment ever since I can remember wanting anything. I didn't have to think about the rest of my life, as everyone said I should do. And then *he* came along. If I could cry off from our drive, I would. He's a most disconcerting man."

Lydia looked at her for a long moment, and then a slow smile lit her face. "Why, Nicole, you *like* him."

"Don't be ridiculous."

"I'm not being ridiculous, although I think someone standing here is. All your plans, your boasts— and all it takes is one man to scatter those plans to the four winds. Now do you understand, Nicole? *You* don't choose. Fate chooses for you."

"Maybe for some people. But not for me. Oh, come along. We shouldn't keep the horses standing, remember?"

"I wouldn't dream of it. Suddenly I'm quite looking forward to this afternoon," Lydia said, turning back toward the stairs, but not before Nicole realized that her sister, seemingly asleep, wandering listlessly through life since last June, had a tiny bit of sparkle in her eyes once more.

"Well, I'm not!" Nicole groused, just to please her twin, and then followed her down the stairs.

LUCAS SLICED ANOTHER LOOK at Nicole, her profile all but hidden by the brim of her fetching straw bonnet.

She'd greeted him rather coolly, climbed up onto the seat almost before he could assist her and had said less than ten words to him as they wended their way toward Richmond.

Her sister and Fletcher were behind them in his friend's curricle, and each time Lucas had looked back to make sure they weren't going to be separated in the traffic, he could see that the two of them were happily chatting together as Fletcher pointed out the sights of the city.

Nicole acted as if she had no interest in the buildings, or the people walking along the flagways. And most especially, no interest in him. She kept her head faced forward, her gloved hands folded together in her lap, and answered him with either nods or in monosyllables each time he attempted to start a conversation.

Thirty minutes of this, and Lucas had had enough.

"Has your brother warned you to behave?"

She turned to him in obvious shock. "What? Why would you say such a thing?"

"I don't know. If I were your brother—and, thankfully, I'm not, for that would be decidedly awkward, considering my less than brotherly attraction to you—I might not let you out at all."

A small smile tugged at the corners of her mouth, but she refused to let it grow. "I don't think you should have said that, my lord."

"Clearly. But if you've decided to take me in dislike, I might as well be honest."

"I haven't taken you in dislike," she said, lifting her chin. "If I had done that, my lord, I wouldn't be sitting here beside you. I never do what I don't want to do."

He couldn't resist teasing her.

"Ah, then you do want to be in my company today. I apologize for thinking you wanted me on the far side of the moon."

She did that thing with her teeth and her bottom lip, and turned her head forward once more. "You can be rather annoying," she said imperiously.

Lucas couldn't remember the last time a woman had said something like that to him. Most probably because no woman had ever said that to him. Not his mother, not his nanny and certainly none of the young ladies of the *ton* who seemed to think they had to be pleasant and charming—and boring—in order to snag him into their matrimonial net.

"Then I apologize again," Lucas said as they left the confines of London behind them and he gave his horses the office to step up the pace. "Is there anything else?"

"Anything else? Oh. You mean is there anything else about you that annoys me?"

Lucas was having some difficulty maintaining his composure. "I don't know if I would have put it precisely that way. But, yes. Please, feel free to open your budget of dissatisfaction and pay all your insults to me at once. It would be kinder."

He wouldn't be surprised if he were to see steam coming out of her nostrils at any moment, but she only breathed rather quickly for several breaths before holding up her hands and ticking off the complaints on her gloved fingertips.

"One, you look at me strangely, which I find unsettling to my customary peace of mind. Two, I am in London for the Season, not to catch myself a husband, so how you may or may not feel about me doesn't matter. Three, I don't like the way I— No, that's it. I'm done now."

"Are you quite sure?" Lucas asked her. "I'm not certain, but I believe I might wish to hear more about your third reason."

"In which case you're doomed to disappointment," Nicole told him firmly. Then she sighed. "Did you ever plan something, my lord? For a long time, thinking about that plan for, oh, months and months. Perhaps even years. Just how you would go on, just how it all would be, and it would unfold exactly as you supposed you wanted it to, because you were so sure of your plan, sure of yourself and your reasons. And then…and then it all goes horribly wrong."

He had stumbled onto something she felt strongly about, obviously. So he answered as lightly as he could, deliberately keeping his father and his own plans and expectations out of the equation, or else his answer would be too serious for the day.

"Not really, no. I seem to have lived a rather

charmed life. I never think I will be disappointed in what I want, and as I already have most everything I want, I don't invest a lot of time in planning for anything else. That might seem greedy."

She looked at him sharply, pain obvious in her marvelous eyes. "Is that it? Am I greedy? Well, of course I am. I care only for myself and my own pleasures. I consider only my own happiness. I want fun, and gaiety, and adventures, and to feel…to feel *free*. And—and I'm annoyed with you because…"

And, suddenly, Lucas understood. Nicole had come to London to enjoy herself, a rare bird indeed, not interested in marriage. And he had stepped in her way.

He sympathized with her, as she had stepped in his way, as well.

If she was willing to be this honest, he wouldn't bother to pretend he didn't know what she was trying to say.

"Shall I go away, come back in two years?" he asked her as he turned onto a less-traveled lane that led through the parkland. "That would probably be more convenient for me, truthfully."

"People don't talk to each other like this, do they? So honestly." Nicole twisted her fingers together in her lap. "Lydia would probably faint if she knew. And Charlotte would roll her eyes and wonder aloud how I always manage to get myself into untenable situations out of my own mouth or through my own actions, and why can't I learn to behave. And Rafe would— No, nobody would tell Rafe. Men are much happier when they don't know anything."

Lucas rubbed at his mouth, massaging away his smile. "And would they all say that you're incorrigible?"

"Among all the rest, yes. But I don't think you should go away. It's too late for that in any case, as you've already ruined all my fun."

If Lucas were to repeat any of this conversation to Fletcher—which he most assuredly had no intention of doing—his friend would probably tell him that Lady Nicole was saying that she had tumbled top over tail in love with him…which would serve him right for teasing with her in the first place. In fact, Fletcher was still mulling the conversation about puddles, sure it had been improper, although at a loss as to how.

But Lucas was too intelligent to believe that Nicole was in love with him. Love didn't happen that quickly, if ever. Their attraction to each other had been instant, yes, but attraction was a far cry from love.

Love wasn't on Lucas's agenda any more than it would appear it was on Nicole's. It wasn't her fault that she was young and inexperienced, and didn't realize in her innocence that their mutual attraction was of a physical nature. And if he told her that, she'd have every right to slap him, and then avoid him.

"What sort of fun were you looking for when you came to London?" he asked her at last, after sorting through and discarding other openings, all of which, he felt sure, would leave him hanging over a yawning pit.

Again, she shrugged, but her silence didn't last long. "All sorts of adventures, I suppose. Everything new and different and…and exciting. I've been stuck in the country for all of my life. For instance, I've never driven a curricle, let alone been driven in one."

"Indeed. And you think I should teach you how to drive a curricle?"

She turned to him in obvious excitement. "I've driven Rafe's coach, at Ashurst Hall."

"Lady Nicole," Lucas said in all seriousness, "if I'm to assist you in regaining the fun you believe I've somehow taken from you, you are to kindly leave off trying to confound me with obvious crammers like that one. Are we clear?"

Her smile nearly knocked him off his seat. "John Coachman let me sit up on the box, and taught me how to hold the ribbons. And I tied some old reins to a chair in my bedchamber, and practiced for months, until I was certain I'd got it right. It's almost the same."

"As chalk is to cheese, yes. Here, let me see what your coachman taught you."

So saying, and with only a quick silent prayer that she had at least told a partial truth, he handed over the reins, and then watched as she expertly took them between her fingers.

His prized pair of matched bays sensed the difference at once, and Jupiter, the left lead, immediately tested the new driver by picking up his pace.

"Oh, no, you don't," Nicole said, drawing Jupiter back in effortlessly. "You don't employ the whip, do you?" she asked, glancing over at the long whip that stood in a holder to Lucas's right.

"Rarely." He then asked her if she wished to try the whip, but she shook her head, concentrating on the roadway. "We're coming to a sharp bend to the left. Are you still game?"

"If you are," Nicole said, her delight obvious. "Behind us, Lydia is probably having a small come-apart, you know."

"Which will leave her in real peril if Fletcher topples off the seat in a dead faint," Lucas remarked, his good humor running full force. "Ah, very nicely done, Lady Nicole. Although I must say that your off wheel came dangerously close to the verge."

"It did? I'll have to work on that. Do many ladies of the *ton* drive their own curricles?"

"A few, yes. None of them, sadly, debutantes."

"Good. Then I'll be the first," she said as he pointed to a wide grassy area and indicated that she should pull the horses off and stop.

Lucas applied the brake as Fletcher's curricle pulled up beside them. "Let me guess. You want me to tell your brother that you should have your own curricle."

She frowned for a moment—delightful!—and then the dimple appeared in her cheek. "I hadn't considered that. Would you do that for me?"

"Not if you held a cocked pistol to my head and had already counted to two," he answered cheerfully. "But, if you consent to drive out with me again, I will allow you to drive my curricle. In the parks, that is. London streets are an entirely different matter."

"Lucas?" Fletcher called out to him. "Did I mistake my eyes, or was Lady Nicole holding the reins a moment ago? Her brother would have your neck if, well, if she broke hers."

"Yes, thank you, Fletcher," Lucas told him, and then asked if anyone would like to stop for some refreshment at a small inn they'd passed, one just off the crossroads a mile closer to London.

Everyone agreed this would be a fine thing, and Lucas turned the team on the soft grass, aware that Nicole was watching his every move, probably committing each maneuver to memory. Clearly she was very serious about her *fun*.

"Thank you," she said as they rode back the way they'd come. "Now if you could see your way clear to locate a place where I might put my Juliet to a good gallop I would most appreciate it. I imagine she is sulking most prodigiously, as I haven't been able to exercise her thanks to this dreadful weather. And I have the most extraordinary riding habit meant to turn heads wherever I go."

"Really? Is that to warn me or to be sure I am suitably complimentary when I see it?"

"My lord?" she asked, instead of answering him. "Do you mind that I'm being so honest with you? Honesty is rare for me, so I may not be doing it right."

"Lady Nicole, I would be willing to wager that there is very little that you don't do *right*. You're most especially proficient in throwing a man who considers himself rather unshakable entirely out of balance."

"Oh." She bit her bottom lip between her teeth for an instant, and then nodded her head. "Good. That seems only fair."

Lucas laughed out loud as they pulled into the small inn yard. "Then we're even?" he asked her. "Leaving us only to ask ourselves what happens next between us."

Nicole shot a quick look past him, to where her sister was being helped down from the curricle by the viscount.

"I think we should be friends, don't you? I think it would be…it would be *safer* if we were to think of each other as a friend."

"For how long?" Lucas asked before he could stop to think, because he certainly wouldn't have said the words if he could think of anything save how much he wanted to kiss Nicole's full, enticing mouth.

"Why, um, I suppose until we don't wish to be friends anymore? Really, this has been the strangest conversation. I may be raw from the country, my lord, but I think you really should know better. And I'm starved. Do you think there will be ham? I adore ham."

Somehow, Lucas restrained himself from saying, "And I fear I am beginning to adore you."

THE INN BOASTED ONLY the single private dining room the marquess promptly engaged while Nicole and Lydia were shown to a small bedchamber beneath the eaves, where they could wash and refresh themselves.

Lydia was still stripping off her gloves as Nicole, her bonnet tossed onto the bed, was standing bent over the washbasin, splashing cold water onto her burning cheeks.

"How did you manage to convince his lordship to allow you to take the reins?" Lydia asked her as she untied the ribbons on her own bonnet. "And, more to the point, do I want to know?"

Nicole rubbed at her face with the rough towel and then smiled at her sister. "Probably not. It was wonderful, Lydia, except that I knew he'd take them away again if I gave the horses their heads, which I truly longed to do. They're a fine pair, not all high-backed and showy like the viscount's team."

"I hadn't noticed any deficiencies in the viscount's horseflesh. We had another lovely talk, by the way. He has a gaggle of younger sisters and a widowed mother, which is why he could not risk himself in the late war, although he feels terrible that he stayed home when so many others risked life and limb for the Crown. So I told him a little about our late uncle and cousins, and how none of them went to war, but ended by perishing anyway. We agreed that safety is a matter of opinion, and that rash actions can lead to unfortunate consequences as easily as facing an acknowledged enemy."

Nicole rolled her eyes. "I'm so sorry I missed that," she said, turning away as she refolded the towel, to hide her amusement. "On the way back to Grosvenor Square you might wish to pass the time conjugating French verbs, which I'm sure would be equally delighting. But, please, while we're at luncheon, do try to find a lighter topic."

"But...but the viscount seemed entertained. What did you and the marquess discuss, then, if you're so much the expert?"

While Lydia washed her hands and then carefully blotted her cheeks with a washcloth dipped in the basin, Nicole perched herself on the edge of the bed, watching her. Lydia, the perfect lady. And such grace and circumspection came so naturally to her, unlike Nicole's less well-thought-out actions.

Lydia, always prudent, carefully *dipped* into life. Nicole unconcernedly *splashed* her way through it. That was as succinct an explanation of the difference between them as Nicole felt necessary.

"The marquess and I," she said, for once watching her words, "have decided to cry friends. We're very...comfortable with each other."

"Really?"

Lord no, Nicole thought, her stomach doing an all-too-familiar small flip. "Oh, yes. He understands that I am in London to enjoy myself, and he is content with that arrangement. You see, I thought it only fair to tell him that, as he may be on the lookout for a wife and to set up his nursery, as are many who come to Town for the Season."

"Nicole! Tell me you didn't say any such thing. To...to simply *assume* that the marquess—any man—should look at you, pay you the least attention, and then have it most naturally follow that he should wish to *marry* you? I know you mean well, sweetheart, and, knowing you, you can't see the enormous impropriety of so much as intimating that his lordship should be…should be…"

"Hot to wed me? Or, at the very least, bed me?" Nicole suppressed a shiver, praying it was one of horror and not anticipation. "Don't tell me you didn't sense that from the moment we first met. I'm not such a gudgeon that I don't know what men think when they look at me. Consider Mr. Hugh Hobart. He—"

"No! We do not discuss Mr. Hugh Hobart. Not ever. You could have been killed. Or worse."

"Lydia, nothing is worse than being killed. Any other condition is only temporary. And, if uncomfortable, even frightening, at least possible to overcome. Or would you rather that I'd withdrawn from life because of what almost happened to me that day, as you did when the captain— Oh! I'm *sorry,* sweetheart."

She hopped down from the bed and ran over to take her sister in her arms, hug her tightly. "You worry so for me, because I reach for everything with both hands. And I worry for you because you refuse to reach even a single hand forward, to take back your life. I love you so much. I don't mean that you should attempt to drive a curricle, or take on a five-barred fence, or flirt outrageously with a dangerous man because it delights something inside you to do so. We're twins, yes, but we're each our own person. You have your own way, you always did. Sweet, and gentle, and loving. Please, Lydia, love *yourself* enough to step out of the shadow you've been hiding in. I want you to *dare* something, sweetheart. Be *alive*. It's what I want for you, it's what the captain would want for you."

Lydia held on to her for long moments, her breathing somewhat shallow and irregular. And then she kissed Nicole on the cheek and stepped back from her. "If I promise to be less careful, will you promise to be more careful?"

Nicole hesitated, knowing her own limits. "In general, do you mean, or with the marquess most particularly? Because I don't know if I could—"

"Oh, no, I'd never ask you to cry off of whatever it is you and the marquess have found in each other. I also am not such a gudgeon. But will you be careful, Nicole? I know you believe it impossible, but even a strong, independent heart can be broken."

"Yes," Nicole said, pinning a bright smile on her face. "We wouldn't want that to happen to the poor unsuspecting marquess, now would we?"

"You're incorrigible," Lydia said, giving her sister another quick, fierce hug.

"Everyone keeps saying that. Mostly, I'm starving," Nicole added, truly believing her sister had at last taken a strong step back into the world. She believed Captain Fitzgerald would have approved. "Now, as we go downstairs, tell me—what do you think of the Viscount Yalding? Does he interest you? He seems to like you well enough."

"Nicole!" her sister exclaimed. "Certainly not!"

"Very well," Nicole said, taking the lead on the

stairs. "Mayfair is fairly well littered with possibilities, I'm sure. I'll keep looking."

Lydia swatted at her sister's head from behind, causing Nicole to laugh in pure pleasure as she continued down the stairs…to see Lucas standing in the narrow hallway waiting for her.

His thick blond hair was slightly mussed from his curly brimmed beaver, a thin red line marking where it had sat on his forehead above those most marvelous blue eyes. He looked completely at his ease, handsome and fit and extraordinarily *alive*. The way he made her feel.

Did he think her smile, her laughter, was for him?

He reached up his hand and she took it, surprised by the frisson of delight that swept up the length of her arm.

And if he did think her smile was for him, what did it matter? After all, Lydia was smiling, wasn't she? And it most certainly was a beautiful day…

CHAPTER FOUR

LUCAS WATCHED, NEARLY mesmerized, as Nicole waved a chicken wing about as she regaled them all with a story about the day Rafe and Charlotte had discovered a nest of baby mice in their bedchamber at Ashurst Hall. Rafe was all for dispatching them forthwith, while Charlotte had demanded they be gathered up and taken outside, to be set free.

Once, of course, Rafe had located their mother, who was probably still necessary to their well-being.

Fletcher was nearly doubled over in laughter as Nicole described Rafe's hunt for the mother, which included a hunk of cheese, a butterfly net and a large pillowcase...only to have Charlotte demand after the capture that he ascertain whether this was the mother or the father, for the father would be no good to those poor babies at all.

"And Rafe declared, 'Madam, against my better judgment I have performed as you asked. Lift its tail and take a look if you must, but I am *done*.'"

And then, as Fletcher roared with fresh laughter, she took another bite out of the chicken wing—her third of the meal—and winked at Lucas.

He only shook his head, silently telling her she was, yes, incorrigible.

She affected no airs, was so obviously comfortable in her own skin, sure of herself and her place in the world, certain that others would like her just as she enjoyed the world at large. Someday she would make a delightful hostess, as well as a real force in Society, setting trends, dictating fashion. If she didn't manage to disgrace herself before she decided just who and what she wanted to be, that is.

Nicole was such a mix of temptress and unaffected delight. He'd noticed when she came downstairs that her cheeks were glowing, and a few of her curls were slightly damp, as if she'd had herself a wash and brush up and her interest had lain more in refreshing herself than in preserving some sense of sophisticated beauty.

She certainly did not apply to the paint pots, or else her freckles would not be in evidence. No, the glow of her skin was pure good health, her lips made pink by nature. Her eyes sparkled with the life inside her, the pure joy of living that shone from her.

Some might find her exhausting. He found her exhilarating, and wonderfully challenging. And if he had any sense of self-preservation, he'd take her back to her brother and then avoid her in future.

"Are you still starving, Lady Nicole," he asked her quietly a few minutes later, "or would you care to take a stroll outside on this so rare a sunny day before we return to Grosvenor Square?"

She looked at him for a moment, her head tipped

to one side, and then put out her hand so that he might help her rise. "Dare we leave these two un-chaperoned?" she inquired in a whisper, those violet eyes dancing.

"You don't wish to invite them to accompany us?"

"Do you?"

Perhaps she could read his mind? Still, politeness decreed that he had to ask the others to come along. "Fletcher? Lady Lydia? Would you care to join us on a small stroll?" he asked as Nicole, her back to her sister, pulled a face at him.

Lydia and Fletcher exchanged looks before both begged off, much more interested in discussing whatever had been keeping them intent on each other these past minutes whenever Nicole wasn't joking about mice and butterfly nets.

"I imagine we can just leave the door open when we leave," she said, taking the bonnet he handed her and placing it on the tabletop. "You know, I've got a solid dozen of these things, a promise I made to myself, yet I have found them more a nuisance than anything else. The brims are lovely, but for the most part I feel like a draft horse with blinders on."

Lucas looked at his curly-brimmed beaver for a moment, and then left it where it was as he offered his arm to Nicole and together they headed for the front door of the inn. "I suppose, since we're only taking a short walk, we can be informal without shocking Society at large."

"If I thought that Society at large had anything to say about whether I wore a bonnet or you your hat,

I should think Society might consider finding something more serious to occupy itself with."

"Do you plan to tell Society that, or shall I? Just before we're both banished, that is."

"And you'd worry about that?" Nicole asked as they stepped out of the inn, turning to the left and a path that seemed to lead into a fairly light woods. "That Society might look askance at you? I would have thought you had more consequence than that. You could even set a new fashion. A hatless fashion."

"I could do that, I suppose. According to Fletcher, I'm fairly dripping with consequence. You, however, would be immediately labeled a hellion, even fast, and mamas would steer their sons clear of you—unless Rafe has set up a large dowry, in which case you could have three ears and no one would care."

Nicole's laugh was a delight, and she unaffectedly leaned her body into his side as she kept her arm through his. "If I had three ears, I'd *always* wear my bonnets."

Lucas looked at the way the sunlight danced off her shining curls, his fingers itching to slide into the thickness, feel their warmth. "And the world would be the less for it. Is that what you hoped I'd say?"

Her smile fled, and she bit her bottom lip for a moment before looking away from him. "No, I didn't. I wasn't angling for compliments, my lord. I thought we were friends now, and only being silly. I am not always, as Charlotte says, on the flirt."

"Your sister-in-law has all the best intentions, I'm

sure, but she clearly can't see you the way I do, the way any gentleman less than eighty and not deaf and blind would see you. You *flirt,* my dear, simply by existing at all. In fact, I'd go so far as to say that if Her Grace is truly worried about either you or the male population at large, she would be doing a service to hang a sign around your neck, warning the unwary away."

Nicole pulled her arm free of his and danced ahead of him along the narrow path. Stopped a few paces in front of him and turned to confront him. "I didn't think you were unkind. But that was a horrid thing to say."

Lucas wanted to kick himself. "Of course it was," he said quickly. "I'm sorry. I didn't mean to insult you in any way."

That imp of the devil was back in her eyes. "Me? Oh no, my lord, I wasn't at all insulted. You insulted yourself, and—how did you say it?—the male population at large. Surely there are gentlemen who care for more in females than appearances."

"At the risk of further insulting my own sex, I have to say that for many of us, appearances aren't just important, but all that's important. We're by and large a shallow bunch."

"So, if I had three ears, and no dowry, you'd turn and walk away from me right now? I see."

Lucas mentally retraced his conversational steps from the moment they'd left the inn, and wondered where he had first gone wrong. And then he realized what she was attempting to do. "Are you deliberately trying to provoke an argument between us?"

Her shoulders slumped for a moment, and then she lifted her chin and looked him squarely in the eyes. "Yes. And it's not working, drat you for being so uncooperative. Why isn't it working? Rafe says I can try the patience of a saint when I put my mind to it."

"I'm not a saint," Lucas said quietly, stepping closer to her. He could smell the sunshine in her hair. "Are you really that afraid of me? Am I that much of a threat to you, Nicole?"

She bit her bottom lip once more, and then quickly raised a hand to her mouth, as if to wipe away some betraying gesture. "I don't even know you, not really. You don't know me, either, when we come straight down to it. So why do you have this effect on me? Because I don't like it, my lord, I truly don't."

"How do I affect you?" he asked intently, daring to touch a finger to the soft underside of her chin, hold it there, mesmerized by the way the sunlight seemed to kiss her lightly freckled skin. "Tell me."

"I wouldn't give you the satisfaction," she said, jerking her head away from him. "This has gone too far. Take me back to the inn or step out of my way."

He couldn't do that.

"Have you spent the past three days wondering what it would be like to have me kiss you, Nicole? Because I have. Sister of a duke, sister of a good friend, and all I can think about is how your mouth might taste, how you'd fit in my arms. From the moment you first crashed into my life, setting my world tipping on its axis."

She shook her head slowly, but didn't turn to run from him. "I'm not afraid of you."

"Really? Because I'm not certain I can believe that. I'm afraid of you. You're everything I don't need in my life right now, just as you've made it clear that you don't want me in your life. And yet here we are, and I still want to kiss you, and I'm more than fairly certain you want me to kiss you. Truth to tell, I doubt either of us will be capable of thinking of anything else until—"

She nearly knocked him off his feet, surprising him by launching herself at him. She took his face between her hands as she stood on tiptoe and pulled his head down and fiercely pressed her mouth to his, her eyes screwed tightly shut, as if she might be in pain.

She released him just as abruptly, stepping back, her chest rising and falling rapidly. "There! Now we neither of us have to think about it anymore."

Before he could respond, she lifted her skirts and ran past him, back to the inn. He decided to light a cheroot and stay where he was for a while, giving her time to recover from her impulsive action.

God, she was magnificent.

And as he smiled, and smoked, and replayed the moment of her impulsive kiss, an idea began to form in his mind. An insane idea, but one that seemed more reasonable the more he thought about it....

WHEN WOULD SHE LEARN not to be so impulsive? When would she finally think first, and then only act afterward?

But Nicole desperately had wanted him to stop talking. To simply shut up, say nothing else that she couldn't deny without sounding like a complete ninny.

It had all seemed so eminently reasonable at the time. And, as it turned out, rather enjoyable.

She should have remembered that she still had to sit up beside the man all the way back to London.

She'd run all the way back to the inn, only skidding to a halt before she took a deep, steadying breath and rejoined her sister and Lord Yalding in the dining room, finding them still deep in conversation, so that neither of them even noticed that she'd returned.

Lucas had entered some minutes later, saying he'd settled their bill of fare with the innkeeper and that they should probably get back to the city soon, before the unpredictable weather took another turn for the worse.

"Don't say a word," she warned him as he joined her on the seat of the curricle after handing her up first. "Not a single word."

"I wouldn't dream of it," Lucas told her. "But may I at least thank you? That was a most…interesting kiss. Daresay your first? I'm flattered."

"That's nothing to the point." She narrowed her eyes as she turned to glare at him. "And, may I add, that's also not what I meant by not saying anything. You're supposed to be a gentleman."

"I am a gentleman. A lesser man would have

grabbed you and shown you what a *real* kiss is, but I restrained myself. In point of fact, I'm rather proud of my self-control, if not actually amazed at my gentlemanly behavior in the teeth of temptation."

"How gratifying for you, my lord, I'm sure. I cannot say the same for myself." Nicole took a deep breath and turned her attention to the scenery on her side of the road. "We shouldn't see each other again, at least not willingly. Although I do suppose we'll inevitably run into each other from time to time, at which point we will of course be civil to each other, especially if Lydia or Rafe is watching. Will you be at Lady Cornwallis's ball?"

"I will be now, yes," Lucas said, infuriating her, except for the traitorous parts of her that were delighted to hear the news. "But I believe I shall be able to restrain myself from tossing you to the floor and ravishing you during the Scottish Reel, if that's what worries you. As for your behavior, I really can't be certain, can I? After all, I wasn't the one who…went on the attack."

"Yes, and I'm glad I did," she said with as much bravado as she could muster, "for now that my perfectly reasonable curiosity has been satisfied, I find that you are not as much of a problem as I'd believed you might be."

"The kiss was a failure?"

As if she'd tell him otherwise—he was already entirely too smug to make her happy! And she'd certainly never let on how happy she was that he seemed to wish to continue…pursuing her. So much easier than her having to chase him, she concluded, while also deciding that she may be her own worst enemy when it came to defending her determined heart-whole plans for her life.

"Since I feel no great need to repeat the exercise, I would rather say it was a resounding success. Watch what you're doing, my lord. You nearly ran us into that ditch."

"Forgive me," Lucas said, facing forward and taking control of his team once more.

Perhaps she'd gone too far? Charlotte was always warning her that her sometimes outrageous speech and actions could drive an anchorite to strong drink. Nicole was silent for nearly the length of a mile, wondering if he'd meant she should forgive him for the kiss, or for nearly running them into a ditch, before admitting quietly, "It wasn't all that terrible."

"I beg your pardon? I'm afraid I've lost track of the last few turns in this conversation."

She rolled her eyes. He wasn't making things any easier for her, was he, and that he was doing it on purpose was obvious. "I said, it wasn't all that terrible. The kiss, I mean. I still like you, much as I don't want to. I think we may both be quite insane, and I know you shouldn't be behaving toward me the way you are, or I toward you, but I still like you. I don't know why."

"You can't help yourself, as I'm naturally charming," Lucas told her, handing over the reins once more. Nicole wondered if he'd made the gesture as a peace offering, but wasn't about to reject his offer. "Cock your wrists just a bit more—ah, that's it. Now, taking into account Fletcher's possible impending apoplexy behind us, take them through their paces, because I know you're dying to. The road is straight here and no one is visible for a good half mile."

She sliced a quick look at him, once more in charity with the man. In truth, she doubted she could ever stay angry with him, which probably didn't bode well for either of them, now that she thought of the thing. "You mean it? I'm good enough? Or are you simply trying to apologize to me?"

"Since I have a healthy regard for the state of my neck and being tossed from this seat is not in my immediate plans simply to make you happy, yes, I mean it. *And* I'm apologizing. Is it working?"

"I think so, yes. I apologize, as well. I'm well aware that I behaved very badly, even if I was goaded into it," she told him, for that was as close to an apology as she could muster. Then she turned her attention entirely to the horses, flicking the reins lightly so that they moved out of their easy canter. She felt the breeze tugging at the brim of her bonnet and smiled. "Ah, heaven."

"And tomorrow, if the weather remains fair, we'll do something about exercising your mare. Juliet, isn't it?"

She nodded, her eyes still on the roadway ahead of them. "Oh, all right, I agree. Only because you're, as you so modestly say, so charming. But don't think that anything will come of it, my lord. There will be no more kisses."

"Well, now I'm crushed. But I agree, there will no more kisses like the one you think we shared at the inn."

Confound the man! She heard his words, but could not help wondering if he was actually saying the opposite of what she might think those words meant. His smile told her she could be right. "We'll go on as we began—as friends."

"Until and unless you want something more or less, yes. But I am not without my motives for agreeing to this, Nicole. After giving the idea far less thought than I probably should have before speaking to you, I wish to strike a bargain between us. One you might consider an invitation to adventure. You did say you wanted adventures while you're here in London."

As they turned at a bend in the road and other vehicles appeared, he took back the reins. She didn't argue with him. She was much too intrigued by the tone of his voice. "That sounds ominous. You have *motives?*"

"From time to time," he said, looking at her rather intently. "Let me just say this quickly before my better judgment rears its head. For reasons I won't bore you with, I believe it might be in my best interests to be considered a love-struck fool for the next few weeks. Or, in other words, harmless."

Now this was interesting, intriguing. "Only an idiot would ever consider you harmless. To what purpose?"

"That's not important. Just hear me out, Nicole, please. We've cried friends, we've warned each other

off, more than once. We neither of us want entangle-
ments at this time. You agree?"

The sun was still shining, yet Nicole suddenly
felt very much in the shade. "That's what we said.
All right, yes, we're…friends."

"So if I agree to allow you to drive my curricle, if
I take you for gallops with your Juliet—and anything
else you might desire, within reason, of course—will
you agree to be my companion in Society? Only for
a few weeks at the outside, I promise. Then you can
be seen to very publicly dash my expectations and
move on to greener pastures in ample time to break
at least a dozen more hearts before the end of the
Season, both of us knowing we'd only been playing
out a charade of sorts, and no harm done to either of
us."

There was something in his eyes Nicole hadn't
seen before this moment. Some sort of determination that made him appear somehow stern, even
forbidding, as well as definitely angry with himself. "I wish I could say I understand, but I don't.
Why would you need anyone to think you a love-
struck fool?"

"Surely I didn't say fool, did I?" If his smile was
meant to divert her, it had sorely missed its mark.

"You did, yes," she said, refusing to return that
smile.

"Then we'll change that to devoted swain, all
right?"

"Not until you tell me *why* you want to look like
a devoted swain, no."

His expression became shuttered. "Then never mind, Nicole. With friends, some things must be taken on trust, as I trusted you with the reins."

He was so infuriating. "Do you always give up so easily, my lord?"

"When I realize I've just made an idiot of myself, yes. Forget I said anything, please. The idea only held merit until I voiced it out loud, at which point it seemed silly, not to mention stupid."

"No, that's not true. As I spout lies so easily myself when it suits me, I can usually tell when someone is attempting to lie to me. You like your idea very much, as it somehow suits your purposes, whatever they are. You simply don't like that I want to know why you feel some need to pretend something that isn't true."

"I have my reasons. That's all I can say."

"All you *will* say." Nicole peered at him out of the corner of her eye, and saw a slight tic working in his jaw. "Are you in some sort of danger?"

His smile nearly dazzled her. "And therefore applying to *you* to protect me? Hardly."

"Don't be facetious," she said without really thinking, her mind still working feverishly. "You can't be a spy, because the war is over and there is no need for spies. Is there?"

"None, no. Nicole, let it go. I shouldn't have said anything."

"You're right, you shouldn't have. But you did, and now I will go out of my mind attempting to discover why you said it and why you obviously feel a need for certain people to believe something that isn't true. Oh! Are you being chased by a particularly persistent mama who is trying to bracket you to her pudding-faced daughter?"

"If I said yes, would you believe me?"

She considered that for a moment. "No, I suppose not. You don't seem the sort to fear petticoats."

"Present company excepted, of course," he shot back, to both her delight and chagrin.

"Yes, yes, I'm ferocious, I know," she quipped lightly, still cudgeling her brain for any reason Lucas would want the world to think he was intent only on courting a woman…and not whatever else it was that he might be doing. "Just answer me this, please. Are you in any danger? Because you didn't really answer me the first time I asked."

He cocked one eyebrow as he looked at her. "You noticed that?"

"I've already admitted that I'm not bookish, like Lydia. But I never said you should feel free to believe me stupid. And you still haven't answered my question."

He was silent for some moments, careful of the increased congestion now that they were back within the confines of London.

She waited, trying not to hold her breath. Because his answer now would decide whether or not she would see him again. She knew that. She was sure he knew that.

"What I'm planning," he said at last, "could perhaps prove minimally dangerous, I suppose. But at the moment, no, I'm in no danger at all. And, if the world has no reason to suspect me of anything, that slight chance of possible danger grows even smaller. Is that enough for you, Nicole?"

Was the man even listening to himself? He'd just dangled a secret in front of her, as well as the prospect of adventure. Did he really think she would be satisfied never knowing what he intended to do? Not that she'd ever know unless she agreed to his plan to use her to cover his intentions.

"Will you tell me when it's over? This thing you'll be doing that you don't want anyone to suspect you of doing, that is."

"When it's over, Nicole, if I'm successful, yes, I'll tell you. I'll tell you everything. That's only fair."

"And if you're unsuccessful?" she asked, her heart beating fast, as she was suddenly quite worried for his welfare, drat him. She wanted adventures, certainly. But both adventures *and* caring for someone else's well-being had not been on her agenda. "What happens then?"

"I don't know," he answered slowly. "I haven't considered failure."

Her smile started small, and then spread into a wide grin. "I never do, either. Consider failure, that is. We're very alike, my lord."

"Lucas."

"We're very alike, Lucas," she repeated, and then she sighed in some small contentment. "All right. Feel free to consider yourself my ardent, love-struck swain. Lydia will be delighted, if full of I-told-you-so's, since she's well aware that I have sworn to care for no man. Rafe and Charlotte will be glad to see me occupied with a suitable person and thus think I'll stay out of trouble, even while I'm having my adventures. And, at the end of the thing, I get to know your secret. Is there anything else?"

"Just one thing. As a gentleman, and considering our friendship, I need to tell Rafe."

Nicole rolled her eyes in exasperation. Did the man know nothing of the meaning of a secret? "Absolutely not. He won't agree to any of it, for one thing. And if Rafe is to know why you want to do this, then I would have to insist on knowing what Rafe knows, or else you'd both have the advantage of me. Which, by the way, I would consider unconscionable."

"He's your brother and my friend. I can't in good conscience deceive him."

"Are you also going to tell him that I kissed you?"

"I don't think so, no."

"But you're a *gentleman*. You're his *friend*. How can you not tell him?" Nicole felt sure she had the advantage now, and she eagerly pressed it.

Lucas's answer deflated her immediately.

"All right. I believe I agree. I'll tell him, saying that it was I who kissed you—to save your blushes, you understand—and Rafe will then announce our engagement in the morning newspapers."

She looked at him, aghast. "You're *threatening* me? After I agreed to *help* you?"

His laughter came and went quickly. "How interesting. You consider the prospect of marriage as a threat, Nicole? To anyone in general, or to me in particular?"

She put up her hands, waving them in front of her to scrub away his words. "Oh, no, you don't. I've said yes, and now that I have you're sorry you asked me, so you want to make me angry so that I'll cry off. Well, I won't do it. Run and tell Rafe about that stupid kiss if you feel some great crushing need for confession. It won't be *my* nose he bloodies."

He looked at her in what she hoped was at least a little bit of amazement. "I think I've just been completely backed into a corner, and by a girl at least eight years my junior. Deny it if you wish to, but you have a very clever and even devious mind, Nicole. Almost frighteningly so."

"Yes, I probably do, but I believe my arguments are sound," she said rather proudly, before remembering the last time she'd been *clever* in what she'd believed was a good cause, which had nearly ended up with her dead.

She'd promised herself then to be more careful, most especially of those she believed she could trust, those she could, yes, even believe she could control, as she'd thought she could control Mr. Hugh Hobart.

Did she trust Lucas? Yes, she had to admit that she did.

Could she control him?

No. She couldn't even control herself when she was in his company.

Still, there was no turning back. Not now. The

carrot he'd dangled in front of her face was too potentially delicious for her to ignore it. Freedom. Adventure. *A secret.*

"I don't know how sound your arguments are, Nicole, but they seem at least to be better arguments than mine."

"I'm very good at making the ridiculous sound sensible, at least to myself," she admitted with a smile. "I practice."

She hadn't even realized that the curricle had turned into Grosvenor Square. He didn't speak again until he'd set the foot brake and a footman ran to assist Nicole down from the seat.

Lucas put his hand on her forearm, holding her in place. "If I had any sense of self-preservation, I'd be running from you right now. But, for my sins, I think we're agreed. Come along and let's ask Fletcher and your sister if they'd care to attend the theater tonight. If we're to convince the *ton* that I'm this love-struck fool I've proposed, we may as well get on with it."

Nicole nodded as he let go of her arm and hopped down from the curricle, hastening around the vehicle to assist her to the flagway.

She put her hands on his shoulders as he cupped her waist, their eyes meeting as he slowly lowered her to the ground. She had to remind herself to breathe. "I'm not simply being nosy, you understand. Or wanting my own way, wanting my own fun. It's…it's more than that. I know you said you're in little danger, but I'm worried about you. As…as your friend. Which makes me very angry with you for some reason."

"I know," he said quietly, his smile delighting her in ways she really didn't wish to think about at the moment. He took hold of her right hand and lifted it to his lips. "Thank you."

Did she blush? Her cheeks felt hot. But that was impossible; she never blushed. Lydia blushed. "Yes…yes, well…you're welcome. And still infuriating," she added when his smile grew and once again twisted her stomach into knots. "And now I'll tell you that I had a lovely time and, if you have a shred of kindness in you, you will take yourself off so that I can go inside and attempt to figure out what happened between us today."

CHAPTER FIVE

LUCAS READ THE FIRST LINE written by the Citizens for Justice out loud—"It is time, friends, to take up arms against an oppressive government determin'd to starve our children and screw honest men into the ground"—and then folded the broadsheet, handing it back to Fletcher.

"Yes, yes, thank you, I've read it. Several times. Quite depressing. She was going to give it to her brother the duke, but he was called away to his estate the morning after we dined in Grosvenor Square, and isn't due back until this evening. So she gave it to me at the inn today instead, having decided not to bother her brother with it. "What do you think, Lucas?"

"Nothing good, that's for certain. And you say Lady Lydia found this in her maid's possession?"

"In the gel's apron pocket, yes. Lady Lydia didn't confront the woman. She admits she may be seeing trouble where there is none, but the fact that she's reading your relative's fiery pamphlets at the moment did set some frightening ideas to percolating in her head."

"He's not my relative," Lucas said offhandedly. "But I can see where Lady Lydia might connect the two in her mind. That broadsheet is speaking sedition, Fletcher. Do you know what that means?"

"Necks will be stretched?" Fletcher offered, shrugging. "When we find out who wrote such nonsense, that is. Citizens for Justice? Citizens for Mischief is more like it. I told Lady Lydia not to worry, but I don't think she believed me. What do you say about this? You're the one who warned of just this sort of possibility not more than a few days ago, after all."

"What do I say about it?" Lucas repeated, subsiding into the leather chair behind his desk in the large private study in Park Lane. He answered carefully. "I think there are no names associated with this nonsense. There's a call to arms, but no mention of when or where the angry populace is to gather, or what they are to do when they do come together. Where do they go? Whom do they attack?"

Fletcher scratched at his cheek. "Well, I… Stap me, Lucas, I don't know. Do you suppose there's a code hidden in there somewhere?"

Lucas smiled. "No, I don't suppose so. No more than I suppose that more than one in fifty of the persons this broadsheet is directed at can even read the King's English, let alone decipher hidden codes. So, what *is* the purpose of this broadsheet, hmm?"

Fletcher screwed up his features, clearly deep in thought. Then he shook his head. "Since we're the only ones who can be counted on to read it, I imagine I don't know."

"But you do know, Fletcher. You just said it. This wasn't directed at the people of London, or wherever-all the thing has been distributed. It was aimed at the people who could read it. *Us*."

"No, sorry, I don't understand."

Lucas wished he didn't understand, either. But thanks to Lord Nigel Frayne, he was sadly sure that he did. It was only Fletcher who believed that Lucas was seeing this particular broadsheet for the first time.

"Think about what you told me the other day. You told me you'd overheard that some in our government believe they've found a way to bring Parliament, Tories and Whigs both, around to the idea of stricter laws and taxes meant to beat down English citizens, correct?"

"I don't believe I said *beat down*. But yes, that was about it."

"All right. And what better way to assure success than to have the populace threatening to rise up against the government? Against *us*, the rich and powerful and, sadly, uncaring."

Fletcher's eyes went wide. "Are you saying— No. That's ridiculous. Why would anyone want that to happen? Riots? Marching in the streets of Mayfair? They throw rocks, Lucas. They rip up cobblestones and use them as weapons. I've heard the stories of what happened not that many years ago. I can't afford to replace all the windows in my townhome, for pity's sake."

"Your glazier's possible bill to one side, we can

none of us afford civil unrest. Calling out the Guard on our own citizens? And I may have actually helped Sidmouth and the others with my impulsive tirade at White's, warning of just such an occurrence if we don't help those among us who are suffering most at the moment. I was unwittingly making their case for them, the exact opposite of my intention."

It also hadn't been his intention to have Lord Frayne approach him. But he had.

Fletcher picked up his wineglass and stared into it, deep in thought. "Let me see if I follow this, all right? You're saying that someone—for the sake of argument, Sidmouth, or some of his ilk—would deliberately goad citizens to rise up against their government? So that the laws that are already oppressive to them can be made more oppressive?"

"Exactly, yes." And, God help him, Lucas knew that he, against all his principles and arguments, was about to become a large part of that effort.

"I'd like you to be wrong. I hope you don't mind. The glazier bills, you understand. Very well, as I see you're set on this—this whatever it is you've clearly decided to do. How can I be of help to you?"

Could he lie to his friend? To clear his father's name, yes. Yes, he could. Especially if confiding in Fletcher could end with the man in trouble. After all, a man didn't do what Lucas was contemplating doing without bending a few of the King's laws. "I don't want to involve you."

"Christ's teeth, it's a little late for that, isn't it? I'm your friend. If you're planning something, I should be a part of it. You'd do the same for me. Now, what do you want me to do?"

"Would it be a hardship for you to continue to pay court to Lady Lydia Daughtry?"

Fletcher sat forward in his chair, his elbows on his knees. "Ah! In case she finds more broadsheets, you mean?"

"No," Lucas said, shaking his head. "I'm sure we can find more of those on our own all over Piccadilly, if we just look."

"Then why?"

It was too late now for the truth.

"That's fairly simple. After, as you call it, making so much of a cake of myself at White's, I don't wish for some people to believe I've taken up the cause of people such as those who supposedly wrote that broadsheet. I need to fade into the background, hoping everyone forgets my...outburst. To help me, Lady Nicole has agreed that I might be allowed to show the world that I'm actively pursuing her, and therefore much too besotted to think about anything as serious as the possibility of civil unrest."

"The devil you say. So you do already have some sort of plan in the works, some way to keep the cobblestones in the streets as it were? Without consulting me, but enlisting Lady Nicole instead? I'm hurt, Lucas. Truly. And she agreed to this, I imagine? Why?"

Why indeed? Lucas had spent the time since his and Nicole's shared afternoon wondering about exactly that, telling himself that she had a real interest in him, and then alternately deciding that her interest was more in the adventure of the thing. The first thought flattered him, the second disturbed him.

He gave a dismissing wave of his hand. "Something to do with curricles and gallops, and probably more I don't want to consider too closely. But never mind that. And I've got no real plan."

"Not yet, you mean, beyond getting people to forget that dreadful speech you made at White's—no offense meant. Again, tell me what I can do to help."

"All right. You could help me by keeping the sister occupied, the two of you acting as chaperones of sorts. Lady Lydia is very protective of her sister and, you'll admit, quite intelligent."

"She is that," Fletcher agreed. "Talks rings around me most of the time, but I don't mind. I think she considers me as harmless as you want whomever you want to think you harmless. Now give me at least a small hint of what you believe you'll be doing that isn't quite so harmless, because I am honest enough to not understand what you *could* do."

"Another time, or we'll be late in getting to Grosvenor Square to squire the ladies to the theater. For now, answer me this. Do you know if Lady Lydia showed that broadsheet to Lady Nicole?"

Fletcher nodded. "Yes, I do know that. She showed it to her. She thinks that's why Lady Nicole read some of Thomas Paine's pamphlet. You remember? *The Rights of Man?* Lady Lydia confided that she'd never been so surprised as when she heard that her sister had read the thing. It's nothing like her, you understand. She believes Lady Nicole has somehow decided that she needs to take more interest in the world beyond her own enjoyments, or some such thing. Lady Lydia is quite proud of her."

"Damn, that could complicate things. I'll have to be careful," Lucas said quietly.

"Careful of what?"

"Of a beautiful woman's curiosity, Fletcher," Lucas said, motioning that his friend should precede him out of the study. "For now, since you've offered to help me, I'd like you to watch over the two of them tonight at the theater when I slip away to meet with someone. Don't turn your back on Lady Nicole while I'm gone, not for a moment. All right? And then, tomorrow, I may be able to tell you more."

"She's only a young woman, barely out of the nursery, and fresh from the country at that. I'm sure I can manage her."

"Yes," Lucas said, turning away from his friend to hide his smile. "I'm sure you think you can."

COVENT GARDEN WAS A MARVEL of architecture and size, dwarfing the small regional theater near Ashurst that Nicole had attended a few times in the company of her brother and Charlotte.

She attempted a sophisticated disinterest in her surroundings, but couldn't maintain the pretense for more than a few minutes. There were simply too many people, too many beautiful people, overdressed people, ladies whose beauty astounded her or whose sausagelike bodies stuffed into corsets and garish silks amused her, gentlemen whose dark, formal clothing distinguished them, youths whose outrageous high-heeled patent shoes, outrageously exaggerated shirt points and dangling lace handkerchiefs made her bite her lip so she wouldn't giggle.

Jewels sparkled on every neck, even when some of those necks looked to be better suited to horse collars. Some laughed too loudly, some appeared desperate, while others seemed to be extremely comfortable in their skin, their clothing and their place in the world.

They sauntered along the flagway in front of the theater. They pranced into the lobby and as they headed toward their assigned seats, their leased boxes. They minced and they dawdled. Everyone was looking at everyone else, measuring the crowd with their eyes. Quizzing glasses and lorgnettes were raised, fans were unfurled and fluttered, expressions ranged from bored to interested to openly curious.

Nicole decided she loved all of them. Caught between her admiration of the heavily gilted carved wood and the brocade wall coverings highlighted by massive crystal chandeliers and unabashed interest in the exotic birds of Society that flitted all about her, she leaned closer to Lucas.

"It's like stepping into a fairy tale," she told him. "Who are all of these people?"

Lucas nodded to yet another couple walking past them, but didn't stop. "Just that, Nicole. They're people. I'd like to tell you they're here to take in the entertainment, but they're not, at least not most of them. They're here to see, to be seen and then to gossip about all they've seen. Which is a pity, for Marie Therese de Camp's play, *Smiles and Tears,* is on the bill for tonight. Would you like to meet her? Does that come under the heading of adventure for you?"

Nicole smiled up at him. "It does, certainly. Is it proper? I mean, to meet a woman of the theater."

"Entirely acceptable, yes, if I send round a note and ask her to join us in our box during one of the intermissions. Not quite as proper if we go to her."

"So of course we'll go to her. Leaving Lydia and Lord Yalding nicely chaperoned in your box by Renée," Nicole said as he gazed down at her rather intently, clearly having dropped into his role of adoring swain. "That is what you meant, isn't it?"

"Thus providing you with another adventure to keep you amused. I do remember my end of our bargain. You look beautiful this evening, by the way. Heads have turned with each new step you've taken."

Nicole had noticed that, but knew she should pretend that she hadn't. "They're looking at Lydia, as well. The men smile and the women frown. Is it too bad of me to say that it's a rather delicious feeling?"

"No, enjoy yourself. Only remember this. The depth of sincerity and true friendliness among those of the *ton,* if you were to step both feet in it, would be no deeper than that puddle we shared the day we met. You and your sister are the enemy to every other debutante, to every marriage-minded mama.

"And the men? Ah, you're too young to know what men think when they look at someone as beautiful and fresh as you and your sister. But not all men. The fortune hunters and pockets-to-let lordships would rather that the sisters of a wealthy duke were homely as stumps, so that their suits might be more easily entertained by your brother."

They ascended a wide flight of stairs, turned on the landing and began to climb again, Lydia and Fletcher and the faithful Renée following behind them. "You're attempting to ruin all my fun, aren't you? I want to be amused, and delighted. Not wary of the motives of everyone I meet. Surely there are exceptions to what you've described as a decidedly unlovely society. You, for instance."

He led the way to one of the red-curtained areas that lined one side of this narrower hallway. "Oh, yes, I'm the exception. Upstanding, entirely trustworthy and without ulterior motives. A simple man, in fact, and scrupulously honest. You could apply to anyone, and never hear a bad word about the Marquess of Basingstoke. You're lucky to have found me."

"So says the man who has asked me to be part of his conspiracy," Nicole pointed out as a liveried attendant leaped forward to draw back the heavy curtains and she stepped first into the back of the private box.

"Mind your step, Nicole," Lucas warned her. "The box is on three descending levels."

She wasn't listening. If the lobby had been wonderful, the theater now opening expansively in front of her was nothing short of splendid. She stepped forward confidently, making her way down the short steps and past the chairs positioned to her left and right, to stand with her gloved hands on the heavy brass rail and look out over the multitude all around her.

There were more people in this one theater than she had ever seen together in one spot in her entire sheltered life. Her heart pounded as she allowed the pure delight of being alive to wash over her.

This is why I was born. For this, to be a part of this, she thought to herself, and then shook her head, unable to believe she'd just had that vain and silly a thought.

She turned to her companions, her smile wide, her eyes dancing with new excitement. "Lydia, come look! The whole world is here!"

But Lydia had already taken her seat in one of the chairs in the front row of the box, Lord Yalding standing behind her, his eyes directed toward the floor. "I see them, yes," she told her sister. "Now sit down, please. If you lean out any farther, you'll be in danger of falling."

"Yes, please, Lady Nicole," Fletcher nearly bleated, still not looking at anything but the floor, his hands holding tightly to the back of another chair. "I can't sit until you do, you know. And ashamed though I am to admit it, I'm never comfortable standing in one of these boxes. The terrifying impulse to leap off the edge and plummet to my death below is most disconcerting."

Nicole sat down immediately, and looked at him in some apprehension. "You think you'd like to *jump,* my lord?"

"No, no, no, of course not. Jumping would be the last thing I'd do. But the *feeling* is there, you understand? That I might do something I know I don't want to do, simply because it would be possible to do it."

"Don't try to understand him, Nicole," Lucas said quietly as he sat down beside her. "He's been this way ever since I talked him into participating in a balloon ascension in Green Park last year. Since then, my friend much prefers solid ground. He won't move from where he's landed now until we're ready to leave."

Nicole peered past Lucas for another look at Lord Yalding. Seeing the white around the man's pinched lips, she said, "Poor man. Oh, look, Lydia is offering him her fan. Isn't that sweet?"

"Not if he takes it, no," Lucas told her. "I doubt Fletcher would feel comfortable in the role of fop. Ah, and we're drawing some attention. Indulge me as I gaze soulfully into your eyes while I assist you in shedding your shawl."

Nicole attempted to remain coolly composed as he reached behind her to help her shrug the soft cashmere shawl from her shoulders even as he did a very good job of finding himself lost in her eyes.

If her breath hadn't involuntarily quickened, if a small, delightful shiver hadn't run down her spine and then wrapped around her to tickle at her lower belly, she would have considered herself safe, considered it all a game.

But this was no game, at least not one whose rules were familiar to her. When his gaze had locked on hers, she could have sworn he meant the near-to-adoring look in his eyes. Knowing he didn't nearly brought her to tears, which was an utterly ridiculous reaction. Yes, she must keep telling herself that, and maybe her treacherous body would begin to take orders from her brain.

Her ivory-sticked fan hung from her wrist and she grabbed at it, snapped it open—nearly taking off the tip of Lucas's nose—and held it in front of her mouth as she whispered, "I think you've made your point, my lord. Unless you're about to begin drooling, which could prove embarrassing to us both."

Lucas sat back in his chair, laughing as if she'd said something terribly clever. As he shifted position, she watched in some admiration the way his intelligent eyes scanned the rows of boxes visible from their own. He hesitated only for a second as he looked almost directly across from them, inclined his head the merest of fractions before allowing his gaze to move on—but it was long enough for her to notice.

She looked out over the expanse of empty air that had set Lord Yalding to worrying he might either leap or tumble from the box, quickly inspecting the occupants of the three rows of boxes that were directly across from where she sat. "Which one?" she asked, still lightly waving the fan in front of her.

"I beg your pardon?"

"Yes, you should. Someone you saw caught your

eye a moment ago and you acknowledged him or her, whomever, with a nod. Someone else might not have noticed, but I am paying most particular attention, you understand. However, if there is anyone else here within sight of this box who is likewise interested in what you do, that person would have seen it, as well. You really haven't had much practice at being devious, have you?"

"Obviously not enough, no. May I also admit to trembling in my shoes to think how much practice you've had?"

Nicole lowered her fan as she felt her smile widen to the point of showing off the dimple in her right cheek. "There, that's it. Not at all fawning, but more astonished and possibly even captivated. Anyone looking at you now would not question your interest. Very good."

His mouth opened slightly, but he said nothing. He only shook his head and then leaned forward to ask if either the viscount or Lady Lydia cared for refreshments.

This left Nicole free to do her own apparently innocent, sweeping inspection of the boxes across the way. No one was looking in her direction at the moment, however, so that she had no way of knowing whom Lucas had seen and acknowledged.

She was momentarily diverted by the sight of a very large woman dressed all in garish purple, a large pink plume waving a good two feet over her head, stumbling down the steps in the box, clearly aiming her bulk at one of the chairs in the front row.

Her aged, too-thin escort, who was attempting to keep both of them from the fearful fate the viscount worried so about, wore a wide-eyed look of complete panic as she pulled him along, the two of them (and those below them in the pit) only saved from certain disaster by the two burly footmen behind them, one clutching madam's purple train, the other with the gentleman's coattails caught in his fists.

Indeed, Nicole was so entertained by the spectacle that, when she turned to point it out to Lucas, she was surprised to realize she hadn't noticed that he'd left the box.

"Where is his lordship?" she asked Lord Yalding just as the crowd quieted somewhat and all eyes turned, at least momentarily, to the stage.

"He's gone to fetch some refreshments," Fletcher told her. He then put a finger to his lips, as if to say it was time to be quiet and attentive.

Nicole was torn. Everyone was applauding quite madly now, and she certainly wished to not miss a moment of her first experience with London theater. But she couldn't help herself. She had to look across the way, to where Lucas had been looking when she'd caught him out nodding.

Keeping her head directed toward the stage, out of the corners of her eyes she did a quick inventory of the half-dozen boxes that could have been the object of Lucas's attention.

Three young ladies and their mother in one; Nicole remembered the rather striking redhead in the middle. The box directly beneath it occupied by two gentlemen, one of them very ordinary, the other impeccably tailored, rather handsome she supposed, but with an expression of such utter boredom that it made her wonder why he'd bothered to attend the theater in the first place.

"Who's that?" she asked Lord Yalding, using her folded fan to discreetly point across the expanse to the facing boxes. "The one wearing the expression of a man who could not be impressed if a herd of wild elephants was to suddenly stampede across the stage?"

Fletcher sighed and redirected his gaze from the stage to the boxes. "Oh. That would be Mr. George Brummell, my lady. He always looks like that."

"Beau Brummell?" Nicole chanced another look at the man. "Oh, my. He is all they say he is, isn't he?"

"If you mean is he out of favor with our Regent, deeply in debt and the man next to him is one of his creditors, as the duns follow him everywhere now to be sure he isn't about to do a flit to Calais to escape them, then yes, he's all everyone says he is. And now, if you don't mind…?"

"Oh, yes. Forgive me. Go back to your…amusement," Nicole apologized, and returned her attention to the inventory she had been doing of the boxes.

The box to the left of Mr. Brummell's had been empty until the purple lady and her terrified escort had stumbled down the stairs, and the box directly below that was still occupied by two plump matrons, a young woman in a lovely shade of blue and—no, the distinguished gray-haired gentleman was gone. Just as Lucas was gone.

Hmm.

"Lord Yalding? *Psst!* Lord Yalding!"

Fletcher sighed again as he tore his eyes away from the rather disorganized ballet taking place on the stage and leaned across the narrow aisle. "How may I be of assistance, my lady?" he asked quietly, shifting his eyes toward the stage as if to alert her that she was once more interrupting a performance he wished to watch.

"My apologies. But there is a young lady in the second row of boxes directly across from us. See her? She's flanked by two older ladies. She's in blue. Do you know her?"

Fletcher followed her gaze. "Lord Frayne's niece? I don't know her name, but that's her. I saw his lordship with them earlier. Yes?"

"Nothing," Nicole said brightly. "I just thought she was lovely, that's all. Lord Frayne, you said. Thank you. Will Lord Basingstoke be returning soon? I'm very thirsty."

"There's a refreshment station just down the hallway. I'm certain he'll return shortly. Now, if you don't mind…?"

"Oh, of course, of course," Nicole said, waving to her sister, who was also looking at her as if she should know better. Everyone always looked at her as if she should *know better,* so this didn't upset Nicole.

Then the two of them returned their attention to

the stage, the ballet concluded and a lone man now standing in the center of the stage, declaiming something or other in fierce tones. Lydia, clearly much impressed, held her clasped hands to her chest and had actually sighed.

Nicole counted to ten, and then counted to ten once again before slipping out of her chair and lightly stepping back up the steps and into the shadows.

"My lady?" Fletcher asked quietly, and perhaps rather anxiously.

"Shh," she admonished him. "The man is orating. There's a draft at the rail. I'm going to sit back here with my maid for a bit."

Viscount Yalding looked at her almost fearfully for a moment, but then shook his head as if to scold himself for whatever he'd been thinking before turning his attention back to the stage.

With a look warning of Dire Consequences if she said anything directed at Renée, Nicole snatched up her sister's reticule and took hold of the edge of the curtain, pushing it aside only as far as she needed in order to slip out into the hallway.

The liveried attendant who had ushered them into the box pushed himself away from the far wall and hastened over to her, bowing and expressing his desire to serve her in any way he could.

"How kind of you," she said, favoring the youth with her most dazzling smile. "My sister is unwell. I'm on the hunt for Lord Basingstoke, who has told me he was off to fetch us some assistance, but he's been gone for ever so long. Did you happen to notice where he went?"

"I did, miss, yes," the attendant said as Nicole reached into her sister's reticule and pulled out a coin, frowning only slightly as she realized the silver reticule clashed badly with her butter-yellow gown with its gold accents.

"How marvelous. And will you now please be so kind as to direct me?"

"Oh, yes. Pardon me. He went that way, miss," he said, pointing with one hand as he pocketed the coin with the other. "Down that way. But there's nothing there, miss, save the last of the boxes and a set of stairs down to behind the stage."

"Thank you," Nicole said, looking to her left now, to see the refreshment station in exactly the opposite direction of where the attendant had pointed. And he wouldn't have gone to visit anyone in any of the boxes, not after nodding to Lord Frayne. "He must have taken the stairs, looking for someone to help my sister. Perhaps you'll escort me to him?"

Nicole knew that she couldn't be seen to be entirely alone in the hallway that was still at least sparsely populated with others of the *ton*. She also felt fairly certain that, even if he discovered her gone, Viscount Yalding wouldn't hazard another trip down the stairs inside the box, which he'd have to do if he left his seat to follow her.

"It would be my pleasure, miss," the attendant said, just as if he was asked to accompany ladies of quality all the time. "I'm Lester, miss."

"Really? What a fine name, Lester. Now please, it is imperative I locate his lordship as soon as possible."

"Yes, miss, the stairs are just this way."

Lester was right, it was not a very long walk to get to another short hallway and the closed door concealing the staircase. When he opened the door, Nicole stepped forward, peered down the poorly lit opening to see that the stairs were the sort that turned on themselves, with a narrow landing not ten steps below her.

"Wait here, Lester," she told him. "Close the door and guard it for me."

"Miss?"

Nicole put her gloved hand on his arm. Lester was at least two years her junior. Easy prey, if she should think of him that way. And at the moment, that's what he was. "Please, Lester. You won't stand in the way of true love, will you?"

"But…but you said your sister—"

"A fib, Lester. In case anyone was listening. This is the only way his lordship and I can steal a few moments alone. They watch us incessantly. I love him *so much*, Lester. May I trust you? Please?"

The boy swallowed and Nicole watched in amazement as his Adam's apple rose almost convulsively in his thin throat. "I, um, I suppose I—"

"Bless you, Lester," Nicole said before he could talk himself out of being dazzled. She looked about quickly, saw no one within twenty yards of them, as indeed this hallway led nowhere once the entrances to the boxes were past, and then quickly entered the stairwell, motioning for Lester to close the door behind her.

She could end up traveling the entirety of the stairwell without finding Lucas, but she didn't think so. Not if Lester saw him go that way, and hadn't seen him return. It was much more likely that he'd gone down one flight, to the next level of boxes, to meet with this man called Lord Frayne.

She had no real plan, she simply wanted to see the two men together, which she was sure she would once she stepped out onto the next level of boxes. How she'd use her new knowledge she had no idea, but she wanted Lucas to know that she knew—even if she didn't precisely know what she knew.

Well, the idea had made sense to her when she'd first had it....

Nicole stayed very still until her eyes had adjusted to the scant light cast by a few tallow candles set into niches in the wall, and then began slowly descending the staircase, her eyes open for the sound of either footsteps or voices.

She made it to the first half landing without incident, turned, and was about to descend to the next landing and exit into the corridor. But then she hesitated.

There was a narrow doorway cut into the wall. How odd that there should be a room stuck halfway between the floors of the theater. And she thought she heard voices coming from behind that door, although it was impossible to make out what it was those voices were saying. Holding her breath, she squatted down and put her ear to the keyhole, feeling rather deliciously like a spy out to discover enemy secrets.

Immediately she heard Lucas's voice.

"…in position before seven o'clock, I'd say, to be safe. I know the place. Saint Giles, just off Fetter Lane."

"No, not the old church itself, the building directly next to it, The Broken Wheel. They're to meet in the cellars below the taproom. The entrance is in the alley behind it. You'll give the password and be admitted."

"And that will be enough?"

"You'd better pray so, yes, or tomorrow night might be your last night on this earth. Then you can directly ask your father who wanted him disgraced instead of applying to me for the information. Listen, learn, and next time, you'll be the one speaking, agreed?"

"Agreed. And I'd be flattered by your concern, my lord, if I didn't know that I'm no use to you if I'm floating facedown in the Thames. And now, jolly as this has been, I need to return to my box. The young lady must be missing me by now."

"I saw her. Quite the beauty. Don't let her distract you."

"There's no danger of that. She's meant only to distract everyone else."

Out on the landing, Nicole pulled a face and silently repeated: *there's no danger of that*. The *nerve* of the man!

"Very well, then. I have another appointment and must get back to my box. You may go."

"A moment, sir. You didn't tell me the password."

Nicole leaned closer to the keyhole.

"I didn't? It's strikingly unimaginative. *Guy Fawkes*."

"Ah, the man who would blow up Parliament. That must be encouraging for you. All right. I'll contact you as soon as possible. Where shall we meet?"

Yes, Nicole wanted to know that, too, but as their voices were getting louder, she knew it was time for her to retreat. Lifting her skirts, she raced back up the stairs as quickly and quietly as possible, knocking on the door to alert Lester that she had returned.

The door opened and the young attendant smiled at her, ready to say something before she roughly grabbed his arm and hastened him back down the hallway. "The ladies' retiring room. Quickly, Lester, where is it?"

"It's, um, it's—there, almost smack across from Lord Basingstoke's box."

"Perfect. If his lordship should ask, that's where I am and have been for ever so long. You're quite worried about me, as I looked pale and told you I was feeling unwell. Can you do that for me, Lester. Please?"

"But I thought you were with— Ah, miss, I understand now. I'm not to know you were with him."

Drat! Caught in her own lies! "It, um, will be better for you if you pretend you don't know, yes," Nicole said, fishing yet another coin out of her reticule. It was a good thing Lydia hadn't spent all of her allowance on fripperies, for Nicole's own allowance had been gone for weeks now.

"He did something terrible bad just now, miss, didn't he?" Lester stood up very straight, clearly eager to avenge any wrong his lordship had done. "I'll take no more of your blunt, miss. I should not have helped you at all, iffen he hurt you."

"He didn't hurt me, Lester, I promise. We argued, that's all. He wishes to elope, but I told him I simply can't do that to my widowed mother. Just remember what I said." Nicole turned and walked as quickly as she could toward the door to the ladies' retiring room, half expecting to hear Lucas calling out her name. But she made it, stepping into the brightly lit square room and leaning her back against the closed door, breathing rapidly.

"*There* you are!"

Nicole's eyes, closed in relief, snapped open in shock. "Lydia?"

Lydia walked over to her, to whisper her next words.

"Yes. Lydia. Your sister, who has been half out of her mind these past ten minutes, wondering what you've done now. How wonderful that you should remember me. Where *were* you? Lord Yalding said you must have come in here. And you've picked up my reticule by mistake, didn't you notice that? I've got yours, but it's empty, without so much as a penny to give the attendant who all but forced a cold wet towel on me so I could refresh myself. I hoped you'd show yourself eventually, as I feel I can't leave here without thanking her. You know Charlotte said we were supposed to do that."

Nicole heard a slight snicker and turned to see that Renée was also in the retiring room, along with several other ladies and their maids. She gave the maid a hard look, and the woman turned her laugh into a cough.

"I'm so, so sorry. I took a wrong turn somehow," Nicole told Lydia. "I was feeling so nauseous, you understand. I was just down the hallway, sitting on a bench. You didn't see me?"

"No, I did not see you," Lydia said, and then her chin lifted slightly and Nicole knew her sister understood. She knew her sister did not also *approve,* but at least Lydia was sensible enough to bite her tongue, with so many interested ears listening to their conversation.

"There was a potted plant next to me, which is probably why you couldn't see me, but I was there all the time," Nicole said, slipping her arm through her sister's. "Forgive me for worrying you. Shall we return to our box?"

Once they were out in the hallway, Lydia stopped walking, so that Nicole had to, as well. "You've done something I don't want to know about, haven't you? You and Lord Basingstoke both."

Nicole did her best to blush, then gave it up as she knew it was probably a hopeless case to even attempt to look remorseful or embarrassed. She'd tell her sister what she expected to hear. "It was only a single kiss, Lydia. Nothing terrible. He *begged* me, you understand. And I was, well, I was curious."

There, she thought. That should get him back for that dismissing remark of his!

"I should have known. You're always curious

over one thing or another. You really allowed him to kiss you?"

And now it was time to tell another lie. Lying to Lester, lying to Lydia—lying to herself. Oh, what a tangled web we weave…that's what Mrs. Buttram would tell her, wagging a finger beneath her nose.

"Only the one, Lydia, I promise. But I upset you, didn't I? I always do, and I'm sorry." She leaned in to kiss her sister's cheek. "I'll make up for it, I promise. You and I, we'll go to Hatchard's tomorrow, and you can poke about the books for as long as you want, and I won't even once ask if you're ready to leave."

"You hate standing about while I'm looking at books."

"I know, and I shouldn't. In fact, I think I shall ask if there are any maps of London for sale while we're there. Especially one that shows all the streets…and the churches. I'm sure there exist any number of interesting churches in London. Perhaps even some where we can take rubbings of ancient graves and such things."

"You also hate poking about in old churches and taking rubbings," Lydia pointed out, eyeing her suspiciously.

"Honestly, Lydia, to hear you tell it, I hate *everything*. I'm trying to make it up to you for frightening you. Why can't you let me do that?"

Lydia, because she was Lydia, immediately blushed and looked upset at her cruelty. "I'm sorry. If you want to apologize, I should be more gracious. But please tell me you won't go sneaking off anymore to meet with the marquess. The man should know better, even if you don't."

With her left hand held behind her back, and as she smiled at Lucas, who was heading toward them from the box, a look of concern on his face, Nicole crossed her fingers as she solemnly swore she would behave from this moment on.

"Lady Nicole," Lucas said, looking at her intensely. "Lord Yalding said you'd taken ill."

"It may have been all the excitement of my first real London outing," Nicole said, immediately knowing she'd chosen the wrong fib, for Lucas Paine wasn't such a fool as to believe that obvious untruth. "But I'm fine now. Shall we return to your box? I want to see this *Smiles and Tears* you mentioned. It sounded most interesting."

"It is. It's also very nearly over." Lucas bowed to Lydia. "If I might escort you back to the box, Lady Lydia, and to his lordship's company? I should like to speak with your sister for a moment, to assure myself that's she's indeed recovered."

"But you were just with—that is, I, um, yes, that would be fine, I suppose. And you'll be right here in the hallway, won't you? Nicole?" Lydia said, looking at her sister in understandable confusion. "Don't be long."

"I won't be. Only long enough to allow his lordship to fetch me some lemonade. It's wickedly hot in here, isn't it?"

"And it will only get hotter," Lucas warned under his breath before following Lydia back into the box to settle her again beside Fletcher. In mere moments he was back, and the smile he'd worn while Lydia was with him was no longer in evidence.

He took her arm at the elbow and directed her back down the corridor, politely inclining his head to passersby also out strolling in the cooler hallway, but not stopping to speak to anyone.

She was fairly certain they weren't on their way to meet his friend, the female playwright, but she wasn't quite ready to give up hope.

"Where are we going?"

"I think you know," he said, and she shot a quick look up at him just before her stomach dropped to her toes.

"Lester," she said quietly, sure she was right. "He told you."

"Is that his name? The boy looked at me as if he wanted to punch me. I'd ask what you told him, but I don't think I want to know."

"He thinks you want to elope and I said no, so we argued. That's all."

"That's *all?* How wonderful. Now I'm a cad on top of a seducer of young women."

Nicole felt a giggle rising in her throat. "Yes, you're quite shameful, actually. How did you manage to have Lester betray me?"

"You gave him copper, Nicole. I gave him silver. Even your most enticing smiles don't carry the weight of a silver piece. You might want to remember that the next time you hope to use your charms to get your own way."

Nicole suppressed a flinch, but only by biting down hard on her bottom lip. He was angry. He was very, very angry with her. She no longer felt herself to be an inventive spy, or out on a delicious adventure. She felt a child, a willful child; even rather ashamed of herself.

But not embarrassed enough to forget what she'd heard!

He stopped in the hallway, quietly instructing her to pretend to be inspecting the hem of her gown for a possible tear in her flounce. And then, once the last couple coming toward them had passed them by after exiting from the last box, and with a quick look both ways down the hallway, he drew her into the smaller hallway, opened the door to the staircase and led her down to the small room off the second landing.

CHAPTER SIX

HE MUST HAVE BEEN OUT of his mind to involve her.

But none of the young women he numbered in his acquaintance would ever have attempted what Nicole had attempted. Following him that way.

Lies rolled off her tongue with seemingly no effort on her part, just so that she could get her own way, indulge her curiosity, chase the excitement she insisted she was searching for, rather than the husband the rest of any year's crop of debutantes was searching for.

Or was there more to it than that? More to *her* than that?

He watched her now as she looked about the small room occupied by only a worn velvet chaise and a small table holding a brace of candles that barely lit the windowless space.

She wasn't frightened. She wasn't ashamed. She was as cool, as confident, as any man, or at least strong enough to give him that impression.

She was so innocent and beautiful and maddening at the same time, his teeth ached.

"What is this place?" she asked him as she made to sit down.

"Don't sit there," he warned sharply.

"Pardon me," she said, looking at him strangely. "I agree it doesn't look very inviting, but you are the one who brought me here. How do you know about it?"

"There are several small rooms like this strategically placed throughout the theater, for private conversations, assignations. This one was already, er, reserved for the evening by the gentleman, so we won't be disturbed."

"Assignations? Really?" She looked about the room once more, with more interest than before. "So you're saying that—"

"I told you, no one really goes to the theater to see the performances," he interrupted quickly. "But never mind that, Nicole. What all did you hear?"

She smiled up at him, the picture of innocence. "What makes you think I heard anything? I merely wanted to know where you'd gone. You didn't even bother to excuse yourself, my lord, which is probably very rude of you."

So saying, she snapped open her fan and began waving it in front of her. "Far be it from me to complain, but this room doesn't smell very good, does it?"

Lucas rubbed at his upper lip, avoiding her eyes. The room smelled of stale sex. The chaise was stained with it. This small room, and the others like it, was used for private conversations, yes, but it was mostly employed for illicit encounters between lovers, straying wives, philandering husbands, and more than the occasional whore and her client. What in hell had possessed him to bring her here?

"Let's do this quickly, then, so we can leave. What did you overhear?"

She sighed and nodded. "All right, I'll tell you. But not here. I don't like it here."

He shook his head. "No, I don't think so. It has taken me longer than it should have, but I believe I'm beginning to understand you, Nicole. We leave here, and you'll find some excuse not to tell me until tomorrow. And tomorrow you'll avoid me, and I'll find myself looking over my shoulder tomorrow night, certain you'll pop up when and where I least expect you to be."

Her sudden mulish expression told him he'd guessed correctly.

He stood with his back against the door, folded his arms across his chest and waited.

"Guy Fawkes," she said at last, glaring at him as if she actively hated him. "Saint Giles. The Broken Wheel. Revolutionaries. I heard it all, Lucas. As would have anyone else who'd taken the time to follow you. You should probably be relieved that it was me, and not anyone else. Now, can we please go?"

"Damn," he breathed, his worst fears confirmed. "And what do you plan to do with this knowledge of yours?"

"Oh, for pity's sake, stop looking at me that way. Nothing! I'm not going to *do* anything. I was worried, that's all. And you won't tell me what's going on, will you, so that you left me no choice but to find out for myself."

She smiled at him. "Yes, that's it. This is entirely your fault at the heart of it. Shame on you."

He slowly shook his head, trying to remember why he'd started this, taken her into his confidence at all.

But then Nicole tilted her head to one side as she continued to smile at him in triumph. Her bewitching eyes sparkled. Her smile set that damned dimple to dancing in her cheek. Her breasts rose and fell above the soft yellow silk of her gown, reminding him of the scattering of freckles on her upper chest that he'd vowed to have a more intimate acquaintance with...and the bloody blazes with the consequences.

"Damn me to hell," he said quietly, stepping away from the door and cupping her slim shoulders as he drew her closer to him. "You think you know what you're doing, don't you? And you have no idea...none at all."

"And that's where you'd be very wrong, Lucas." She gazed straight up into his eyes, hers never wavering. "I know you're doing something very dangerous. I know that you seem to think you need me to help you pretend that you're not. I know you're blockheaded enough to think I'm so young and silly that I'd be content with a few tame adventures in exchange for helping you possibly get yourself very badly hurt, or worse."

"Blockheaded? Did you just call me blockheaded?"

"I could call you a lot worse." She lifted her hands and carefully removed his hands from her shoulders. "So we're done. Finished. No more play-acting. No more silly pats on my head meant to amuse me while you and Lord Frayne plot whatever it is you're plotting. I'm through, Lucas. Now let me pass."

Any small amusement Lucas was feeling—and he wasn't all that amused!—evaporated instantly. "Lord Frayne? Christ! You even know his name?"

"Yes, I do. I'm very good at learning things when I apply myself," she said, still looking at him without a trace of embarrassment for having followed him. "He knows something you want to know, and he's making you do something dangerous for him so that he'll tell you what it is you want to know, about your father. And I don't think you're precisely happy about the bargain you made with the man, either."

Lucas rubbed at his temples, astounded. "All right, all right. You know everything. Or at least you think you do. So I repeat, what are you going to do about it?"

"Nothing," she told him again hotly. "I'm not going to do anything about anything, because I'm not going to see you again, I'm not going to be any part of something that could end with you floating facedown in the Thames."

"What did you do, Nicole—commit my every word to memory?"

"Never mind that. You should have told me when I asked, Lucas, that's all. I warned you. Anyone who knows me would have warned you. I don't like secrets. Now either take me back to my sister or step aside. I can find my own way. I don't think I can look at you any longer."

He didn't move. "Because I didn't tell you what your rampant curiosity insisted you know? Or because you're worried about me, worried enough to be angry with me? Why, Nicole, I think I'm flattered."

Lucas wasn't a stupid man, and he was able to catch hold of Nicole's wrist as she aimed a slap at his face.

"Let me go," she demanded quietly, her magnificent eyes so deeply purple with her anger they were very nearly black.

"I can't," he told her honestly, to his surprise and amazement. "Let you go, or keep you here…either way, I'll probably never forgive myself."

"Lucas…"

She was saying his name, not in protest he told himself, but in question, perhaps in anticipation. Or was he merely flattering himself to believe that she was attracted to him, their blood running hot with their anger? He decided this was no time to delve too deeply into such things.

His mouth came down on hers as he held on to her wrist, his other hand moving to her waist, sliding around her back as he pulled her toward him.

He would have been gentle, if she'd allowed him to be gentle.

She didn't.

She pressed herself against him, scalding him

through his evening clothes with the heat of her soft, yielding body that curved so perfectly into his.

He felt her sigh against his mouth and deepened their kiss, educating her even as she taught him that innocence had a taste more glorious than nectar.

He dragged his mouth away from hers, promising himself he'd let her go. But her smooth neck beckoned and he couldn't resist the siren call that drew his head down…to kiss her slim throat, to allow his tongue to lightly drift over her freckled skin.

Somewhere in the back of what was left of his mind, he realized that this was how men, emperors, kings, had been helpless in the clutches of beautiful, intelligent women for centuries. Anne Boleyn, Madame de Pompadour, Emma Hamilton. Nell Gwyn had been younger than Nicole when she had captured the heart and mind of King Charles II.…

"Lucas…"

Reluctantly, he reined in the passion that had taken him so by surprise. He had been about to cede her powers she didn't have. She was a mere child in her first Season; wild and impulsive and passionate, yes, but not calculating. He was, or so he'd thought until this moment, a sophisticated man of the world.

He lifted his head and looked down into her eyes, now soft with an emotion she probably didn't understand. "You're right. We shouldn't see each other again. We're complicating each other's lives. Neither of us wants that right now. And I, for one, can't afford the distraction."

Were those tears standing in her eyes? Was she

that upset that he'd agreed they shouldn't see each other again? Was she worried for his safety?

Was there ever another man so stupidly arrogant as he?

She bit her bottom lip as she nodded her agreement. And then, just when he thought she understood, she said, "I want to go with you tomorrow night. You shouldn't go alone."

"Go with me? When pigs fly, madam. This conversation is over."

He grabbed her hand, holding her back as he opened the door just enough to assure himself that no one was present in the stairwell, then pulled her with him. Out of the room, back up the stairs and out into the main corridor once more, only releasing her hand once he knew they might be seen.

They'd come back to the hallway during an intermission, clearly, for the hallway was crowded with people once again intent on seeing and being seen. They blended in with the promenade without drawing attention to themselves.

"Lucas?" she whispered even as she pretended an interest in those around her. "You heard me. I know where you're going tomorrow night. I know when. Thanks to Lydia and her seditious pamphlets, I almost think I know why. Let me go with you. I listened when Rafe and Captain Fitzgerald spoke of the war, and how it was always important to have someone you can trust watching your back. You need someone to watch your back. You can trust me."

"No," he whispered even as he nodded to Lady

Cornwallis, who had waved to him while speaking to Lord Gordon. "Absolutely not."

"Very well, then, you've been warned. I'll find my own way," she said, her words daring him, her tone politely conversational, a smile on her face as she continued to look about as if eager to see everything she could as they walked along.

"The devil you will," Lucas said as they slipped past a small knot of people standing smack in the middle of the hallway, oblivious to the congestion they were causing. "Good evening, Lady Baldridge, Lord Baldridge. A fine evening, indeed it is."

"Yes, Lucas, the devil I *will*. You can't undo what's done and I can't unlearn what I've learned. The Broken Wheel at seven o'clock. I haven't forgotten."

"I'll bring Rafe into my confidence, have him lock you in your chamber." Would this hallway never end? He wanted her back in the box, back with her sister. Lady Lydia. The normal, sensible sister.

"You wouldn't do that," Nicole nearly purred as Lucas snagged a glass of lemonade from a passing servant and handed it to her. "You already threatened to tell Rafe and haven't, so you won't do it now. Besides, he was detained in the country. He isn't here. And you can't tell Charlotte because she's increasing, and you wouldn't want to upset her. But there is something you can do to dissuade me."

Lucas looked at her sharply. The minx! She had been threatening him in order to bargain with him. Or, more likely, blackmail him. And he thought she was innocent? As innocent as Eve offering up the apple! "Name your terms," he said tightly.

"I was just going to do that, yes. One, let there be no more of this silliness of us not seeing each other again because we both know we don't want that, much as I wish we did. That was only my temper speaking out of turn. So you will take me out tomorrow morning so Juliet can have a good gallop."

The box was within sight, and Lady Lydia and Fletcher were both standing in front of it, scanning the crowd, looking for them.

"I'd already agreed to that."

"And you've just agreed again, so there's absolutely no way you can break your word now. Two, you will tell me all about The Broken Wheel and Lord Frayne while we're out for that ride tomorrow. And your father. Every last thing."

"And then you'll be satisfied? I won't turn around tomorrow night and see you and some poor harassed Ashurst footman believing you can both walk into a place such as The Broken Wheel with none the wiser? God! Do you know I can almost imagine you being hare-witted enough to actually attempt such a dangerous stunt?"

"*You're* doing it," she pointed out, waving to her sister. "Or are only men allowed to be hare-witted?"

Lucas didn't bother pointing out that he *was* a man, and capable of defending himself, while she was only a woman and couldn't possibly— Oh, good Lord. "Nicole?"

"Yes?"

"Do you know how to shoot?"

"Of course. Pistols. And archery as well, although I doubt there's any need for that here in London, is there? What else is there to do in the country if one doesn't care for needlepoint or watercolors? I'd like to learn how to fence, if you're willing. Oh, yes, that reminds me. And number three—we continue our charade, as you call it. It's clear to me now that you want others to believe you're as harmless as…well, as harmless as Lord Yalding, I suppose. So you will continue to pretend to adore me. You look silly, but I rather like it."

They stopped just six feet away from Lydia and Fletcher and she turned to face him. "Quickly, Lucas. Do you agree to my terms?"

Again *her* terms? And, suddenly, Lucas understood. He had come to her with his plan. Now, somehow, she'd managed to turn it all around so that it was *her* plan. It was her plan because that's what Nicole wanted: to be in charge, calling the tune to which he would dance. She was once more what she insisted she needed to be, her own mistress.

He'd been wrong to compare her to Eve. Young as she was, country-raised as she was, she was miles ahead of anything that woman had managed when it came to feminine wiles.

But she'd been at least partially caught up in her own web, because she cared for him, cared what happened to him. He'd felt her response to his touch. No wonder she was angry with him!

"Agreed," he said at last, and they joined Lydia

and Fletcher, apologizing for having been delayed so long in a truly stultifying conversation with Lady Hertford about the woman's ball.

Nicole fell so neatly into backing his lie with a quick, amusing story about Lady Hertford's intention to drape her ballroom all in pink netting that Lucas would have believed her if he didn't know better.

Then again, since first laying eyes on Lady Nicole Daughtry, Lucas wasn't sure he still could be counted on to know his head from his heels. It was easier just to watch and enjoy her.

Except Nicole's smile, so bright and unaffected, suddenly froze in place as she looked past him, to the crowds still milling about in the corridor.

"Is something wrong?" he asked her quietly.

"You might not think so," she said, turning her head as if to hide her face. "I suppose it would depend on how happy you'll be to know that Lord Frayne's other appointment seems to be with my mother."

CHAPTER SEVEN

THE THRICE MARRIED and widowed Lady Helen Daughtry—Dowager Duchess ever since her son's ascendancy to the title, but as the word *dowager* was repugnant to her, she had settled for Lady Daughtry—advanced on the small party as she clung to Lord Frayne's arm.

She was dressed all in deepest pink, her favorite color, the style of her gown really more suited to her daughters than to a woman on the shady side of forty. Her blond hair was piled high on her head and woven through with pearls; diamonds winked at her earlobes and from the heavy gold necklace that looked as if it weighed several pounds. Her makeup was artful, but obvious to Nicole, who had seen the woman once—only once—before Lady Daughtry had done some sort of magic with her pots and potions that managed to erase full decades from her face.

Nicole wondered if her mother drenched herself so in perfume and powder because she wished to smell good, or if she did it to cover the scent of desperation, the sick anxiety her daughter could see in the woman's clear blue eyes.

She would not be her mother, never be her mother. Desperate to be loved, terrified to be alone and uncared for. The woman was pathetically reliant on others to prop her up, her entire happiness dependant on the adoration of those others.

"There you are, my darlings!" Helen Daughtry trilled as she came to a halt much too close to Nicole for her comfort. "Shame on you, that I should have to run my own daughters to earth here at the theater." She turned to Lord Frayne. "My son has given me the most lovely house in Grosvenor Square, you know, right next door to his own residence, but I could remain moldering there for weeks on end without having a hope of my own daughters stepping next door to visit their loving *maman.*"

Maman, was it? Not mama, not mother. *Maman.* Nicole supposed that if her mother couldn't keep her daughters in the nursery any longer, and with her son the duke firmly into his majority, she would try to use them all to her advantage. Helen Daughtry, doting mama. It was very nearly laughable.

"A thousand apologies, *Maman,*" Nicole said as she curtsied to Lord Frayne. "I had not until this moment realized that you've grown so ancient as to not be able to *step next door* to visit your children. Why, I'm surprised you can get about at all."

"Nicole, don't," Lydia whispered quietly.

"Oh, nonsense, Lydia," she answered brightly. "Our mother knows I'm only funning. Don't you, *Maman?* Now it's time for you to tell your companion that you have nurtured serpents at your bosom, I believe. I always enjoy that part."

"I spared the cane, Nigel, for my sins," Lady Daughtry said with an exaggerated sigh. "But she is amusing, isn't she?"

"Yes, um, yes, and a belated good evening, Lady Daughtry," Lucas said, jumping in to fill the breach as the woman glared at Nicole, her smile glacial even as she laughed at the small joke. "Lord Frayne, please allow me the honor of introducing Lady Daughtry's daughters, Lady Nicole and Lady Lydia. You remember Lord Yalding, of course."

Nicole beat down her unexpected anger at seeing her mother and curtsied once again. "We're delighted, my lord. I believe I saw you earlier, in one of the boxes across from Lord Basingstoke's. And your lovely niece as well, Lord Yalding told me when I inquired as to her name."

She watched as the man's gray eyes went cold. "Yes, my niece. I would introduce you, save that she is leaving for the country early tomorrow morning. Helen? You wished to stop by Mrs. Drummond-Burrell's box, I believe, before Intermission is over?"

"Of course, Nigel, darling." She winked at her daughters. "In truth, he only wants me all to himself for a few moments. Naughty man," she said, lightly tapping Lord Frayne's forearm with her fan.

They all watched as Lord Frayne and Lady Daughtry moved off, the woman's perfume lingering behind so that Nicole made a statement by unfurling her fan and moving it rapidly beneath her nose as she turned to ask Lucas, "What was that all about? She looked at him just now as if she would be delighted to see a knife sticking out between his shoulders. Lucas?"

"It's my fault, Lucas," Fletcher said miserably. "I said she was his niece. It was all I could think to say."

"And she's not?" Lydia asked, peering past the viscount to watch as her mother and Lord Frayne continued on their way, her mother talking to him nineteen to the dozen. "Where are they going?"

Nicole turned to watch, and as the crowds had begun making their way back to their seats, it was easy for her to see the couple pass beyond the last of the boxes, and then quickly turn into the small hallway she already knew too well.

She looked at Lucas, who seemed to have developed a strong itch directly in the middle of his forehead, for he had half covered his face as he scratched at it.

"Lydia, let's return to our seats," Nicole said, trying not to be ill. "What with one thing or another, I've barely seen any of the performances."

"And whose fault is that?" Lydia said in a rare show of temper before she allowed Fletcher to assist her through the curtain and back to their chairs.

"If she isn't his niece," Nicole said quietly as Lucas offered her his arm, "then I'd have to suppose that she's really his—"

"Mistress, yes," Lucas told her as they settled into their seats. "And, before you ask, I think the young lady has just been usurped by…well, by your mother. Which, by the way, you can't know, because you have no knowledge of that staircase or of the room off the half landing. We're agreed?"

"I suppose you are," she said in some disgust. "I'm simply revolted. She'll not rest until he marries her, you know. They all marry her. And then they die. Rafe says they want to—die, that is, not marry her."

"Your mother is a beautiful woman. I see more of your sister in her than I do you, but perhaps you favor her more in other ways."

Nicole shot him a look that should have had him jumping from the box just to escape her. "You said that to be mean."

"Probably. And it was small and petty of me. Please accept my apology."

Nicole sighed and sat back in her chair, so embarrassed for her mother that she may have been looking down at the stage, but she neither saw nor heard anything. "My mother marries often, and also badly. My poor father, second son to a duke and with a fatal failing of wagering huge sums on everything, according to Rafe, from marked cards to which raindrop will first reach the bottom of a windowpane. And then the others, each worse than the last. Please at least tell me Lord Frayne isn't two steps from debtor's prison."

"His lordship is quite well-heeled, Nicole. If he weren't, I would have paid him handsomely for the information he has promised me and there would be no intrigue right now. But he won't marry your mother, if you believe her hopes lie there. His only son died last year in a coaching accident, as I heard it told. Frayne is on the lookout for a young wife who can give him a new heir."

"Then why is he…" She rather helplessly waved her hands in front of her, unable to find the correct words. There probably weren't any correct words, or at least proper ones.

"When something is freely offered it is often accepted, even when the person doing the taking has no plans of returning the favor."

Nicole looked at him for a long moment, and then redirected her attention to the stage. She wasn't like her mother—she wasn't. *Oh, please God, I'm not, am I?*

Only when it came time to applaud did she realize that her gloved hands had been clenched into twin fists in her lap.

IT WAS AFTER MIDNIGHT when Nicole finally threw back her covers in disgust and slid out of bed, deciding she needed a glass of warm milk or else she'd still be awake to usher in the dawn.

She'd tried to blame Lucas Paine for her sleeplessness, but when that didn't work she'd had to confront the fact that she had behaved badly tonight, very badly.

Even worse, now she didn't know how to do anything else but continue behaving badly—because otherwise he wouldn't tell her anything anymore, and if she had to spend the next days and even weeks worrying about whether or not he was going to be hurt, or worse…well, how dare he do that to her!

Circles. Her mind was going in circles she

couldn't seem to straighten out into anything even vaguely resembling a straight line that would get her from one place to another—preferably far away from the notion that Lucas Paine was becoming more and more important to her.

How dare he do *that* to her, as well!

She slid her bare feet around on the floor until she located her slippers, and then jabbed her arms into her dressing gown before heading for the hallway and the servant stairs that led down to the kitchen.

As she made her way down the dimly lit corridor, she saw light spilling out from beneath the doors to Rafe and Charlotte's bedchamber.

With Rafe still at the estate—which one, she didn't remember—Charlotte was alone in the suite of rooms. The babe wasn't expected until July, when they'd be back at Ashurst Hall, but Charlotte had been spending quite a lot of time in bed lately, claiming fatigue.

Nicole looked at the light for a few moments, biting her bottom lip as she decided if she should be worried, or just worried that she was worried, and then knocked on the door. "Charlotte? Charlotte, it's Nicole. Are you all right?"

She heard some sort of answer, but couldn't make out the words, so she depressed the latch and stepped inside, closing the door behind her. "Charlotte?"

"I'm right over here, Nicole."

Nicole stepped carefully, remembering that there were several carpets in the room and she didn't want to trip over any of them, passed beyond the small antechamber and into the brighter light of the bed-chamber. Charlotte was sitting on one of the chairs flanking the fireplace, her feet propped on a low footstool, an open book on what was left of her lap.

"Why aren't you sleeping?" Nicole asked, sitting down in the facing chair and tucking her legs up beneath the hem of her dressing gown. "Lydia and I would have told you all about the theater, but we thought you'd gone to bed."

"I did," Charlotte said, marking the page in her book with the embroidered ribbon Lydia had made for her last Christmas and putting it down on the small table beside the chair. "But Rafe's son had other ideas, I suppose. Do you think it's possible he'll be born wearing little riding boots? With *spurs?*"

Nicole laughed, as she imagined she was expected to, but then a sigh escaped her.

"Nicole? What's wrong, sweetheart?"

"Wrong?" Nicole looked at her sister-in-law, a woman she considered to be one of the most intelligent persons she knew. After all, she hadn't been able to outwit Charlotte, not ever, hard as she'd tried. "There's nothing wrong. I just…I just wish I knew me as well you know me, I suppose."

"Oh, dear," Charlotte said, "that sounds ominous. Now tell me what you mean."

Nicole looked at her friend, their onetime neighbor who had known her since they'd all been children. Charlotte was so beautiful, even more so than before she and Rafe married, before she'd become pregnant with his child.

With her sun-streaked brown hair tied back in a blue ribbon, the light from the fire casting her all over in a soft, golden glow, she epitomized everything Nicole supposed was perfect about womanhood. Charlotte was happy in her skin, in her marriage, in her impending motherhood, adored by her husband and adoring him in return.

In short, Charlotte was everything Nicole had vowed to herself she would never be.

Nicole needed her freedom, did not wish to acquire any *hostages to fortune.* She didn't want anyone to live for her, or to live for anyone else. She would never cry the way Lydia had cried for her Captain Fitzgerald. She would never be the figure of fun her mother had become, certain that there was no happiness without a husband to adore her.

Her happiness would depend on her, never on anybody else.

She'd never look so well-loved and content as Charlotte did tonight....

"Nicole? You're frightening me, sweetheart. Here, take this."

Nicole looked up to see that Charlotte was holding out a lace-edged handkerchief. Only then did she realize that her cheeks were wet. "I'm sorry," she said, sniffing as she wiped at her face. "I didn't mean to…"

"No, I suppose you didn't. I don't remember the last time I saw you cry, or if I ever did, for that matter. Even when you fell off your pony when you were ten and broke your arm, you never cried."

Nicole smiled soggily. "Yes, I did. I just didn't let anyone see me. Lydia had already shed enough tears for both of us, thinking it was her fault I fell."

"And was it? I know you said it wasn't."

"She couldn't have known I was going to take Jasper through the gardens that way and surprise her on the path. It was my fault. I had only been thinking how much fun it would be to go where I wasn't supposed to go. I didn't think of the consequences." She looked at Charlotte. "Why do I do that?"

"You were a child, Nicole. Ten years old. You don't act so rashly now."

"Yes, I do. I just did tonight. I'm just what my mother has always called me—I'm nothing but a willful child."

"This has something to do with Lord Basingstoke, doesn't it?"

Nicole nodded, and then blew her nose. She hated crying. Crying was for children. "I thought I was teasing him, having fun and maybe an adventure. And now...and now I realize how wrong I was, and how dangerous it can be to...to care about somebody else." She banged her balled fists against her thighs. "He makes me so angry."

"The Marquess of Basingstoke," Charlotte said quietly. "He makes you so angry. Because it's dangerous to care for him. How very interesting. Dangerous for whom, Nicole?"

Nicole knew she wasn't making any sense, but now that she'd begun to unburden herself, she couldn't seem to stop.

"For both of us. Because it's dangerous to care for him, because he's doing something dangerous and I know it would be even more dangerous for him if I were to try to help him. Not that he *wants* me to help him in any case. Not in any way that really matters, anyway.

"And then he looks at me—you know, *looks* at me? And I know he doesn't really mean what his eyes are saying, that it's just part of everything else, but I find myself wishing he *did* mean it, and then I get so mad at myself for wanting what I always said I didn't want and…oh, what am I going to do? This has to be how Lydia felt when Captain Fitzgerald went off to Brussels. I feel so totally *powerless*. Captain Fitzgerald went off to war, to something dangerous…and he didn't come back, Charlotte."

"Are you going to tell me what Lord Basingstoke is doing that's so dangerous?"

Nicole shook her head. "No, I'm sorry. It's not my secret, which is something else he made very clear, up until the moment I found out even the little bit I do know—which I'm kicking myself for doing, because now I'm really frightened. Not that I can let him know I'm frightened, of course, because he thinks I'm just this…this silly pest he asked to help him but didn't really want to have help him because, well, because I was flirting with him, I know I was, and being shameless, and so he thought he could make a game out of pretending he was infatuated with me."

"Why…why would he think he could make a game out of pretending an infatuation?"

Nicole waved a hand in front of her, as if the answer wasn't important. "I really can't say, except to tell you that we both agreed to the idea for our own reasons. Charlotte? What should I do?"

Charlotte laughed softly. "Oh, I'm sorry, sweetheart. I know this isn't at all funny. But how can I offer you any advice when I still don't have the vaguest notion what you're talking about?"

"But you aren't going to insist that I tell you everything, are you? That's the difference between you and me, Charlotte. If Rafe were to tell you that he couldn't tell you something just yet, you'd say that was fine, as long as he assured you he was all right. You'd stand behind him and wait for him to tell you when he felt he could. But not me. I have to know everything for myself, and I have to know it immediately. I have to poke and prod until I'm satisfied that I know everything, because maybe I can…no, *definitely* I'll have a better idea or an easier way, or *something*. Oh, I don't know what I mean."

"I do. You need to feel that you are in control of every situation, Nicole. In control of your own destiny, and maybe everyone else's, as well. Since the day you and Lydia were born, you never knew if you'd be with your mother at Willowbrook, or shuttled off to Ashurst Hall as the poor relations begging charity and a roof over your heads while your mother married yet again and wanted you and Lydia and Rafe out of the way. You'd all think yourselves happy and settled one day, and the next there was another stepfather taking charge of Willowbrook, running it further into the ground and all of you deeper in debt. Rafe hated it, too. That feeling of being powerless to control his own life, his own destiny."

"But not Lydia, never Lydia. She just accepted all of it," Nicole said, sighing. "Accepted it and made the best of it."

"Did she, Nicole? I wonder. I think of Lydia as staying safe in her cocoon, but destined to emerge someday into the beautiful butterfly who will surprise us all as she takes to the skies."

Nicole sniffed and smiled. "I'd like to think so. When the captain died, I thought she'd die, too."

"Fitz was her first love, barely more than infatuation on her part, although she won't realize that until she falls in love as a woman, not a young girl. I think Fitz would have made her happy. I know he loved her. But would she have flown with him, ever spread her wings fully? I'm not sure. But, someday, someone will waken her, and we'll all be amazed at how high she can soar."

"That would be wonderful, wouldn't it?"

"It will be, yes. Just as I long for the day you let go of the armor you've worn for so long, and allow your heart to open. To joy, to pain, to life as it is, not the way you think it should be. That one day you'll stop dashing here, dashing there, looking for something you think will make up for whatever you believe is still missing in your life. In the meantime? I don't know what to say to you, Nicole, other than to trust your heart to know what's right."

"And if my heart tells me that it can't just sit back

and watch, and wait, and do no more than hope for the best? If my heart tells me that to do that would be to chance losing everything?"

Charlotte looked at her for long moments, until a log burned through and fell in the grate. "You're more like Rafe than I realized. You go after what you want, and damn the consequences. When your brother decided I was keeping something from him, he wouldn't let go until I'd told him everything I'd promised myself I'd never tell anyone. But he did that, Nicole, because he loved me and wanted to help me. Not just to satisfy his own curiosity."

Nicole blinked back fresh tears. Honestly, she was soon going to be a watering pot. She searched her mind for something to say, and could only come up with, "He makes me *so angry.*"

"Yes, you've said that. Now you have to decide why that is, don't you?"

CHAPTER EIGHT

LUCAS HAD BEEN FORCED to drag himself out of bed at seven, not having found sleep until nearly dawn. He'd seriously considered sending round a note postponing their ride, but that wouldn't be fair to Nicole, who was probably already dressed and fed and waiting for him to arrive in Grosvenor Square.

A fine bay mare already wearing a sidesaddle was giving a groom fits as Lucas rode up on the newest addition to his stables, an unfortunately nervy four-year-old black stallion he'd picked up at Tattersall's last week thanks to Sir Henry Wallace's bad luck at Faro that had him selling off his horseflesh.

Thunder—a dreadful name, but the animal did seem to know it belonged to him—almost immediately attempted a closer acquaintance with the mare, challenging Lucas as to who was the master here, man or horse.

Naturally, for that was how his luck had seemed to be running lately, the stallion decided to rear up just as the door to the Ashurst mansion opened and Nicole appeared on the portico.

Lucas brought the stallion under control, but not until Thunder had reared a second time and then danced in a tight circle as if showing off for the mare.

As one of the Ashurst grooms dusted off Lucas's hat and handed it back up to him, Nicole called out, "I can have Lydia's Daisy saddled and brought round, my lord, if you can't manage that beauty. Daisy wouldn't say boo to a goose."

The groom, who'd had his hand out for a copper, snickered at the insult before backing away, clearly understanding that his chance for a tip had just disappeared.

"You're too kind, Lady Nicole," Lucas drawled as she gracefully descended the marble steps to the flagway.

"No, no, I'm never kind. But I am easily amused," she answered, approaching the stallion with a bit of carrot in her gloved hand. "He's gorgeous. What's his name?"

"Thunder and Turf," Lucas told her reluctantly, giving the animal its full name. "I acquired him only last week, and have been putting about ever since, trying to come up with a better name."

"I should hope so, poor thing. Here you go, you handsome boy." She held out her hand, palm up, and Thunder took the carrot with a light touch that would have amazed the Basingstoke groom whom the horse had bitten just yesterday. She then stroked Thunder's white-blazed face as the damn animal tried to nuzzle at her neck.

The bay whinnied almost plaintively.

"Oh, and now you're jealous, aren't you, Juliet? I have one for you, as well. But just one for now, if you really want a gallop." She fed the mare and then put her booted foot into the handhold the second groom made for her and lightly vaulted up onto the sidesaddle in one fluid motion.

The first groom mounted a brown gelding that looked as if it couldn't keep up with either horse, and then the three of them turned toward the entrance to the Square, the groom dutifully falling into place some distance behind them.

"And now, belatedly, good morning, Nicole. May I compliment you on that splendid riding habit?"

"It is, isn't it," she answered, touching a hand to the military shako hat that dipped fetchingly on her forehead. "I warned you that it was magnificent."

She was wrong. The midnight-blue military-style jacket and split skirt fit her like a glove, accentuating all of her enticing curves. But it was not magnificent. *She* was magnificent. Lady Nicole Daughtry would be magnificent in rags.

He'd seen the gentlemen looking at her, openly or covertly, last night at Covent Garden. She would make her first formal appearance at Lady Cornwallis's ball this very evening, having attended the Queen's Drawing Room the previous week to receive the Queen's blessing to enter Society, and Lucas knew that if he didn't quickly demand she let him write his name on her card for the opening waltz and at least one other dance, he would not see her all evening.

Not unless he took his sword with him to the ball, to slice his way through her admirers.

"We're early enough to ride in Hyde Park, if you would like to show off your ensemble," he said, already knowing her answer. Nicole was frank, almost cheeky, but she was not vain.

"You promised me Richmond, where we would have no constraints. Juliet desperately wants a long gallop, and so do I. Or are you going to renege on me now, afraid you won't be able to handle your own horseflesh?"

"I suppose I'm to take that as a challenge?"

"I most certainly hope so, yes," she said as they made their way along streets populated only by early-morning delivery wagons and a few street hawkers crying out their wares as they rode by. "Oh, look—that woman has strawberries!"

Lucas shook his head, knowing that the street vendor needed no further encouragement to run into the street, carefully balancing her large wicker tray on her head as she approached them. "And I suppose you'd like some?"

"I would, yes. We can carry them with us, and eat them while the horses are resting after their gallop. Don't you like strawberries?"

He had a moment, an unsettling moment, wherein he envisioned his head lying on Nicole's lap as they relaxed on soft green grass beneath a shady oak and she fed him a strawberry....

"I like them well enough," he said, fishing in his pocket for his purse and handing over more than the strawberries were worth before instructing the woman to deliver the small basket to the groom riding behind them. How the servant would carry them without spilling the basket, Lucas did not care. As long as there were at least two strawberries left when they arrived at Richmond.

As ragged urchins began appearing from no-where, holding up dirty paws in hopes of a coin, and vendors juggling towering poles stuck through with pastries or tied with lavender showed all intentions of crowding around the two horses, Lucas told Nicole it was time they moved on.

The last time they'd ridden this way, in his curricle, Nicole had evinced no interest in her sur-roundings, as she had been too busy—he realized now—being angry with him while devising ways to pry his secrets from him.

This morning, however, she was full of questions, and they spent their time discussing architecture—which he knew much about and her very little—and the people passing by them, whom she seemed to delight in making up stories about to amuse him.

"That man, over to your right," she said, point-ing with her pert little chin as they were forced into keeping the horses at a walk in the early-morning traffic coming into the town from outlying farms. "He may look like a draper on his way to open his shop, but he's really a deposed prince from some long-forgotten country in Europe. Poor man, to be brought so low. But he retains his dignity."

"If that means he's prancing down the flagway as

if he's got a pole up—what about those three men lounging on the corner up ahead?" he asked quickly.

Her smile faded. "Oh. Soldiers, most certainly. See? One is still wearing his torn and faded uniform jacket, probably because it's the only coat he has. And the one next to him, with the empty sleeve—he lost his arm in the fighting. They're all so thin and stooped, as if the world is pressing down on them from every side. Rafe says it's unconscionable, the way we're treating our brave soldiers now that our government doesn't need them for cannon fodder anymore."

Lucas watched as one of the men lifted his head and looked at them, as if he'd heard what Nicole had said. The man's vacant eyes took in the fine horse-flesh, the finer clothing, and the vacant look turned to one of disdain, and then naked hatred before he stepped into the street, his expression carefully blank once more, his hand held out in the way of all beggars. "A penny, kind sir," he whined plaintively. "For the starvin' kiddies, yer ken?"

The burly Ashurst groom eased his mount forward as if to put himself and his horse between the marquess and the beggar, but Lucas held him back by raising his arm. "Your regiment, soldier?" he asked smartly, and the man reflexively straightened his posture.

"Thirty-third Foot, sir. All o' us. Bertie there got his arm lopped off by some damned Frog durin' the worst of it, and Billy can't hear no more fer spit, seein' as he was workin' the cannon. Me, I'm jist hungry, sir. We're all always hungry. That's what fightin' in the Thirty-third got us."

"The Iron Duke's own regiment? In the thick of things more than once, weren't you," Lucas said, reaching into his purse once more. He came out with three gold crowns, more than any of these men had seen at one time in their lives, he was sure. "One for each of you. I only wish it could be more."

The soldier looked at the gold pieces, looked up at Lucas, his eyes wet with tears. He reached for the coins before the man on the huge black horse could change his mind. "God keep yer, sir, and yer lady, too! God bless and keep yer both!"

Lucas watched as the man hustled back to his companions, handing a coin to each of them. He wished he could feel good about what he'd just done, but he didn't. He felt hollow, empty. A traitor to those three soldiers, to all of the desperate people he longed to help. He could try to console his conscience any way he could, but at least for a while, he would be betraying these men.

Now it was his turn to be silent as they rode on, at last breaking free of the congestion of the city and entering almost abruptly into a green, lush countryside.

Nicole hadn't said a word, hadn't told him he'd done a good thing, hadn't commented at all. She allowed him his silence, as if she knew words would be woefully inadequate.

There were other early-morning riders already exercising their mounts across the expanse of softly rolling hills when they arrived, mostly grooms with their employers' horseflesh, as their employers were still abed or just waking to their morning chocolate.

There was a mist hugging the lowest spots in the distance as Lucas pulled up his mount and pointed straight ahead. "That mist masks a narrow stream. Normally I'd say we could walk our mounts through it, but with all this rain, it's probably running fast, so stop before we get there."

"You always walk your horses through it? When it isn't running fast, that is?"

He answered without thought. "No. With Victor, I'd jump it, if that's what you mean. I don't know if Thunder would take the jump or dig in his forelegs and send me sailing over his head."

"There's only one way to find out, you know," she said cheerfully, and he turned to look at her, sure she had just dared him.

"Nicole…"

"You know, Lucas," she interrupted before he could finish, "sometimes when Juliet and I are out for a run, I whoop."

"Pardon me? You *whoop?*"

Her smile was an invitation to God only knew what. "Yes. I *whoop.* I yell. At the very top of my lungs. There's something…something very *freeing* about racing with the wind and letting it snatch away anything bad or sad inside you. I just open my mouth and let it all out."

"Like a hussar charging into battle," Lucas said, nodding. "Their yells are meant to both inspire fear in the enemy and rid themselves of their own."

"I suppose it's very much like that, and it works for anger and frustration, as well. You might want to try it. Today seems like a very good day to *whoop,* for both of us. Don't let Thunder think he's in charge. I'm off!"

She touched her heel to the mare's flank and the horse broke into an immediate gallop down the long slope that led to a flatter area before dipping again toward the stream and the uphill slope on the other side.

Thunder, obviously surprised by what had just happened, reared and turned in a circle before Lucas could point him in the correct direction.

"Damn her!" Lucas shouted, watching her progress. "And now I'm supposed to chase her."

He heard the Ashurst groom chuckle behind him. "She'll dare the stream, m'lord, 'cause you said not to," he warned. "Lady Nicole dares everything."

"Yes, thank you," Lucas said, cursing himself for not being aboard the reliable, fleet-footed Victor even as he consigned the idea of Nicole feeding him strawberries to the fantasy it had been in the first place. "Oh, bloody hell!" he shouted, and dug his heels into the stallion's sides.

Thunder surprised him immediately, the horse's thirst for speed overriding its more belligerent behavior.

There were other riders visible on both the grass and the lanes that wound through the landscape. But none of them were putting their mounts through their paces in any way even marginally resembling the neck-or-nothing pace Nicole and her mare had set.

In fact, most of the other riders had reined in their

horses and were now simply watching Nicole's progress as she flew down the long grassy hill, Juliet's hooves tossing up clumps of soft earth as the mare seemed to almost float above the ground.

But Thunder clearly wasn't about to be left behind by a mere female. The stallion's stride lengthened, its powerful muscles bunching and releasing beneath Lucas's thighs even as his curly brimmed beaver flew, unlamented, from his head, leaving him bareheaded, his hair blowing across his forehead and into his eyes.

He could be riding into battle, swinging his sword above his head, his heart pounding, the wind in his face as it blew away all the cobwebs that cluttered his mind, the worries and the shadows, his thirst for revenge and the memory of those soldiers and their collective despair that mirrored the despair of so many others.

For these few precious minutes he would live in this moment, this one magnificent moment, and the devil with yesterday, the devil with tomorrow. He'd catch up with Nicole and race her to the very end of the earth. He'd glory in her laughing eyes, allow himself to be swallowed up by her youth and beauty, and leave consequences for another time, another Lucas Paine, a more sober, careful Lucas Paine who was so happily absent at the moment.

Looking ahead, he could see what he already knew: Nicole had no intention of pulling up her mount before they got to the stream. She was going to unhesitatingly put her horse to the jump—the two of them eagerly flying through the mist and into the unknown.

And she'd make it safely to the other bank.

Because she wouldn't have it any other way. Because she never planned for failure. Because she was part child, part witch, and the most *alive* creature in creation.

Which did not mean he'd let her lead the way.

"Go, Thunder!" he shouted, leaning over the stallion's neck to shout in its ear. "You're not going to let a woman best you, are you?"

Thunder responded as if he understood, his pride stinging him into greater speed, so that in a few more strides they'd pulled abreast of Nicole and her mare.

She turned her head toward him and grinned in her delight. Lucas felt what seemed like an actual physical blow to his midsection.

He punched his left arm high into the air and shouted. It felt so good the first time that he did it again. *"Waa-hoo!"*

"Waa-hoo!" Nicole shouted back at him as Thunder pulled past the mare, heading straight into the mist and toward the stream.

Once inside that mist, the ground became visible. Otherwise the coming jump would be suicide, which luckily hadn't seemed to occur to the stallion.

Lucas dared a quick look behind him, knowing he'd see Nicole there, and then concentrated once more on the leap into the unknown.

He gave one more exhilarating shout, and then Thunder planted his front legs for a heartbeat in time before bunched muscle catapulted them both into the air, the rushing water of the stream passing by below them before the thunder of the stallion's hooves struck flat rocks and harder ground on the other side and, without missing a stride, they were off and running once more across the soft spring grass.

Lucas looked over his shoulder in time to see the bay mare gather itself for the leap. Nicole's head was down, her entire body levered forward, showing her to be the expert rider he'd known she was.

And then she was safe, the mare's neck stretching out as it chased after Thunder.

"We did it, Lucas!" Nicole shouted to him. "We did it! *Waa-hoo!*"

Was her heart pounding the way his was? He felt nearly drunk with exhilaration. Young again, the way he hadn't been ever since his father's death. And all because of a wild, hey-go-mad girl he was rapidly believing he did not wish to live without in his life.

He slowed Thunder over the course of the next several hundred yards, Nicole doing the same with her mare once she was abreast of him, and the horses were down to a walk by the time they reached a line of trees at the crest of the next hill.

"We need to rest them before heading back," he told her, pointing to his left. "But not here. There's a spot over there where we'll be out of the way in case there are any other maniacs out for an all-or-nothing gallop this morning."

Her breath still coming fast, her cheeks pink, her eyes shining with happiness, she merely nodded her agreement. Nicole couldn't hide her emotions if she tried with all her might, that was clear. He wondered how she would look lying beneath him, as he wakened her to a whole new set of emotions....

They followed along the front of the line of trees that looked very natural where they grew, even if Lucas knew this entire area had been cleared and cleverly planted especially to look as if Nature had planned it that way.

When they arrived at a small copse Lucas led the way inside the concealing greenery before he dismounted and took the reins Nicole tossed down to him, leading their mounts over to tie them to a large branch that would allow them to graze.

"You lost your hat," she said as he raised his arms to encourage her to trust herself to his care as she unhooked her leg from the pommel and slid to the ground.

"I've lost much more than that, and by that I mean any sense of dignity I previously believed mine. But I don't seem to mind," he told her as she placed her hands on his shoulders. He responded by cupping her waist as she slid forward and down, searing him from chest to knee with her touch.

Her smile curved the edges of her bee-stung mouth, centering all his attention on how her lips might taste today. Perhaps they'd taste of sunlight and freshly scythed grass. Or of laughter and youth. Adventure.

"They'll say I'm leading you around by the nose, you know. Those people we tore past as if the hounds of hell were after us," she told him, stepping out of his reach. "Is that still what you want Society to think?"

He watched as she walked over to a recently coppiced tree trunk that had begun to sprout new greenery at its base and sat down on its broad, angled surface, looking rather like a forest nymph perched on her woodsy throne.

"It's what we agreed again last night, yes. Just as I agreed to answer your every question. Although I believe I'd like to amend that, having given the thing some thought. I will still agree to tell you whatever you want to know—as long as you promise to behave."

She drew off her gloves and laid them in her lap. "Meaning?"

"I'm not sure," he said, planting one boot on one of the several smaller trunks that had also been cut back in order to encourage new growth and leaning in close to her. "Meaning, Nicole, I can't be sure what you might take it into that head of yours to do, so I want to be prepared for any eventuality. Which, as it turns out, requires an all-encompassing promise from you to not do anything about whatever I might tell you."

She reached up to extract the pair of silver pins that held her shako hat in place, pulling them out one by one and then lifting the hat from her head.

"Nicole?"

He watched as she removed a few more pins and her dark hair fell down around her shoulders. She shook her head as she ran her fingers through the mass of ebony waves.

"Oh, that's so much better. You know, I used to think I couldn't wait to put up my hair, because that would mean I was all grown up. Now I've realized that all it does is give me the headache. I think I'll have Renée cut it all off."

"No!" Lucas mentally slapped himself for his near-violent reaction to such a potential disaster. "That is…short hair is no longer in fashion. Now what are you doing?"

She'd pulled a black grosgrain ribbon from her pocket and was busily tying back her hair at the nape, so that it trailed down her back. "I think that should be obvious," she said, getting to her feet, the shako hat in her hand. "I won't promise."

"Pardon me?" He was so caught up in looking at her, at the few tendrils of hair that hadn't been captured by the ribbon, but hung in loose corkscrew curls around her face, that he realized he'd lost track of their conversation. "You won't promise you won't do what? Drive me to drink?"

"No. I won't promise you anything. I've thought about it, Lucas, long and hard, and I simply can't do that. I'm sorry." She went to move past him, clearly believing their conversation over, which he'd be damned if it was!

He took hold of her arm and swung her around to face him, watching her as her eyes flashed darkly purple, warning him of God only knew what. Of something simmering inside her, ready to explode.

"What happened?" he asked her. "Last night you were full of questions and demanding answers."

"Yes, but I've decided I don't want any more answers. More answers would only lead to more questions, and if I can't do anything to help you other than to let you look at me as if I'm some delicious lemon tart—well, then I'd rather live with my questions. It's enough to know what you're doing tonight. After that—if you live through tonight—I can't think about what you're doing whenever you're out of my sight."

Lucas didn't know what to say. He hadn't wanted to tell her anything more than she'd already overheard, already guessed. But that had been last night. Today he wanted to tell her everything. Today he felt he needed her to understand the reason why he was doing Lord Frayne's bidding.

"Nicole?" he asked her quietly, trying to think through what he was saying even as he was saying it. "I want to tell you."

Her eyes flashed again and this time he was certain of what emotion he saw in those deep purple depths. Anger.

"Well, then isn't that unfortunate for you. You're going to war—don't raise your eyebrows at me like that. In a way you are, going to war, that is. If I can't go into battle with you, and you've made it clear that you don't want my help, then I'd rather not know about those battles until they're over. Or does the idea of me sitting up nights, pacing the floor, worrying about your silly, stupid neck thrill you in some way? I imagine it does. I imagine men who go off to war are always comforted to believe that there's someone left behind to pray for them, to mourn them, the way Lydia did with her captain."

"Nicole…"

"No! I'm going to finish this. Other women can sit and wait—and knit socks, I suppose. But not me, Lucas. Not *me*. I can't do that. I *won't* do that. I've given this a lot of thought—a lot of thought—and I know myself well enough now to know that I can't be like those—"

He wasn't surprised at himself when he cut off her tirade with his mouth. But was he destined to only kiss her when she wouldn't shut up?

He reveled in her anger, because it meant she cared, even as she'd never admit that to him…or to herself. Her anger brought a passion with it, one that had her clinging to him as he plundered her mouth, the two of them each giving as good as they got.

He ran his palms down her sides as she reached her arms around his neck, pulling him down to her. His fingers sought and found the narrow gap between her riding skirt and her jacket, now raised up because she was standing on tiptoe to get closer to him.

When he touched her bared skin she moaned low in her throat, pushing herself more tightly against him, which thwarted his nearly insane urge to rip open the embroidered silk frogs holding her jacket closed.

He insinuated his knee between her thighs, pulling her closer, grinding his arousal against her in a move so elementally carnal she should have pushed him away, shocked by the intimacy.

But she wasn't. Nicole was nothing she was supposed to be.

He knew she was innocent. Her reaction to him might be highly passionate, but it wasn't at all practiced. She simply went where her feelings took her, eager to experience everything life had to offer, and the world and conventions be damned.

This much he knew, had concluded during his long sleepless night.

The one question he still asked himself and had not yet been able to answer was the question that perversely decided to repeat inside his head now. *Was he another adventure for her?*

"Nicole, enough," he said as he pushed her away from him far enough to be able to look down into her eyes, the darkness he saw in them now one of passion, not anger. "Your groom will be looking for you."

"That's all you have to say?"

"No. It's nothing that I have to say. I need to speak to Rafe."

"Why?"

Lucas smiled at her naiveté. "Because, sweetheart, if I'm going to keep compromising you at every turn—and there's so far little doubt that I won't continue this way—I have to ask for your hand in marriage. Or else your brother, who is a very good shot, is likely to put a pistol ball between my eyes."

"Don't try to change the subject, Lucas. We'll argue about that another time." She reached up to push his hair out of his eyes, her touch seeming so natural to him, a casual intimacy he welcomed. "Tell Lord Frayne no. Tell him you've changed your mind, that you aren't going to do what he wants you to do, tonight or any other night."

"I can't do that, Nicole."

She dropped her hand to her side. "Then let me go with you tonight."

They were back to that? "I can't do that, either."

She closed her eyes for a moment, and when she opened them again they were cold, determined. The soft, yielding Nicole was gone, as was all her innocent passion. They could have been two strangers, for all she looked at him as if he meant nothing to her.

"Then don't bother applying to Rafe, for there's no fear that you'll ever again be close enough to me to even consider compromising me. Now take me home."

Now he was angry, with what he believed was good cause. "You're what your mother calls you, aren't you? A willful child. You expect everyone to dance to your tune, and if they don't, then you turn your back and walk away. Is that it, Nicole?"

"Yes!" she said emphatically. "That's exactly what I am. And you're nothing but trouble to me, when I came to London to be amused, to enjoy myself. Not to worry about some determined idiot intent on getting himself killed and too stubborn to ask for help except in the most ridiculous way possible. I wish I'd never heard anything I heard last night. I wish you'd never come to me with any part of your preposterous scheme. And then you joke about *marrying* me? Ha! I wish I'd never met you!"

She turned her back on him and stomped over to her mare, waiting impatiently until he made a step with his laced fingers, at which point she mounted with much less grace than she had in Grosvenor Square.

He untied the reins and handed them to her, knowing she wouldn't wait for him to mount before she and the mare were already on their way back to the stream. They'd ride back to Grosvenor Square side by side, not speaking.

She was right. This was his fault. He had come to her with his stupid scheme, not thinking it through, but just spouting the idea because it served to keep him in her company—he was honest enough with himself to admit that much. He'd taken one step along the road to putting his own interests first, and that had made it easier to take the second. If he kept this up, he'd soon not be able to find his way back.

He'd like to comfort himself with the thought that she worried about him, cared for him. Felt some passion for him. But that was only a small comfort at best.

It was over. Barely begun, what they had, might have had, was over.

Nicole was young. She would most probably lock herself in her chambers in Grosvenor Square and have herself a good cry, and then forget him.

Lucas felt as old as time. He'd repair to Park Lane,

lock himself in his study and drink himself into a stupor, knowing he'd never forget her.

And the groom could eat the damned strawberries…

CHAPTER NINE

"Oh, come look at this, Nicole," Lydia said, opening yet another book she'd picked up from one of the many tables at Hatchard's. "It's all about flowers. See the beautiful watercolors. Here's one of daisies, and another of nettle—oh, and heather. I wish I could paint half so well. What have you found?"

Nicole looked down at the slim volume in her own hand. "Nothing, really. Just a series of drawings depicting the streets of London. I found Grosvenor Square, and Rafe's mansion is marked off, as are all the others, with *Ashurst* printed right there for anyone to see. I now have a much better idea of precisely where we are."

"How interesting," Lydia said, taking the book from her and opening it. "And there's Carleton House, and Covent Garden, where we were last night, and Saint Paul's. Nicole, didn't you say something about touring some of the churches with me? With these maps, we could assemble a plan, decide which churches to visit first. I think we should buy this."

"If you want," Nicole said, shrugging her indifference to the idea.

"If *I* want? Visiting churches was all your idea. What's wrong? Ever since you returned from your ride with Lord Basingstoke this morning, you've been moping about, even as you say you're not. Are you unhappy with his lordship? You seemed to be very happy with him last night."

"He's amusing enough, I suppose," Nicole said, retrieving the book of flower paintings from the table and handing both purchases to Renée as they headed for the counter to have the books added to Rafe's bill. "Now don't frown or lecture me, but I told him this morning that I wish to feel less…encumbered as you and I enjoy our first Season."

Lydia leaned in close to whisper, "You sent him away? Is that what you're saying? Nicole? I thought you liked him. You *kissed* him."

"He kissed *me,* Lydia. There's a difference."

"There is? How?"

Nicole didn't remember her sister ever being quite so inquisitive. "I don't know. There just is. In any event, you should be happy that I've realized I was behaving badly. So yes, I've sent him away."

The girls stepped outside onto the flagway, the maid in tow, to be met by one of the Ashurst grooms who held up a large umbrella above their heads, for the afternoon had turned wet.

"Did you break his heart, Nicole? You said you thought it might be fun to break a few hearts while we're here. That it might be delicious, I think you said."

"I said quite a few things before we came to

London, and it would please me very much if you did your best to forget them all. I can be exceedingly silly and childish sometimes."

"Well, yes—but you're never mean," Lydia said, slipping her arm through her sister's, "so I knew you were just attempting to shock me. Other people may not realize that, but I do."

"Thank you," Nicole said quietly as they climbed into the coach. "In any event, his lordship and I agreed that we really do not suit, and that's the end of it. Our parting was very…amicable."

Lydia sat herself down on the facing seat and looked intently at her sister. "But it has left you sad. Will you still wish to go to Lady Cornwallis's ball this evening? Because if you feel the need to cry off I'll certainly understand, and I wouldn't mind at all sitting home with you."

Nicole pinned a bright smile to her face as she brushed a few raindrops off her cloak. "Stay home? Nonsense! I would not think to miss our very first real ball. And how different it will be from the tame country dances we've attended. Only imagine, the ball doesn't even open until ten o'clock. At Ashurst Hall, we'd just be saying our prayers and climbing into bed."

"Lord Yalding offered to escort us, you know, thinking that the marquess would as well, I suppose. But now that Rafe is back, perhaps he'll take us instead."

Nicole delivered a mental slap to her unthinking brain. How very like her to act, and only later consider the consequences of her action. Now she had ruined her sister's chances with Lord Yalding.

"But you like Lord Yalding."

"He's a very nice man, yes, if rather young, I suppose," Lydia told her. "But it is only you who thinks there is more to our friendship than that. I'm sure we'll see him tonight, in any event. So we'll ask Rafe."

"No, we can't ask him to do that, not when he's just back from the country. He'll want to stay with Charlotte. But I understand what you mean. If Lord Basingstoke isn't to accompany us, then Lord Yalding might feel awkward. Will you pen him a note?"

"I should do that, yes. But who will accompany us? Mrs. Buttram's gout is giving her fits," she said, mentioning their hired chaperone of last year who had returned to them for the Season since Charlotte didn't wish to go into Society in her current condition. "I suppose there is always…Mama."

Nicole's stomach dropped to somewhere in the vicinity of her damp shoes. So this was what penance was like. Her willfulness, her stubbornness, her need to protect herself even as she knew she had opened herself to more hurt by trying to shield her heart—this was her punishment for all of it.

"Yes, I suppose there is always our dear *maman*," Nicole said, each word an effort. "Aren't we fortunate."

LUCAS LISTENED, NOT REACTING, as his friend told him about the note that had been sent around by

Lady Lydia, explaining that while she would be delighted to see him that evening at Lady Cornwallis's ball, she and her sister had decided it would be more fitting if their mother, Lady Daughtry, accompanied them.

"You know what's queer, Lucas? I didn't think they much liked each other," Fletcher said, sipping on his wine. "You know, the mother and the daughters. Lady Nicole said they were just teasing, but it didn't feel like teasing to me. It felt like when my sister Sophie and our cousin Jane are forced to be nice to each other during Christmas holidays, when we all get together as a family. Like daggers-drawn, behind the smiles. Could make you want to hide behind the couch, out of the line of fire. Females frighten me, Lucas, and I don't cavil to admit it."

"It's my fault, Fletcher. Lady Nicole and I argued, and I imagine she asked her sister to find a way to avoid me."

Lord Yalding immediately relaxed. "Oh, well that's all right, then. I thought it was me, but it's you. You argued, you say? That's very bad of you, Lucas."

"I'm a bad man," Lucas told him, getting to his feet. "And now, if you don't mind, I have a few things to do before I meet you at the ball."

"We're not going to dinner?" Fletcher put down his wineglass and also stood. "I thought we were going to dinner together. Stap me, Lucas, I told my cook not to bother. Now what am I supposed to do?"

Lucas glanced at the mantel clock. It was already

after six. "I'll have my housekeeper put out something for you. But I have to leave now."

Fletcher looked at him curiously. "Does this something you have to do have anything to do with what we were discussing the other day?"

"Do you really want me to answer that question?"

"No, I suppose not. Unless, that is, you want me at your back. I might not be very good at skullduggery, but if you need someone at your back, well, I'd do it."

Lucas had a quick memory of Nicole offering much the same service, but with more enthusiasm, and definitely more conviction that she could actually be of help to him.

"I'm humbled, Fletcher, I really am. But no. I'll be in no danger."

Fletcher nodded, looking at his friend. "You know, Lucas, your father has been dead for a very long time. You'll probably never find the answers you believe are out there, waiting for you. And I have to ask you—what does it matter anymore? Nobody else remembers."

"I do. My mother does. My father's death nearly destroyed her. For too long we both believed something that wasn't true. I've been offered real answers, and I can't turn my back on that chance. If I have to make a deal with the devil to do it, I will. I did."

Once again, Fletcher nodded. "Lord Frayne."

"How—"

"I'm not entirely blockheaded. Lady Nicole wasn't the only one who noticed that he was gone from his box just as you disappeared from ours. You're playing a dangerous game with that fellow, my friend."

"Yes, I suppose I am. And not the only dangerous game I seem to be playing at the moment," he added, thinking of Nicole.

Thirty minutes later, clad now in baggy brown trousers, a seaman's rough wool sweater, a shapeless sack of a jacket and a pair of boots that had probably last seen service at Waterloo and not been cared for since, all purchased by his valet at a bow-wow shop in Tothill Fields, Lucas approached the rear door of The Broken Wheel.

Two burly men, beefy arms crossed on their chests, pushed themselves away from the wall to challenge his entrance.

Lucas, his blond hair dulled by ashes from the grate in his bedchamber and shoved beneath a greasy cap, his face and hands looking as if they hadn't seen soap or water in months, lifted his chin belligerently and glared at them. "What? I'm too pretty for you?"

The guard closest to him turned his head away, probably catching wind of the breath Lucas had fouled by chewing on a large boiled onion. He'd figured the aroma would go well with that of his clothes, which had spent the day wrapped around a large fish his valet had procured at Billingsgate, paying only half price because it was already three days old.

"Step yerself back, fer chrissake," the guard

ordered. "Yer smell worse'n m'wife durin' her time. Now be on yer way! There ain't nuthin' here fer the loiks o'yer."

"My good friend Guy Fawkes would not say that," Lucas told him quietly.

The guards exchanged quick looks, and the second one stepped forward.

"Seems ta be a mouthful of pretty English fer a man what looks an' smells like yer," he said suspiciously.

But Lucas was ready for just such a response, having practiced several different patterns of speech before his valet told him he'd be caught out for an impostor using any one of them.

"A man can't fall on hard times?" he asked, his gaze never wavering as he looked at the guard. "A man can't lose his living through no fault of his own? We're all of us ground down by the same government heel, my friend. But the hell with you, that's what I say."

He turned his back on the man, only to feel a large hand come down on his shoulder. "Yer knew the right words. That means yer knows somebody what trusts yer. Go on in."

For just a second, Lucas closed his eyes in relief. Then he shook off the man's hand, muttered a curse and headed into the cellar of The Broken Wheel.

There were only a few candles lit in the windowless brick room that smelled of damp and sweat and stale ale. He could barely make out the faces of those standing closest to him, which made sense, as nobody would wish to be identified once free of this place.

Taking a seat in the middle of the last row of rough wooden benches, between a small man holding a homemade crutch and a very large woman who took one sniff of him before going in search of another seat, Lucas waited for his eyes to adjust to the dimness before daring to look around him.

The room was more crowded than he would have thought, with more than seventy people, mostly men, all sitting quietly, not looking at their neighbors. Waiting.

There was a small commotion at the door a few minutes later, and three men made their way through the crowd to a table set up at the front of the narrow room.

All three were roughly dressed, down at the heels and out at the elbows, and the largest among them pressed his palms against the tabletop to announce, "Citizens for Justice will come to order!"

He then turned to the man at his left, who nodded and stepped forward.

What followed was, to Lucas's mind, a recitation of all the sins known to man—the blame for them all being placed at the Prince Regent's doorstep—followed by the second man's angry diatribe that could be nothing less than a recipe for certain disaster.

And the desperate men and women in the room cheered every seditious word, agreed with every risky portion of the plan. They would gather on Westminster Bridge with their pikes and their pitchforks and their wooden clubs, and better weapons—swords, rifles—would be provided. Once fully armed, from there they would march on Parliament, to tack up their list of demands on the very front doors to the chambers.

Lucas knew what he was supposed to do when he presided over another meeting like this, in some other tavern cellars. He was to stand up and repeat much of the same things he'd just heard here, combining them with those he'd spouted so spontaneously just a few days ago at his club. As Lord Frayne had told him, he'd been very persuasive in his concerns for the common man. He'd simply been speaking to the wrong audience.

And Lucas had agreed. In exchange for learning who had attempted to destroy his father, he had made a pact with the devil who was Lord Frayne. He would play the role of *agent provocateur,* help to incite riots that would prove to the populace that new repressive laws and sanctions were necessary to keep England safe from its own version of the late Revolution in France.

Tonight he was present mostly to watch and learn. He knew that both of the men who had spoken so passionately were in the pay of Lord Frayne and those like him. The next time he heard from Lord Frayne, it would be with the time and location of the next meeting, held in some other place like The Broken Wheel, where he, Lucas, would be the one to take center stage, to inflame and inspire and betray another room filled with hopeless, hopeful human beings who wanted nothing more than coal in their hearths and food in their children's bellies.

And for that he had been promised the name of the man who had destroyed his father. His father, the man he'd hated for so many years, only to receive an anonymous communication a year ago in which he was told his father had not been a traitor who ended his own life, but a true patriot destroyed by another man's lies.

For this past year, Lucas had tried to find answers on his own, but he had failed. But one impromptu, impassioned speech, and suddenly Lord Frayne had appeared to offer him the answers he sought. Lord Frayne, who had hated Lucas's father, but now would appear to hate someone else more. Enough to expose the man's name to the son who had sworn to avenge that father, while Lord Frayne stood back, out of the fray, his hands clean.

Yes, it was a devil's bargain, one that made all of the men and women in this room, and all the others like them meeting in secret all over the city, all over the countryside, nothing more than pawns in a much larger game they would never understand.

Could he do it? Could he really become what Lord Frayne was in order to clear away the lingering suspicions about his father's death?

Could he justify his actions to himself in the belief that once he knew all of Lord Frayne's plans he could then somehow thwart those plans before it was too late, console himself with the notion that he wanted the truth about his father for his mother's sake, and not his own?

Could he look Nicole in the face ever again if she knew the dangerous game he was playing with other people's lives?

Could he look at his own face in the mirror?

No. No, he could not. He must have known from the beginning that he could not do this.

Before he could stop himself or consider the consequences, Lucas realized he was on his feet, pointing toward the men still spouting promises of full bellies and jobs for everyone just as if they had the power to grant either.

"Show us!" he shouted. "Show us these weapons! Why should we believe you? Do we go to Westminster Bridge on promises, face the king's troops with only your fine words to defend ourselves? Where will *you* be standing when we march?"

It wasn't, as Lucas realized almost instantly, the most brilliant thing he'd ever done. If his acquaintances at his club had smiled weakly and found reasons to excuse themselves from his presence the other day, those in attendance tonight were not quite so subtle in their response.

"Coward!"

"Better we die men than starve like animals!"

"Throw the damn'd bugger out!"

"Coward! Coward! Coward!"

People heard what they wanted to hear, believed what they needed to believe. Lucas had always known that. The occupants of the room, united in their need to believe, turned on him as one, showing him a precursor of the mob they could become if the march on Parliament ever took place.

He ducked as he sensed more than saw something thrown in his direction just as someone grabbed his arm and began pulling him toward the door.

He tried to shake himself free, but a quick "Best be movin' yer dewbeaters, guv'nor" shocked him enough that he simply bent low and allowed himself to be led toward the stone steps leading up to the street.

"This way, guv'nor," the man who had rescued him said.

Lucas needed no encouragement to break into a run, following the three men who led the way down one alley and into another, and then another, until, when they stopped for a moment, there was no longer the sound of shouts or footfalls behind them.

Only then did Lucas look at the men who had pulled him to safety.

"Name's Johnny, sir," the soldier from that morning said, indicating his friends. "Billy. Bertie. Billy here thought it wuz yer. Yer doesn't belong here, sir."

"Clearly not, no," Lucas said, looking around and trying to get his bearings. "My coach is waiting for me at Lincolns Inn Fields."

"That way, sir. We'll see yer safe there."

"Don't you want to know why I was here tonight? Dressed like this?"

Johnny shook his head. "Don't matter. My kiddies gots meat in their bellies tonight, sir. Real beef. We ken we don't needs ter know much more'n that."

"You do know that those men back there—the ones who spoke—aren't really your friends, Johnny. They're only here to incite you to riot. They want civil unrest to frighten Parliament into passing new laws to keep you down."

Johnny looked to his companions, who only shrugged, and then back at Lucas. "That's the way of it, sir. There's always those what listen."

"I suppose you're right. I was probably very foolish back there, wasn't I?"

Johnny rubbed his hand beneath his nose. "Not m'place to say, sir. Yer knows what, sir? Yer smells worse'n Billy here. And that's powerful bad."

Lucas laughed, the tension broken. He looked up at the sky, gauging that it would be fully dark soon and that he had a lot of scrubbing to do in his tub before he could present himself at Lady Cornwallis's ball.

But he felt better, better than he had in days, since making a devil's bargain with Lord Frayne.

The three men accompanied him back to his coach, all of them skulking along from shadow to shadow in the midst of tumbledown buildings with no smoke coming from fireplaces, no smells of roasting meat floating on the air, and only vacant or hostile stares from those sprawled across doorways or leaning against drainpipes.

When they arrived at the coach, Lucas made Johnny promise to present himself at the servant's entrance of his mansion the next morning at ten.

"Don't have no fine tick-tock, sir, or knows how to figure one iffen I did."

"No, of course. I apologize. Be there when you can be there, my friend. I'll let my man know you're coming. By tomorrow night I want to know that the three of you, and your families, are all on their way to my estate. I want you out of this, out of whatever might happen here."

"Sir?"

Lucas rubbed at his head, his hand coming away smeared with ashes and grease. God, he was a mess! And fairly giddy—which was an odd reaction, he thought.

"It's all I can do, Johnny. I'd be a fool if I thought I could right every wrong, a fool to think I could right a wrong with another wrong, and a fool is exactly what I've been. Just let me do what I can do." He held out his hand to the man. "Will you give me your word?"

The soldier looked at Lucas's hand in disbelief. He looked to his companions who stood there with their mouths hanging open. No one of the quality shook the hand of men like them. Even their own Iron Duke had called them the scum of the earth.

Johnny wiped his hand on his trousers and then shot out his arm. "My word yer be havin', sir, an' my life iffen you should ask it."

Lucas found he had nothing to say after that. "Then we're done here."

Bertie nudged Johnny with his elbow and whispered in his ear.

"Sir? Bertie here says what we mayhap should know yer name?"

Lucas laughed ruefully. "And Bertie would be right. I'm Lucas Paine and, for my sins, the Marquess of Basingstoke."

Bertie spoke for the first time. "Coo-*ee*..."

His heart feeling considerably lighter than it had an hour earlier, Lucas climbed into his coach and headed back to Park Lane to literally soak his head.

After that, he'd find Nicole and tell her he had no more secrets, there was no more danger, so she could stop avoiding him or worrying about him.

Then he thought about Lord Frayne, what the man's reaction would be to what he had done tonight at The Broken Wheel, what he knew now about the man's plans, and he changed his mind....

CHAPTER TEN

NICOLE LAUGHED BRIGHTLY as she looked back and forth between the glasses of lemonade being offered to her by the pair of handsome young gentlemen, each vying for her attention.

"The only polite thing for me to do, I imagine," she teased, "is to either profess a most prodigious thirst, or none at all. Which do you suggest, gentlemen?"

"If you might allow me a peek at your dance card, my lady," the redhead with the smiling green eyes said, "I should then allow Freddie here the honor of presenting you with his glass."

"The devil you will," Baron Frederick Bayslip countered, and for a moment Nicole wondered if the two men would come to blows. They stepped off to one side, lemonade sloshing in both glasses as they gestured in their argument, leaving Nicole to realize that it had been the former: she was prodigiously thirsty. And very unlikely to get anything to drink.

At which point she raised one kid-gloved hand to her mouth and yawned.

"Nicole, don't," Lydia whispered to her. "You're supposed to be delighted."

"Really? Then why am I thinking this is all so silly, and that I would only be *delighted* if they'd all just go away? Lord Hemmings very nearly ripped my flounce during the quadrille. Viscount Walbeck's breath tells me the man has a great love of boiled cabbage. Mr. Timmons vows an ode to my eyes, already enamored of rhyming violet with frigate—I believe he was in the Royal Navy for a time—and that redhead over there—"

"Mr. Sunderland," Lydia supplied helpfully, trying not to giggle.

"Yes, thank you. And Mr. Sunderland has promised me a ride in his new high-perch phaeton tomorrow, directly after telling me about a bad spill he took just last week. But he's fairly certain that won't happen again, now that his father has hired a coachie to teach him how to drive. Oh, and how to whistle. Whistling, it would seem, holds more interest for him than finding ways not to be tossed into a ditch."

"You won't go with him, will you?"

"No, I won't. But now that I've made an excuse I'll have to stay very clear of the Park tomorrow or else be caught in my lie. It's the same with dancing, you know. If I turn down a single gentleman tonight, I cannot dance again all evening. Mama was quite clear on that when she delivered her loving lecture on how we're to behave. All while she's prancing about as if she's more on the lookout for a husband than any of the dozens of debutantes here. She makes herself a laughingstock."

Lydia sighed. "I know. I've been watching her. And I overheard Lady Cornwallis herself telling another woman that if that coarse Lady Daughtry cast out any more *lures* as she travels the fringes of the ballroom, well, Lady Cornwallis wouldn't be surprised if she were to see entire schools of little fishies flopping about on the floor."

Nicole laughed at this rather tame joke, but then became serious once more. "You do know, Lydia, that she'd be welcomed nowhere if it weren't that she's now the Dowager Duchess. But if she continues on like this, no one will come near either of us, either, thinking we're like her."

"That hasn't happened so far," Lydia pointed out just as the redhead—Mr Sunderland?—clearly having won the battle of the lemonade, approached once more, his smile triumphant.

"My lady, your servant," he intoned gravely as he made her a deep bow, sweeping out his arm as he did so, which resulted in his hand, and the glass, coming into contact with one of the marble pillars, sending the glass to smash on the floor.

"Well, hell." Mr. Sunderland colored in embarrassment. "I…that is…I'll be right back," he said weakly, and took himself off.

"Reducing all the eager gentlemen to blithering idiocy, I see," the Duke of Malvern said moments later as he bowed in front of the sisters. "Although, with Sunderland, you shouldn't consider that too great an accomplishment, as he is, as my late father would have said, already next door to a yahoo. Good evening, Lady Lydia, Lady Nicole. You're not dancing this evening?"

Nicole could sense Lydia's body stiffening beside her even as she heard her sister's sharp intake of breath.

"Oh, yes, we have both been dancing, Your Grace," Nicole told him before Lydia could say anything to contradict her. "My partner for the next set should be presenting himself any time now. As soon as his fond mama clips his leading strings, I imagine."

The duke laughed, as he was supposed to do, and then turned to Lydia. "Would I be dashing all my hopes if I were to ask your hand in the next set, my lady?"

"No to one, no to all," Nicole whispered as she pretended to lean in toward Lydia to adjust the ruffle on her sleeve.

"Why, I... No, Your Grace. It wouldn't be dashing your hopes," Lydia answered quietly, and with all the enthusiasm of someone being asked if she preferred a hood or no hood before facing the gallows.

"And your partner will be returning shortly?" His Grace asked Nicole, clearly not wishing to leave her standing alone on the fringe of the ballroom.

Nicole nodded as she made shooing motions, and then watched as her sister and the duke made their way onto the floor, to join in a set forming for the quadrille.

Poor Lydia. Her sister knew it was not rational for her to hold the Duke of Malvern in such dislike. Yes, he had been the one to deliver the terrible news about Captain Fitzgerald to them all. Yes, Lydia had all but pounced on the man, declaring

him a liar, ordering him out of the mansion in Grosvenor Square until he drew her tightly to him,
holding her against her will until she collapsed,
sobbing, into his arms.

The man was a constant reminder of all Lydia
had lost.

But he was also Rafe's friend, had been Captain
Fitzgerald's friend, and Charlotte had confided in
Nicole that the captain had in nearly his dying breath
asked the duke to "take care of my Lyddie."

Lydia would be horrified if she knew that....

Nicole watched as her sister moved through the
dance with her usual grace, her beauty so under-
stated, so fragile to the casual observer, although
Nicole knew Lydia had strengths few could imagine.

Then she looked at the duke. There was no denying that he was a well-set-up gentleman: tall, straight
and clad impeccably. His dark blond hair had a bit
of curl to it that kept his features from looking too
severe. Yes, a handsome man.

As the movements of the dance brought the two
of them together, Nicole decided that he and Lydia
made a most attractive couple. Not that she'd say any
such thing to Lydia.

"Why aren't you dancing?"

Nicole squared her shoulders and turned to her
mother, who had appeared out of nowhere, or out
from under a member of the peerage, or wherever
she'd been this past half hour or more. As usual, she
was dressed all in pink, her bodice cut full inches too
low, in Nicole's opinion, and the overly flamboyant

design of the gown better suited to a woman half her age. "My partner seems to have been detained."

Helen Daughtry unfurled her ivory-sticked fan and began feverishly waving it beneath her chin. "Thank goodness. I was half-convinced you'd said something incredibly outrageous to someone and thoroughly put yourself beyond the pale, which would have been so like you. Besides, your gown may be a pretty color, but it pales beside my own, and I shouldn't be casting my own daughter so very much in the shade. I vow, I pace the floors at night, so worried for the both of you. The sooner you and dearest Lydia are betrothed and married, the happier I will be. As your *maman,* you understand."

"And if Lydia could find a husband who would take her off to the wilds of Scotland, and if I were to marry an American adventurer and sail away across the Atlantic, you'd be positively ecstatic. But what to do with Rafe, *hmm?* And that grandchild he and Charlotte will be presenting to you in a few short months? Oh dear, oh dear. How will you explain *them* away?"

"I don't know what you're talking about," Lady Daughtry protested, the fan moving even faster. "I am delighted in my children."

Nicole sighed, wondering why she couldn't seem to exchange more than a few words with her mother without rancor. "I'm sorry, *Maman.* Lydia and I are so grateful that you agreed to accompany us tonight."

"As well you should be. It does my own plans no favors, you know, to be forced into the role of nursemaid. And I suppose I'll have to leave the ball when you do. Yes, of course I will. Though I imagine you two could find your own way home if I were seen to escort you to Rafe's coach."

"That would be fine, *Maman,* yes. Even preferable."

"For both of us, darling, I agree. Oh, and here comes an even better answer," she trilled, playfully nudging Nicole with her elbow. "And look at him looking at you. I should offer the man a spoon, the better to eat you up. My congratulations, dearest. Basingstoke is the catch of the Season. And quite the talented lover, or so I've heard it whispered. Just don't allow him his fun too soon, or else you might lose him."

Nicole longed to take out her handkerchief and stuff it into her mother's mouth. "That's disgusting."

Helen Daughtry laughed, giving a toss of her blond head. "You'll change your mind soon enough, unless you pick some cowhanded dolt. At least Basingstoke is said to know what he's doing. Ah, and he comes closer. Stand up straight, darling, you're here to show off your merchandise, you know."

Nicole looked in the direction her mother had indicated, unable to stop herself from reacting, and saw Lucas heading toward her, making his way past those still standing on the fringes of the dance floor as if they didn't exist. Lord Yalding trailed in his wake, his expression torn between confusion and apprehension, not that Nicole believed that to be out of the ordinary for Lord Yalding, poor man.

She'd known Lucas would make an appearance here eventually. If he wasn't floating facedown in the Thames, that was. But he was safe, appeared to be all in one piece, so his interlude at The Broken Wheel must have been a success. How very wonderful for him.

Not that she cared.

He looked magnificent in his evening clothes. His blond hair shone a light gold beneath the many chandeliers. His blue gaze was perhaps more intense than usual, but she could easily pretend not to notice.

She could turn her back on him when he bowed in front of her, give him the cut direct. *That* would prove to him that she'd meant what she said this morning.

Could she do that? Could she really do that to him…to herself?

Damn him, no, she couldn't!

"Lady Daughtry," Lucas said as he bowed in front of the woman, who immediately snapped her fan shut and held out her hand to be kissed. "For a moment I thought I saw Lady Lydia standing here. My congratulations, my lady, for it is clear that you have discovered the secret of eternal youth."

"You're too kind, my lord," Helen gushed as Nicole did her best not to roll her eyes in disgust at the woman's eagerness to believe any flattery. "And, Lord Yalding, good evening to you," she continued, holding out her hand to the viscount, as well. "And how is your lovely mother? And all those daughters. We'll pray they turn into beauties, won't we, as we all know there's no hope for dowries."

"Mother!"

"Oh, don't sound so shocked, Nicole," Helen Daughtry said as Fletcher's ears turned bright red. "His lordship knows I'm only speaking the truth. Don't you, my lord? I would be suffering the same poor fate with you and your sister were it not for your uncle and cousins cocking up their toes so conveniently, so that Rafe could step into their shoes."

"Mama," Nicole whispered, squeezing the woman's elbow. "You're being incredibly rude, even for you."

"No, my dear, thanks to those fool patronesses at Almacks and such, the world has grown incredibly missish. We all used to be much more frank—and *frankly,* much more fun. Oh, look, there's Lord Frayne. And he's coming our way. I do hope I've saved him room on my dance card."

Nicole looked to her left and saw Lord Frayne indeed advancing toward them with some determination. But then he was detained by a gentleman wearing a puce waistcoat. Lord Frayne looked none too happy, whether with the man or his waistcoat she couldn't be sure.

Lucas reached out his hand and grabbed on to Nicole's arm. "Come outside with me," he said. Ordered. Commanded.

Nicole wanted to wrench her arm free, refuse him, but something in his eyes stopped her. "It's raining," she said, realizing how ridiculous that sounded.

"Yes, but it's considerably *cooler* out on the balcony, my lady," Lucas told her.

She wanted to be stubborn. "But my dance partner should be looking for me at any time."

"Fletcher? If Lady Nicole's dance partner shows himself, tell him the lady had better things to do than wait on him. Either that, or dance with him."

Lady Daughtry laughed, clearly not understanding what was going on, not that she'd ever admit to not being awake on all suits.

Nicole persisted. "And…and Lydia will be back soon."

"Fletcher?" Lucas prompted, his gaze still on Nicole.

"I'd much rather dance with her, yes, Lucas, I understand. But where are you—"

Nicole shook her arm free as Lucas tried to lead her toward the nearest set of French doors. "I won't be dragged along like some sack of meal, Lucas," she warned him.

"You'd rather stay in the ballroom and watch your mother embarrass you as she flirts with her new lover?"

"You already know the answer to that," she told him as he opened the door and motioned for her to precede him onto the balcony.

"Stay close to the wall and out of the rain," he instructed her—honestly, as if she were so harebrained as to not think of that herself!—as he looked to his left and right, as if trying to catch his bearings. "This way," he said, taking her hand and leading her to the right.

"Where are we going? Or does Lady Cornwallis also have small hidden rooms she leases to amorous gentlemen, erring wives and the occasional conspirator?"

Lucas looked back at her, grinning. "I see you're in fine fettle this evening, Lady Nicole. You look gorgeous, by the way. Pink suits you."

"I loathe pink. I only ordered this gown to upset my mother, who lives in the color. You cannot know how annoyed I am to have received so many compliments tonight. I may actually have to wear the dratted thing again."

He stopped in front of the last set of French doors and laid his hand on the handle. "Yes, I can see why that bothers you. But to be truthful, it's that fetching neckline that probably elicited so many compliments, although even the rawest of greenhorn admirers would have the sense to stop short of saying that your bosom looks quite delectable this evening, ma'am."

"You just said it."

"I know you like honesty. I was being honest. Honest enough to add that I find your freckles more alluring than any string of diamonds any other woman is wearing this evening."

Nicole fought down the urge to cover her neckline, and her dratted freckles, with her forearm. "You're the most impossible man I know."

"And how many men do you know, Nicole?" he asked her, depressing the handle and pushing open the door enough to peek inside. "Come. We can talk in here."

"But that's just it, Lucas," she told him mulishly

even as she followed him into the room, watching him as he crossed the room and locked the door that led to the rest of the mansion. He then repeated the action with the French doors. "I thought I made it very clear this morning that I don't want to talk to—"

The next thing she knew her back was pressed against the wall just inside the door and Lucas had her face cupped in his hands. "You're right, Nicole. We shouldn't talk, you and I. We shouldn't ever talk."

A joy she didn't know existed exploded inside her as his mouth came down on hers, a fierce, sudden hunger for this man that had her opening her mouth to him, had her arms sliding around him, her fingertips digging into his back as she took all he gave and returned it with everything that was in her.

His response was to drag his hands down the sides of her neck, over her bared shoulders. And then he stopped, just where her off-the-shoulder flounced neckline covered her skin. Leaving her feeling curiously frustrated, mildly angry that he was tantalizing her with a secret he didn't mean to share with her.

She hated secrets.

Remembering how he had felt pressed against her that morning, Nicole dared a forwardness she couldn't have conceived of even a week ago, before Lucas had stepped into her orbit and turned her world upside down with his very first smile. She dragged her hands down his back, all the way down past his waist, and then pulled him closer to her as she ground her lower body against his. She felt his hardness against her belly, and something inside her tightened almost painfully. But deliciously.

Lucas made a sound low in his throat—delighting her—and pulled back from their kiss to look down into her eyes.

"You don't know what you're doing," he told her, sounding slightly breathless.

"Then teach me, Lucas," she told him, so breathless herself it was difficult to give voice to her blatant dare. "Teach me."

He picked her up then, holding her close against him, walking with her until she felt the edge of a table against the backs of her legs. He lifted her so that she now sat on the edge and they were eye to eye, their breath mingling, their very heartbeats joined.

"When I'm with you, all I want to do is touch you. When I'm away from you, all I can do is think about you, and how much I long to touch you. To kiss you. To hold you. You feel it, too, Nicole, don't you? That's why you're so angry with me. I'm inside your head, just as you're inside mine."

She didn't look away from him, her mouth slightly open as she took shallow breaths, all she could manage as she watched his eyes darken, filling with some emotion she couldn't name, but that only added to the building pressure low in her groin.

"Yes…" she admitted, knowing neither of them would believe her if she lied. "I think about you all the time. Touching me…"

Nicole felt the tug on her neckline as Lucas worked the bodice of her gown lower, the material trapping her arms at her sides even as she felt the cool night air on her bared breasts.

Still, she concentrated on his face, on the way he looked at her, the hunger she now saw there, the way his eyes closed as she felt his hands cup her soft flesh.

She bit her bottom lip between her teeth when he opened his eyes once more, his expression now one of question. Was she all right? his eyes asked her. Was she frightened? Should he stop?

She wet her suddenly dry lips with the tip of her tongue. Her mother's words came back to her, nearly ruining this most wonderful moment. But the woman had also sanctioned this, hadn't she? Implying she had much to learn. "Teach me…"

He lowered his gaze, looking down at her, and she felt her nipples tightening in response, which amazed her. She didn't know what was happening to her, but clearly her body did. She gasped aloud as she felt his thumbs graze over those taut tips, calling up even more strange, delicious sensations.

Lucas dipped his head closer, pressing kisses against the side of her throat so that she lifted her chin, allowing her head to fall backward, offering him anything he wanted. His lips left a trail of fire across her chest, between her breasts, his thumbs still working their magic even as she knew there had to be more. She wanted more.

And then his mouth was on her, open over her nipple, warm and wet. His tongue was doing things to her she hadn't imagined possible, and when he sealed his mouth on her, drew her into him, his tongue moving faster, faster, she thought she might cry, the feeling was so intense.

Nicole's eyes shot open when she realized he'd somehow managed to inch up her skirts. How had he managed that without her noticing? How did she still breathe, think, when all she could do was feel?

His fingertips teased the sensitive skin of her inner thigh, just above the top of her silk stocking.

And then moved higher.

She didn't care. She couldn't care. She just wanted more. Whatever he wanted, she wanted. If that meant she was her mother's daughter, then so be it. Everything she had, she would give to this man, in this moment. She could no more deny him than she could deny the need to breathe.

She knew he wanted her to spread her legs for him, just instinctively knew it. Her body knew it.

And then he touched her. Intimately. Unbelievably. Insanely…incomprehensibly…indelibly.

The damnable design of her gown still trapping her arms to her sides, her body singing, soaring, Nicole buried her head against the side of Lucas's neck…and bit him. Holding him in place as his mouth incited her, as his fingers teased her and drove her and at last took her up and over some magical five-barred fence, so that she was flying, soaring, no longer chained to the earth or any of its constraints.

But she didn't come floating back down to the ground when it was over. She came down in a crash of need, still longing for more. She managed to free herself long enough to pull her bodice back up, releasing her arms…and then she was holding on to Lucas with all her might, wrapping her legs around his waist, trying to get inside him, become a part of him.

"Shh, shh, it's all right, sweetheart. It's all right," he soothed her, as she would soothe Juliet when the mare was frightened by a storm. But this storm had been inside Nicole herself, and although fading now, still held the power to keep her heartbeat racing out of control.

"Don't let go," she told him fiercely. "Please don't let me go. Not yet."

"I won't," he told her. "I can't.…"

He held her not for hours, only for minutes, perhaps. Time had no meaning for Nicole. She simply needed him to hold her, to stay with her. She wanted everything she'd sworn she never wanted, and she wanted it forever.

But nothing lasted forever.

"Hey. Hey, you in there! You think you're the only ones looking to get out of the rain?"

The question, called through the wooden door, was followed by a practiced, high-pitched giggle Nicole recognized instantly.

"My mother," she said in real horror, drawing back from Lucas, who helped her get down from what turned out to be a desk, probably Lord Cornwallis's desk. "Is that Lord Frayne with her?"

"I don't think so, no," Lucas said as he helped her smooth down her skirts and fix the flounce at her bodice that was half tucked into itself.

"It's *not?* But that would mean that—"

"Yes, I think it would. Nicole, are you all right? I didn't plan… I didn't bring you in here to— Oh, bloody hell."

The knocking had begun again, along with the jiggling of the latch.

Lucas took Nicole's hand. "Come on. We'll leave the way we came in."

"You're not going to unlock the other door?"

"So you can say hello to your mother? Hardly." He smiled, and the embarrassment Nicole had begun to feel creeping in as her passion at last cooled disappeared. She was still Nicole, and he was still Lucas. Something had changed. Something very important and extremely elemental to both of them. But they were still the same people.

"You're right. Let them stand out there. Where do we go now?"

"Back to the ballroom. You've already been gone too long."

He unlocked the French doors and they stepped outside, staying close to the wall once more as they made their way along the deserted balcony.

Just before they reached the set of doors they'd used to leave the ballroom Nicole asked him, "What happened tonight? You were going to tell me, weren't you?"

"I was, yes. Tomorrow, Nicole. I'll tell you everything tomorrow, and you can either turn from me in disgust, or forgive me."

"I don't understand."

"No, I know you don't. But I do, at last."

Clearly he wasn't going to tell her anything else, not now. She followed him back inside the overheated ballroom, the two of them stepping straight behind a wide pillar fronted by a concealing palm.

"You go first, and then I'll join you. Your sister is right over there, with Fletcher. If anyone asks, you were with your mother, who felt ill from the heat. God knows she's not in the ballroom to make liars out of us. Go on."

Nicole did as he said, stepping out from behind the pillar and walking quickly over to her sister. "Well, *here* you are," she said in some exasperation. "I've been looking all over for you. Our dearest *maman* says the heat had made her ill and insisted I accompany her to the front doors, where she could stand under the portico and cool her agitated brain, or whatever. Personally, I think she's simply had too much wine."

"You were with *Maman?*" Lydia looked confused. "But...but Lord Yalding said you left with Lord Basingstoke."

"You did?" she asked the viscount, who immediately took a great interest in his shirtcuff. "Oh, yes, I remember now. I was with him, for a moment, arguing with him, as usual. But then *Maman*...well, let's just say that the next time she decides to suffer an attack of the vapors, Lydia, she'd be wiser to apply to you for sympathy."

"Lucas! There you are," Lord Yalding exclaimed, rather like a drowning man who has just spied a longboat packed full with rescuers. "Lord Frayne was looking for you earlier. He seemed hot to see you."

"Yes, I can imagine he might be," Lucas said quietly. "What did you say to him?"

Fletcher shrugged. "Nothing much. Just that you were probably around here somewhere, since you brought me here in your coach and you wouldn't have gone off and left me here. You wouldn't have, would you?"

"I wouldn't even consider such a shabby thing. I am, however, famished. As it would seem the musicians have signaled an intermission, would anyone else care to go down to supper?"

"You're not going to go look for Lord Frayne? I told you, he was most anxious to speak with you. Most anxious."

Nicole looked at Lucas, waiting for his response.

"And that, Fletcher, would be Lord Frayne's problem, not mine. Ladies, shall we?"

Nicole slipped her hand through Lucas's offered arm, wondering if anyone who looked at them could tell what they had been doing not ten minutes earlier—she felt as if everyone should be able to see *something* on her face.

"Why are you avoiding Lord Frayne?" she asked him as they followed several other couples down the marble stairs to a large chamber below the ballroom that had been set aside for refreshments.

"I'm not ignoring Lord Frayne. I'm paying outrageous court to you. And I'd be extremely gratified if you would look up at me adoringly, since I find I'm in no mood to let you out of my sight for the rest of the evening and otherwise I might be forced to punch some poor fool in the nose for daring to interrupt us."

And with those supposedly light and teasing words, Nicole knew. "You're still in danger, aren't you?"

"Yesterday I would have lied to you and said no. Perhaps I would have lied to you this morning, although I believed at the time I was prepared to tell you the truth, even if it damned me in your eyes. Tonight? Ah, tonight I can say very honestly and openly—yes, it's possible."

"Lord Frayne," Nicole said, and sighed. "Oh, Lucas, what did you do?"

He was silent until they had found an empty table and he'd helped her into her chair. Then he leaned down toward her and told her quietly, "Tomorrow, Nicole. We'll talk more tomorrow. What I will say now is that what I've done today, earlier this evening, is to learn the difference between what is important to me, and what is really important. Now I have to decide what I'm going to do about it."

She watched him as he and Fletcher went in search of plates of food for them all, sighing quietly as she remembered his touch, her tumultuous reaction to that touch. She felt so close to him, and yet still so far away.

Intimate strangers, that's what they were now, which sounded almost poetical but was, in reality, exceedingly disturbing.

CHAPTER ELEVEN

LUCAS LIT A CHEROOT with a paper spill from the fireplace, glancing toward the mantel clock before tossing the spill back into the flames.

The clock had just chimed twice.

The note Lucas had penned to Frayne, to be delivered to the man by one of the Cornwallis servants, had been clear: *Discretion and cool heads are strongly suggested, my lord. I will be your guest one hour after midnight.*

Frayne was keeping him waiting, undoubtedly in retribution for the way Lucas had avoided him at the Cornwallis ball. He could only wonder if the delay had been planned in order to show that he, Frayne, was the one in charge, or if he expected Lucas to spend the hour quaking in his evening shoes, fearful of the man's power.

Either way, the man was doomed to disappointment.

Lucas turned toward the door to the study as he heard the latch depress, and watched dispassionately as Lord Frayne entered, his waistcoat undone, his cravat loosened. His age showing.

"I've just spoken to the men you saw tonight, and it seems I misjudged you, Basingstoke, gave you credit for an intelligence you do not possess. You're as stupid as your father before you," he said without preamble. "I thought you understood our bargain."

"I thought I did, as well," Lucas told him, sitting down in one of the wing chairs flanking the fireplace, crossing one long leg over the other. "As it turns out, I was wrong. I find now that I have other priorities, as well."

Lord Frayne shrugged his shoulders before crossing to the drinks table and pouring himself a glass of port. Glass in hand, he walked across the carpet, to stand directly in front of Lucas's chair, to glare down at him, a sneer on his face. "You probably believe your outburst tonight at The Broken Wheel changed things, don't you? That you damaged your government's plan."

Lucas drew on his cheroot and then slowly blew out a stream of smoke, making the man wait for his answer.

"You mean *your* plan, Frayne, yours and whoever else may be involved. I believe I understand you now. You mean to draw even more power into your hands. More than our mad king, more than our proliferate Regent. More even than Sidmouth and Liverpool, who might share some of your beliefs and even think they understand your plan, but lack the ability to see beyond control of Parliament."

"Small men, small minds, limited ambitions," Frayne said dismissively. "As for our brain-addled

German king and his wastrel sons? They are all clearly superfluous."

Lucas hid his surprise at Frayne's honest statement of his intentions. It was knowledge Lucas would be safer without, clearly. Yet he pressed the man for more information.

"It's all you think you need to gather all the power to yourselves, don't you? One good show of insurrection. A few hundred dead, the good citizens of London frightened half out of their wits that there will be full-fledged revolution, guillotines set up in every square."

"You didn't seem so squeamish when I asked you to join us."

Lucas stood up, knowing he stood a full head taller than Frayne, who backed up several paces rather than be forced to tip his head back to look up at him. "No, I didn't. And I have to live with that. I was willing to trade my beliefs, my integrity, for the dangled promise of learning who is responsible for my father's disgrace."

"A favor for a favor. You understood that well enough. You were quite articulate, defending the downtrodden. You could have been brilliant at rousing them to action. I couldn't have hoped for a more effective *agent provocateur* to set the cat amidst the pigeons. Those men you heard earlier this evening? They, and the others like them, are serviceable, but they none of them think too quickly if forced to vary from the script they've been trained to recite. They tell me that after your outburst some of their audience began questioning them, doubting their ability to arm them and protect them from the king's troops. That wasn't helpful to me, Basingstoke."

"I'm sure you'll find some way to overcome that small defeat. Men like you always do. But, as you now know, it will be without me. We're done, you and I."

"Your father meant that little to you?"

Lucas didn't answer. He tossed the cheroot into the fireplace and turned his back, eager to be out of the man's company.

But Frayne obviously didn't plan on being dismissed so easily. "I saw you skulking off with that black-haired bit tonight, you know. A lady in name, but obviously with the morals of a whore," he called after Lucas. "Just like the mother. I could have her as easily as I've had the mother."

Lucas stopped where he was, turned and retraced his steps until he was inches from Lord Frayne. "Have a care, old man."

"Oh, so it goes deeper than I imagined. Splendid. You keep your own counsel, Basingstoke, about what you know, and I'll keep mine. Otherwise…" He let his words fade away as he shrugged.

"Say what it is you're so anxious to say."

"Very well, if I have to lead you by the nose, I will. I can destroy the mother. She writes letters, you understand. Very, shall we say, *frank* letters. And, as she's as enamored of the idea of trapping me into marriage as she is her new title, she also signs them."

Lucas felt his stomach clench. "So?"

"*So,* my idealistic friend, she's barely tolerated now, our dearest Helen. If the letters were to fall into the wrong hands, the lady would go down, and her daughters with her. There are already those who question how convenient it was for the late duke and both his sons to have perished the way they did, opening the way for Helen's brat to come into the title. Oh, Basingstoke, if ever I saw a family more ripe for destruction, I can't remember it. Unless—" he paused, smiling "—I think back to the day your father killed himself in order to spare his wife and son seeing him publicly hanged."

"My father was not a traitor to his country. You said as much yourself."

"Did I? I say a lot of things. And do you know what, Basingstoke? People believe what I say. *You* did. You should believe what I say now, however, you really should. One word, a single word of what you think you know, and I'll begin talking. Do we understand each other?"

So it had been a lie? All of it? Frayne knew nothing about his father's disgrace, his death or the men who as good as murdered him? It had been a lie, and he'd been so eager to believe that he'd tossed his own integrity to the four winds and agreed to do Frayne's bidding?

Frayne's smile answered Lucas's silent questions: *Yes, yes, yes.*

Lucas could imagine his hands around Frayne's neck as he slowly squeezed the life out of the man. He could see Frayne's mocking eyes bulging half out of his head, and then going flat and empty. Lucas had never felt so close to violence in his life. It would be so easy.

"We understand each other," he said at last, and quit the room.

"BUT YOU CAN'T," LYDIA SAID, panic evident in her voice as she followed her sister into her dressing room. "You simply can't."

Nicole found the gloves Renée had sworn she couldn't find, and turned to her sister. "Of course I can, Lydia. I rode out with Lucas yesterday with Charlotte's approval. There's no reason I can't *drive* out with him this afternoon. It's perfectly proper."

Lydia walked over to a chair and sat down heavily. "I know *that,* Nicole, even though I am finding it difficult to know when you like his lordship, when you loathe him and when you want me to believe you feel nothing at all for him. The drawing room is stuffed full of so many flowers from your admirers—"

"*Our* admirers, Lydia. Several of those posies and bouquets were meant for you, as you well know. As are at least half of the cards gentlemen left here since we decided—*you* decided, as I remember it—that we weren't receiving this morning. The Duke of Malvern, I noticed, both sent around a lovely bouquet and left his card."

"Yes, and that's it, Nicole, that's the whole of it, and why you can't leave me. He's coming back. He was speaking to me during the movements of the dance—impossible to do, really—and I found it easiest just to agree with him as if I'd really been paying attention to all he said, and…and, somehow, I agreed to take in the Elgin Marbles with him this afternoon."

Nicole leaned against the high bureau, grinning at her sister's obvious panic. "Lydia, sweetheart, what terrible thing do you suppose is going to happen? You'll go, you'll say something excruciatingly intelligent about each silly broken bit of marble, and then you'll return here. All in all, a pleasant, if boring, afternoon. The man doesn't bite, you know."

Lydia looked down at her hands, which were twisting in her lap. "I never said he did."

"No, but you act as if he's some terrible bogeyman, when he's really just a man."

"Every…every time I see him I'm reminded of…"

Nicole went down on her knees in front of her sister's chair, her heart aching for her twin. Still, some things had to be said. "It isn't the duke's fault that he lived, Lydia, and Captain Fitzgerald died. Like Rafe, he was the captain's friend. Unlike Rafe, he was there when the captain died. Do you think you're the only one who lost somebody very dear to them that day?"

Lydia raised her head, her huge blue eyes shining with unshed tears. "I don't know what happened that day. I don't want to know. But when I see the duke, I find myself longing to ask him. I…I wonder if he feels the same. If he wants to tell me. It's why I try so hard to avoid him."

"But you can't avoid him, Lydia. He's Rafe's

friend. I happen to know that His Grace has been invited to dinner tomorrow night, for one thing. If you cry off today, it will only be to see him tomorrow."

Lydia sighed and got to her feet, taking hold of her sister's hands and squeezing them. "I'm not ready, Nicole. A single dance, a guest at the dinner table. They're very different from being with the man for an entire afternoon. He's very kind, and I never seem to have anything to say to him. Please. Please say you and the marquess will come with us. *Please*."

THE DUKE OF MALVERN had arranged for a private showing of the Elgin Marbles so that Lydia could spend as much time as she wanted touring the extensive collection.

Nicole was liking the man more and more.

They entered the building quickly, doing their best not to notice the poorly dressed people, men, women and children, milling about outside, crying out to all who would listen: "We don't want stones! Give us bread! Give us bread!"

"We can thank Cruikshank for that," the Duke of Malvern said as the door closed behind them and a guide led them toward the collection of sculptures, chiseled bits of inscription, even entire sections of the frieze that once adorned the Parthenon. "I saw the cartoons he's put up in his shop window."

"'John Bull buying stones at a time his numerous family want bread,'" Lucas said as he cupped

Nicole's elbow, guiding her up the stairs in the nearly windowless building that temporarily housed the collection. "I imagine it's difficult for the people in the streets to see the need for Parliament to have just authorized the expenditure of thirty-five thousand pounds for *stones*. Not when their children are going to bed hungry."

"Don't forget the ten thousand pounds just allocated to construct proper housing for the collection," the duke added, and then turned to Lydia. "And now we're ruining your enjoyment, aren't we? Keep in mind, Lady Lydia, that what may seem folly to so many is at the same time preserving treasures that could otherwise be lost to us, and to future civilizations. We probably owe Lord Elgin a debt of gratitude. For the moment, however, all the man has is debt. Mountains of it."

They began walking around the perimeter of the first large room, only to see that much of the collection housed there was still concealed in wooden crates.

"Not all of his debt comes from shipping half of Greece here," Lucas told Nicole as he steered her away from the other couple. "The man's wife tired of watching the Elgin coffers go bare on, as John Bull says, *stones,* and abandoned him for another man a decade ago. The divorce was very public and quite scandalous. More than Greek and Roman statuary, more than most any work of great art you can imagine, our countrymen love a scandal."

"You say that as if in warning," Nicole told him, pretending an interest in a headless statue that also was missing one arm and most of one leg. She was hard-pressed to understand how this particular ruined creation could be considered a boon to future civilizations.

But her sister was clearly enamored, which probably made her, Nicole, a hopeless Philistine. That was usually the case, she knew, with Lydia's interests intellectually high, and hers more attuned to admiring superb horseflesh and perhaps a perfectly prepared joint of beef.

"Are you planning a scandal?" she asked him teasingly. "Lucas? I asked you a question."

He seemed to mentally shake himself before he answered her. "No, at least not today. Come with me. There are several more rooms to wander through. Your sister won't miss us."

Nicole looked over her shoulder to see Lydia, an open pamphlet describing the pieces in her hand as she bent down to inspect several lengths of marble frieze that had been pieced together to re-create the design of horsemen all in a row. "You're probably right. She's completely forgotten she didn't want to come here today. Where are we going?"

"Somewhere I can kiss you, if that's all right with you," he told her, opening doors and peeking into rooms until he at last seemed to be satisfied that he'd found the right one. He made her an elegant leg, sweeping his arm toward the doorway, inviting her to go inside. "If madame is so inclined?"

"Madame would say no, except then madame would be lying through her teeth," she told him quietly, looking behind her once more before stepping into the dimness of what appeared to be a storage room.

He closed the door behind them, nearly reducing them to total darkness, and put his hands on her shoulders. "Are you all right?" he asked her. "Last night…I didn't mean for what happened to happen. I didn't take you there for that to happen. I was so…so full of myself, I suppose I should say, after what I'd done. Still with my blood running stupidly hot. And then I saw you standing there. So beautiful, so perfectly wonderful, and with me knowing I could have lost you, knowing you could just as easily turn away from me as say hello to me, and I— Oh, never mind. How can I apologize for something I can't regret?"

She wished she could see his face. "I'd say very prettily, although you certainly have my permission to stop now. You said you wanted to kiss me."

"I did, didn't I," he said, and she sensed him moving closer to her. She put her hands on his waist as he brought his mouth down on hers, and it was like returning home after years and years spent away. She fit in his arms perfectly, their bodies had been fashioned for each other, the fates had ordained them.

He ran his hands over her familiarly, and her body responded instantly, melting against him, encouraging him.

"Enough," he said, carefully pushing her away from him. "No, that's not true. That wasn't nearly enough, but we need to talk. I need to tell you so many things. I'd hoped we could be alone this afternoon. I'd engaged a private dining room at an inn not often frequented by the *ton*. Damn! All this sneaking around has to stop, Nicole. I must speak with Rafe. We need to marry. You understand that."

Of course Lucas would think she'd agree with him. He'd compromised her, not without her help and agreement, and they both knew that convention dictated he was obliged to marry her now, whether either of them wished it or not.

Life was so much simpler for men who were not titled, for women who were not sister to a duke. Momentary madness or truest love, whatever had brought them to this point—neither mattered. Society would say that they'd made a decision with their passions that they would have to live with for the rest of their lives. The man was then free to take mistresses and the woman, once she'd produced a few male heirs that at least nominally resembled her husband, could take lovers. Her mother had explained it all to her with some glee, and it was all fairly depressing.

Nicole sighed and stepped away from him. "You keep saying that."

"And I keep meaning it."

"Yes, I'm sure you do," she told him, folding her arms across her waist, feeling herself retreating from him and sure he knew what she was doing. "You…um, you can't resist me. And before you laugh at me," she went on quickly, "I can't seem to resist you, either. And that's all very nice, Lucas, but—"

"Pardon me?" he interrupted, not without humor. "You're objecting to our attraction to each other?"

She was becoming exasperated. "I have from the very beginning, if you'll remember. It—this *attraction* we seem to have—has all been very inconvenient, for both of us."

"Because you didn't come to London to catch a husband."

"Yes! It's all so tawdry, Lucas. Being dressed up and put on parade. The gowns, the parties, the rides in the Park. They should be delicious fun, but in the end, they're all so…so calculated. How large is her dowry? What do you think, are her hips wide enough to be a good breeder? Gad, look at those teeth—I wouldn't want to saddle any son of mine with those higgledy-piggledy chompers, not even for twenty thousand a year. And before you laugh, I heard someone saying that just last night at the ball."

"All right. I'll agree with you. The Marriage Mart, if examined too closely, is rather an embarrassment to civilized people. But what has that got to do with us?"

Did he have to ask such intelligent questions? "I don't know! I just know this wasn't why I came to London. I never planned to marry anyone. *Ever.*"

"Would it help at all to say that I believe I'm most probably falling in love with you?"

"No, because I wouldn't believe you," she answered honestly, even as she couldn't deny a delicious tingle running through her at his words. "I'm not a very lovable person. I'm shallow, and I'm silly, and horribly stubborn. And selfish. When you're not kissing me, you're arguing with me, and usually for good reason. I can't help it that I'm…that I'm pretty, and that you want to kiss me. I *wanted* you to kiss me. I wanted…I wanted everything. People shouldn't marry for *wanting,* Lucas."

"So what you're saying is that I have been dazzled by a shallow, willful child, and I'd be a bloody fool to ask for your hand in marriage? I see."

Oh, she could hit him! "You didn't have to say it just that way, but yes, that's what I mean. And…and I thank you very much for caring so much for my reputation, except that I highly doubt you're about to climb to the top of Saint Paul's and call out to all and sundry that you have compromised me. What we did, what we may still do unless you've either taken me in disgust now or decide to never see me again? That's *our* concern. It's what we want. What *we* do should have nothing to do with anyone else."

"And you believe all of this," he said, turning for the door. "You really believe that what two people do has no effect on anyone else."

She felt tears stinging at her eyes. "No," she said quietly, at last admitting the truth. "I can't have lived so much of my life at the whims of my mother and believe that. I just need to know I'm nothing like her."

He'd opened the door a crack, but then immediately shut it.

"You're *nothing* like your mother," he told her, cupping his palm against her cheek. "My God, Nicole, how can you even think that?"

"Perhaps…perhaps because we did what we did at the theater. Perhaps because of what we did last night. And both times, Lucas—both times!—there she was, doing the same thing. Casting out her lures, attempting to reel in yet another fish, a fourth husband to tell her that she's young, and beautiful, and exciting. She as good as told me to allow you whatever you wanted. Not too soon, of course, as you might not wish to buy what you can get for free."

"Damn the woman," Lucas swore quietly, "is there no end to the trouble she can cause?"

"Lucas? What are you talking about? What other trouble has she caused?"

"No, not right now, sweetheart," he told her, taking her hand and heading for the door to the storeroom once again. "Your sister will be looking for you. But we're not done with this. I need to see you tonight. I'm imagining you're invited to Lady Hertford's rout?"

"Among other events, yes. But I won't change my mind, you know," she told him, knowing her tone lacked conviction.

"I'm sure you believe that," he said, kissing her cheek, leaving her wanting so much more. "I'd be disheartened, if I didn't believe I'm going to very much enjoy showing you the error of your thinking."

They stepped out into the larger room to see Lydia and the duke just entering it, Lydia still with her booklet open, clearly on the hunt for more bits and pieces of statuary.

"You sound very sure of yourself, my lord," Nicole told him, blinking as her eyes readjusted to the sunlight spilling in through windows high on the wall. "It's very annoying of you."

He smiled down at her as he offered her his arm. "And I'm looking forward to *annoying* you more this evening. But I'm tiring of closets, aren't you? If the weather stays fine, perhaps tonight I'll *annoy* you in Lady Hertford's garden."

Nicole was about to respond to that laughing threat, but she found she had nothing to say. After all, agreeing with him wouldn't help matters at all, would it?

"I'd rather, I think, we talk about what you did last night at The Broken Wheel."

"I'm sure you would," he said.

"That was no answer," she told him, tugging on his sleeve as he tried to guide her back to her sister.

"All right then. Yes, I'll tell you. I'll tell you everything. And then you may feel free to turn down my proposal again, this time for good reason."

CHAPTER TWELVE

WHITE'S WAS RATHER THIN of company, probably because the cold and damp had been joined by a thick yellow fog that entered the fashionable club each time the front door was opened, so that it now clung just above the floor like a malicious cloud.

Lucas passed by an older gentleman who was being helped to the foyer by one of the servants. The man was coughing violently into a large handkerchief.

"Good afternoon, Lord Harper," Lucas said, expecting the man to cut him dead, for he had been one of those who'd been quite vocal when he'd made his impromptu speech about the volcano, the weather, its threat to the harvest and the need to assist those who would suffer most from all of it. "You look unwell. May I assist you to your carriage?"

Lord Harper pulled the handkerchief from his mouth and glared at Lucas. "You can bloody well go to hell, Basingstoke, that's what you can do. This damnable fog is all your fault. A man can't breathe!" He replaced his handkerchief as another round of coughing took him.

Lucas did his best not to smile. "I beg your pardon?"

"Yes, you bloody well should! It's as if you *wished* this poisonous weather on us, what with your doom and gloom predictions. I'm packing up and leaving for the country, away from all these chimneys belching smoke that never seems to go higher than a kite before coming back down on us."

"It will still be cool and rainy in the country, my lord," Lucas pointed out, still not without humor.

"Is that so? Then I'll know who to blame for *that,* too, won't I!"

The servant rolled his eyes at Lucas, who inclined his head in a small bow—to the servant or his lordship would be his secret. He handed his hat and cloak to another servant and continued on to the club room, to meet with Rafael Daughtry, Duke of Ashurst.

"Thanks for meeting me, Rafe."

"How could I resist, when your note included a warning not to let anyone else know? And by anyone, I'm fairly certain you meant Nicole." Rafe stood up and the two men shook hands before a servant brought over another glass and placed it on the small table set up between the pair of wing chairs closest to the fireplace.

"Fletcher left for the country this morning, summoned by his mother, and complained that his coach was sure to get mired in the mud at least a dozen times on its way to Hastings. How was your trip?" Lucas asked, pouring himself a glass from the decanter.

"Other than the mud, you mean? Because Fletcher's right about that. Better than it would have been a year ago, thanks to my dear wife, who has schooled me in how to behave as a duke should when confronted with a dilemma such as the one I faced at our Kent estate. I dismissed the estate manager, hired another, was able to straighten out the account books—a year ago I would not have had a harlot's prayer at deciphering them—and ordered a new stone for the grist mill. There are still moments when I think of myself as the soldier I was, the poor relation I was, a man with few expectations, but they're becoming fewer."

Lucas hadn't been looking for an opening quite so soon in their conversation, but now that he had it, he asked, "How did your uncle and cousins die? I'm afraid I'm woefully behind on much of what occurred while I was with Wellington."

Rafe raised his glass and took a healthy sip of his wine, not quite meeting Lucas's eyes as he answered. "It was a boating accident. A new yacht, a sudden storm, and everyone aboard was lost. No bodies were recovered. I received word from my aunt Emmaline while I was still in Paris."

Sensing he wasn't hearing the entire truth, Lucas put down his wineglass and leaned forward in his chair. "Then there's no one who saw the yacht go down?"

"No. Why?"

Lucas sighed. Rafe was his friend. The man's wife was soon to give him his first heir. Their happiness was evident, he'd seen that for himself on his visit to Grosvenor Square. Rafe was a good man, a good soldier. There had never been a hint of wrong-doing attached to his name, Lucas was sure of that. But this story was ripe for any sort of scandal when someone like Lord Frayne was doing the telling.

"I should begin at the beginning," Lucas said, motioning for the servant to bring another decanter.

"Perhaps you should," Rafe said, eyeing him with some suspicion. "I thought you asked me here to apply for Nicole's hand. Or at least Charlie—my wife—did. What do my late uncle and cousins have to do with anything?"

"Nothing, Rafe. They have nothing to do with anything. Or at least they shouldn't. I'm afraid I've managed to put all of us into a dilemma. Let me explain."

He began with the death of his father, a death he and his mother had believed a coward's suicide to escape his traitorous actions, and went on quickly to the anonymous letter he'd received a year ago, telling him that his father had been innocent of any wrong-doing. He quickly passed over his year-long search for the person or persons responsible, instead re-counting his scolding of his contemporaries right here in White's not even a week ago—it seemed years ago now—and the subsequent offer to trade information for assistance.

"I was fully prepared to help the man, Rafe, make no mistake about that. I was being offered answers I'd been looking for, something to ease my mother's pain, which has been constant for fifteen years. She has refused to come into Society ever since my father's death, and her health is none too good. If I could give her answers? I wanted to believe what I was being told, Rafe. But when it came down to it, as it did last night, I couldn't do what I'd promised. Not for myself, not even for her."

"That doesn't surprise me. You were always a man of honor, Lucas. Now tell me the rest. How does this concern my uncle and cousins?"

"And your mother," Lucas said, refilling both their glasses.

"My *mother?* Christ, Lucas, should I be calling for another decanter?"

Again Lucas explained quickly. His silence about the plans and motives of the man who had approached him in exchange for the man's silence on the supposed questionable circumstances of the late duke's drowning and that of his sons. Lady Daughtry's unfortunate letters kept safely locked away. Nicole, Lydia, all of them, kept free from a scandal that could, at the very least, effectively banish them from Society.

"And you believe him, this man whom you seem curiously reluctant to name?"

"I believe he's capable of most anything to protect himself, to further his ambition, yes. I also think that as long as the man has ammunition in his pistol— your mother's letters—none of us can ever feel entirely safe."

"I agree," Rafe said, a muscle working in his cheek.

"I thought you would. In addition, there's his plans for this country. Which is why I asked to meet with you today. A march on Parliament, Rafe, with the government's troops informed, and waiting for them as they cross Westminster Bridge? How do I turn a blind eye on that plan? The blood shed on that bridge would be on my hands. I don't fool myself, believing there won't eventually be riots if the weather doesn't improve, if the harvests are as poor as we all think they're going to be. Our country has seen such civil unrest before. But I could stop this one march, this one riot."

"I won't ask you how you could stop it, but I believe you. I also agree that you have to do everything you can to prevent what could very well become a massacre."

"Thank you for that. At the same time, how do I proceed, knowing I would be opening you and your family to such dangerous scandal and supposition if I did? That you murdered, ordered murdered your own uncle and cousins in order to claim the title? Brand your mother a whore?"

"Give me his name," Rafe said tightly.

Lucas had been expecting the question. "For you to do what, Rafe? Confront him? I'd go with you, if I thought that would do any good."

"No, directly confronting him wouldn't work for us, I agree. But as my friend Fitz used to say, if you dig a grave for others you may fall into it yourself. It sounds to me like this man needs a small push into this grave he's so industriously digging for others."

"All right," Lucas said, remembering yet again why he'd always liked Rafe Daughtry. "Let's talk about how we're going to do this pushing. Oh, but before we begin, I probably should tell you that I'm going to marry Nicole."

"Really," Rafe said, his fierce expression softening. "Does she know?"

"She knows. She's refused me. Twice—or perhaps that's three times. I think I've lost count."

Rafe nodded. "That sounds like Nicole. Charlotte's told me a lot about what Lydia and Nicole's lives were like while I was gone. Lydia adapted very well to being shuttled back and forth between our small holding of Willowbrook and my uncle's estate as our mother's whims decreed. But Charlie couldn't say the same for Nicole. Emmaline, my aunt, gave up trying to control her wild starts. I don't know what all she dared, and don't think I want to, but I do know this—my sister has told everyone, repeatedly, that she will never marry. Probably because our mother has married so often."

Lucas decided to keep his own counsel about Nicole's reasons, her fears, real or imagined. "I do love her, Rafe. I think I've loved her since the day we met, crazy as that seems, and she nearly knocked me over, in more ways than one. I can say without modesty that she shares my feelings—although she would rather bite off her own tongue than agree with me. I've considered throwing her across my saddle and riding her to Gretna Green to marry over the anvil, not that I believe it will come to that. I just want you to know that she's safe with me."

"I would never doubt that for a moment, my

friend," Rafe said, holding out his wineglass for a toast. "I only wish I could say with the same conviction that *you're* safe with her."

NICOLE FELT RAFE'S EYES on her as she faced him on the velvet squabs of his town carriage. She even fussed with her thin shawl for a few moments, attempting to surreptitiously draw it closer over her breasts, fearful that he'd think her gown too mature for a debutante. After all, how could one explain to one's own brother that sometimes nature dictated fashion, and no amount of clever tailoring could hide what was simply *there*.

Finally, when she could no longer ignore his looks, his small smile, she lifted her chin and addressed him in her usual frank way.

"What's so amusing, Rafe? Or are you simply hoping I'll break into song at any moment?"

"Nicole!" Lydia exclaimed beside her.

Nicole ignored her. "Rafe?" she persisted. "Are you going to tell me, or do I have to guess? Let me see, all right? Charlotte told you that I've overspent my allowance again. No, that wouldn't have you smiling, would it? Very well, then, what would have you smiling? Would it be too much to ask that our mother informed you that she is leaving for Paris in the morning, prepared for a stay of at least a year?"

"I didn't know the former, and we could none of us be so fortunate as to be gifted with the latter, no. I was merely thinking about a conversation I had earlier today with our friend the marquess."

Nicole's stomach knotted. "He came to you? I told him not to do that, and he did it anyway? What's *wrong* with that man?"

"He doesn't shake in his boots when you give orders?" Lydia suggested, suddenly both her sister and her brother sharing their own small joke at Nicole's expense. "How extraordinarily courageous of him."

"We should consider petitioning the king to issue the man a commendation for bravery," Rafe agreed, nodding.

"Oh, aren't the pair of you amusing," Nicole spat, turning to look out the window of the carriage, not really seeing anything save her own anger. "I won't marry him, you know. So it doesn't matter what you said to him."

Rafe didn't answer her, and Lydia had decided to check her reticule to make sure her maid had tucked a clean handkerchief in it, or some such thing.

The carriage inched forward in the crush of vehicles all making their way to Lady Hertford's rout.

When she couldn't stand the silence any longer, Nicole said, "So? What did you say to him?"

"I didn't say anything to him," Rafe told her, once again showing her hints of a smile she knew was very like her own—so she also knew that he was enjoying himself mightily at her expense. "He didn't come asking for my permission to marry you."

"He didn't?" For the very first time in her life, Nicole knew she was actually blushing, hot color running into her cheeks. "Well…well then, why did he come to see you?"

"Did I say that he came to see me? I don't think I did. We met at White's. We may meet there again, or somewhere else, as we travel in much the same circles. Unless you want to forbid me from speaking to the man?"

Nicole's eyes narrowed as she glared across the carriage at her brother. "You did that on purpose. You made me think something when that something wasn't what I should have been thinking at all. Didn't you?"

Rafe folded one long leg over the other as he looked at her. "Charlie's right, your mind is a corkscrew, and following it on its journey is a recipe for exhaustion. I have no idea why the man would want to marry you."

"He doesn't! You said he didn't ask you."

"Ah, yes. But I didn't say he didn't *tell* me. As his friend, I should probably have attempted to talk some sense into him, but he seemed determined, poor deluded fellow. And we're finally here."

He leaned forward and undid the latch, hesitating as a groom prepared to lower the steps so that he could descend to the flagway and then assist his sisters.

"Ladies, I'll escort you upstairs and then retire to the gaming room, as I'm promised to a few friends for whist. I'll come searching for you at midnight. In the meantime, Lydia, I understand Viscount Yalding would like to hear all about your

visit to the Elgin Marbles. As for you, Nicole—
behave yourself, and if you can't do that, please be
discreet. In other words, when the marquess pre-
sents himself to you, as I already know he will,
don't immediately begin yelling at him like a
fishwife, all right?"

Nicole thought about refusing to leave the carriage, but what would that prove, other than that she
could be exceedingly stubborn, which everyone
already knew. Besides, Lucas was most probably
already inside, and she couldn't very well strangle
him from out here on the street, now could she?

The wide marble steps leading up into the public
areas of the Hertford mansion were clogged five
across with guests waiting to be greeted by their host
and hostess. Nicole wanted to tell them all to go
home, or go do something at least mildly productive.
All they were doing now was delaying her confron-
tation with Lucas.

The cloying scents of too many perfumes mingled
with the sweat of those who gave perfume more credit
than it commanded when compared to the frequent
application of soap and water. Feather plumes began
to wilt in the heat caused by the close proximity of
so many bodies, and conversation dwindled to
nothing more than complaints that their hostess might
believe a "sad crush" was the epitome of success for
her rout, but for her guests the whole thing was beginning to seem more like a colossal failure.

By the time Nicole and her siblings had
mounted the last step, she had considered and dis-

carded any number of ways she would greet Lucas when she saw him. As twenty minutes stretched past a half hour, her anger had disintegrated into embarrassment and then, finally, all feelings deserted her save wanting to grant him anything if he would rescue her from this crowd and get her something cold to drink.

She spied Lucas and Viscount Yalding nearly at once after smiling at her hostess, who also seemed to have passed beyond being delighted with the great number of the *ton* who had chosen her rout as their premier event of the evening, and wanted nothing more now than to go somewhere and sit down. Rafe's greeting and compliments to the woman were met with a slightly harassed, "Yes, yes, thank you, Your Grace. Keep moving, please."

"Come on, Lydia," Nicole said to her sister, taking hold of her elbow and only nodding to Lord Hertford as they brushed past him. "See them? They're holding glasses of lemonade for us. I can forgive any number of sins in a man that considerate."

"Then you aren't going to tear a strip off his hide for telling Rafe he's going to marry you?"

"I said forgive, Lydia, not forget. You won't be appalled if the marquess and I sneak off somewhere for a while to be private, will you?"

Lydia's smile was back. "Since he's going to marry you? No, I suppose not."

Nicole looked at her sister, the quiet, well-behaved, never troublesome sister who would never say boo to a goose. "You're enjoying my frustrations, aren't you?"

"Not enjoying them, Nicole, not precisely. But I will admit it is rather pleasant to see you befuddled. You've always been so sure of yourself, so very much in charge of yourself, and everyone around you. And, yes, you did always seem to have a way of making everything happen just as you wanted it to happen. Now, thanks to his lordship, you can perhaps understand how we lesser, less sure mortals feel. It will probably do you good."

Nicole forgot about her thirst, pulling Lydia to a halt, which nearly sent the couple behind them crashing into them, until she could take her sister aside. "You make me sound terrible. And *bossy*. How have you put up with me all these years?"

Lydia squeezed her hand. "No, no, it's not like that. I've always thought you *splendid*. You dare anything. You dream everything. I'm just this boring bluestocking who wouldn't even dream to do anything outrageous."

"You're not boring, Lydia."

"Don't argue with me, please, just listen. This is neither the place nor the moment, but perhaps you'll understand when I tell you that the captain and I…were never even alone together, not for a single moment. We never spoke freely, although we both knew how the other felt. We never touched hands, we never kissed. He went off to war, off to die, and I'll never know what it would have been like to feel his arms around me, holding me close. Do you know how much I regret that, that I never *dared?* So I would be the last person, the very last, to tell you not to dare what your heart desires."

Nicole saw the tears standing in her sister's eyes and knew this wasn't the moment to correct her, to tell her that she didn't know what her heart desired, just what her body craved. If the two, heart and body, were vying with each other for control, she had no idea which was winning, or why.

"You're so wise," Nicole said instead, pulling her into a quick, fierce hug. "I'm so very lucky to have you as my sister."

"Hear, hear now," Rafe said, coming up behind them. "What am I missing?"

"Nothing," Nicole said, blinking rapidly to dry her eyes. "How long will we stay here? Midnight, you said?"

"Charlotte told me I was to keep you here for two hours, and then make sure you also appeared at Mrs. Drummond-Burrell's, where we are to most profusely thank her for securing your vouchers to Almacks. Either plow your way through the rooms like the rest of the sheep, or find quiet corners for your conversations with the gentlemen I see approaching us now. I'll meet you back here. We're agreed?"

"Good evening, ladies, Rafe," Lucas said as he and Lord Yalding handed over the glasses of lemonade before bowing to both women. "Fletcher and I thought some refreshments might be welcomed after that stint on the stairs that probably is delighting our hostess down to her toes but has put the rest of us in mind of what it must be like crossing the Atlantic in steerage. Sorry, Rafe, you'll have to get your own."

He once again looked marvelous in his evening clothes, of course. Smooth, unruffled, cool, the exact opposite of how she felt. As it would be beyond foolish to punish herself by denying her thirst, Nicole thanked both gentlemen, and then drank down the lemonade in a few probably unladylike swallows. "Thank you," she said, looking at Lord Yalding while handing the empty glass back to Lucas. What he did with it, she really didn't care.

Naturally, as if by magic, a servant appeared out of the multitude of milling guests, holding out a silver tray so that Lucas could deposit the empty glass on it and at the same time deftly pass full wineglasses to Rafe and the viscount while reserving one for himself.

Nicole decided that Lucas could at least possess a single flaw. She might be happier with him if he had a temper, or if he chewed with his mouth open— Nicole *hated* that!—or if his smiles weren't always so wonderfully reflected in his eyes....

"Why, yes, that seems fine, Rafe," Lydia said, obviously in answer to something their brother had said. "Nicole, you agree?"

Caught woolgathering, Nicole smiled and nodded. "Yes, fine. Of course. Why would I object?"

"In that case," Lucas said, holding out his arm to her, "what do you say we be on our way."

On their way where? she asked herself, looking back over her shoulder to see that Rafe was now speaking to Lord Yalding, and looking completely unconcerned that he'd just sent his sister off with...well, it wasn't as if he were sending her off with some stranger, now was it? Honestly, was the entire world plotting against her?

"Where are we going?" she asked at last.

"Weren't attending, were you?" Lucas asked her as they made their way beneath an archway and into a second large, crowded chamber.

"No, I wasn't. I was much too occupied planning your demise in sundry painful ways," she told him as she attempted to pretend a disinterest in the stir being caused as a rather large woman was led, half-swooning, to the side of the room by a pair of clearly struggling gentlemen. The elderly lady following after them could be heard telling anyone who would listen that if her sister would only leave off her stays, she wouldn't be fainting every ten minutes. "Could you please tell me the point of all of this?"

"I would think that would be obvious. There is no singing, no dancing—there would be no card room if Lord Hertford hadn't put his foot down—and damn little in the way of refreshments. The hostess invites twice the number of people her rooms can comfortably hold, and the affair is a success if enough of them show up to cause a crush. Or fainting. Or both, I suppose."

Nicole felt her mood improving with each word Lucas said. "Go on."

"A successful rout is one that combines lines of coaches that stretch for blocks, a long wait on the stairs, followed by a slow, painful progression through rooms specifically set aside for that purpose, and then a trek down another set of stairs and a lengthy wait for your coach. And the object of it all is to see, to be seen—paraded, as I believe you term the thing—and then move on to the next party, the next rout, the next ball, and at each one you make sure to recount that you just left Lady So-and-So's utterly boring gathering, but what can one do, when one is invited everywhere?"

Nicole was doing her best not to laugh out loud as he told her all of this, and only realized they were on their way toward a second flight of stairs when she felt cool night air coming toward her.

"We're leaving?"

"That would be the part you weren't paying attention to when the rest of us were making our decision, yes," he told her. "Rafe is meeting with his friends in the card room, the ever-cooperative Fletcher and your sister are staying close by while they discuss Elgin's fascinating marbles and friezes, and you and I are wandering the rout for the next hour. As we are bound to miss each other if we attempted to meet again here, we are going to travel separately to Mrs. Drummond-Burrell's residence."

"But we're not wandering the rooms. We're leaving."

"You'd rather go back up there?"

"You know the answer to that," Nicole said as he led her down the flagway and around the corner, to where his carriage waited out of the crush.

Lucas helped her inside before following after her. The interior was completely dark once he'd closed the door, the curtains drawn tightly against prying eyes. Nicole realized that this was the first time the two of them were together without any fear of someone walking in on them, knocking on a door or otherwise interrupting them.

Which probably shouldn't have thrilled her as much as it did.

"We now have less than two hours for me to tell you everything I want to tell you, everything I need to tell you, and so much more I wish I didn't ever have to tell you," he informed her as he settled beside her. "How much of those nearly two hours is taken up by you as you berate me for meeting with Rafe this afternoon is up to you. But first—"

She knew what he was going to do before he did it, so that she was already moving toward him, her arms sliding around his neck as she parted her lips, welcoming his kiss.

For reasons only her treacherous mind could explain to her, she suddenly thought of all the years that stretched ahead of her, years without Lucas's kiss, his touch.

And she held on more tightly, knowing all she had to do was agree to his proposal and she'd never have to leave him again, never have to miss his kiss because she'd never be without it. Without him.

It would be so simple to say yes.

She was not her mother. Lucas told her that, her sister told her that, Charlotte told her that. It would be so easy to believe all of them.

It was so easy to believe she loved this man, completely and totally, and that he loved her completely and totally in return.

But she'd seen the power of lust, of desire…of *wanting*. And she'd seen its just as sudden death and the unlovely consequences.

Her mother had wanted each of the two men she'd brought into her children's lives to their father's place, and all of the other men who had, as Rafe had termed it, "auditioned, but didn't make it to the final act."

And her mother had sworn she'd loved each and every one of them. Until she'd gotten them to her bed, or to the altar. "Always the bird in the sky, girls," she'd warn them when she was alone again, and feeling maudlin. "Once the bird is in your hand, you notice that they're really rather dirty, messy things, and not nearly so exciting as you'd imagined. It's the curse of men, and most certainly the bane of marriage."

Nicole held on tighter as the carriage moved through the dark streets, reveling in the way Lucas roamed his hands over her body, sighing into his mouth as he slid a hand up beneath the hem of her skirt, to hold the heat of his palm against her thigh.

She was her mother's daughter, in so many ways. She had wants, and desires, yearnings Lucas had wakened in her. Lydia had been content to love from afar, had been willing to wait for her captain to return, had believed in the conventions that dictated behavior for those of their station. Lydia, as their uncle, the late duke, had often said with a sneer, was a good girl.

There had been no question as to what that had made Nicole. It had made Nicole her mother's daughter.

Stop it, stop it, she warned herself as the coach came to a stop and reluctantly she let Lucas pull away from her. He gave her one last kiss and then arranged her shawl back around her shoulders.

"And that is going to have to keep me for tonight," he told her, running the tip of one finger down her cheek. "Tonight, finally, we talk."

CHAPTER THIRTEEN

"WHERE ARE WE?" NICOLE ASKED as Lucas helped her down from the carriage.

"We're in the mews behind my residence in Park Lane. I didn't think it a good idea for you to possibly be seen entering with me, unescorted."

"You're getting very good at intrigue," she told him as he led her down a narrow path and into the kitchens of his mansion. "And you've ordered the staff to stay in their rooms?"

"For the most part, if you must know, I've given them the evening free. But if you're hungry, I can summon someone."

Nicole took off her shawl and hung it over one of the chairs arranged around a large, rough wooden worktable. "Don't be silly. What would you like?"

Lucas leaned a shoulder against the door frame. "I'd like to take you upstairs, with the two of us staying up there for at least the next week, actually. But, barring that, are you telling me that you know what kitchens are all about?"

He watched in some amusement as she lifted a heavy white apron from a hook on the wall and tied it around her waist, covering her glorious lightest-green silk gown. "I wasn't always sister to a duke, remember. As our mother's tendency was to burn through in a week the allowance my uncle sent quarterly, both Lydia and I were often called upon to assist in the kitchens, and elsewhere. I can also start a fire tolerably well, and refresh the bed linens. Your cook keeps an extremely neat kitchen, which bodes well for your never having to worry that the food on your plate will make you ill. Now," she said, looking around the room, "where is the larder?"

Lucas pushed himself away from the door frame, also looking around the room, noticing three separate doorways that led Lord only knew where. "This house has been in my family for three generations. Would it disappoint you terribly if I were to admit I don't have the vaguest idea?"

"No, I don't think so. Why should you?" She left the kitchen, returning moments later. "I think that hallway must lead to the housekeeper's quarters," she said, and then tried the next doorway.

When she didn't return at once Lucas decided she'd located the larder, and went to see what she would do next. He imagined that if they both lived to the ripe age of one hundred, he still couldn't be certain what she might do next. She was a constant source of amazement to him.

She greeted him with an order. "Hold out your hands."

He did as she said, and soon they were returning to the kitchens, his arms loaded down with a platter containing what looked like the remainder of the beef he and Fletcher had shared for dinner, and half a loaf of bread Nicole had tucked under his arm.

Nicole plunked down a large wedge of cheese she'd unearthed from a cabinet, and then went on the hunt for some crockery. She also found a large, dangerous-looking knife she handed him along with the suggestion that he do his best not to slice off a finger.

"You can talk when you're done," she told him, and by the time he was done, she had poured milk into two earthen mugs, carved off hunks of the cheese and bread, discovered a rough linen square to use as a serviette, and arranged everything on heavy white plates he assumed were normally used by the servants.

It was clear to him that she planned to remain in the kitchen for their impromptu meal, but a man needed to draw the line somewhere, and he did. He spied out a wooden tray and loaded it with their meal. Having eliminated two of the doorways, he chose the third, and told Nicole to follow him.

She did, but only after returning the meat and cheese to the larder, and without removing the apron, which he found to be the most alluring thing she could have chosen to wear. He didn't know why he thought this, and the whole notion might not stand up to too much scrutiny, but all he wanted to do was pull her close and kiss her senseless.

Instead, he led her up the stairs and through the mansion to the drawing room, which was well-lit and prepared for them. He placed the tray on the table between a pair of couches, one usually reserved for a highly polished tea service and bone china cups—pleased with himself to see he hadn't spilled more than a few drops of the milk—and indicated that Nicole should sit down.

"No, not yet," she said, walking straight to the fireplace and the large portrait that hung above it. "That's you, isn't it? Is your father's hand on your shoulder in pride, or to hold you in place so the artist could paint you?"

"In my defense, the weather was fine, and I would much rather have been running the fields with my dogs than posing by a stream." Lucas joined her in front of the portrait. He remembered when it had been painted. "My father had just returned from Russia and Copenhagen, where he had traveled on a mission from our government. He'd been gone for over a year, and was rather proud of his accomplishments. We were to travel to London the following month at which time, as rumor had it, the king himself would honor him for his service in assisting Emperor Paul of Russia to convince Denmark to join the League of Armed Neutrality. There was also talk that he would be favored as the next Prime Minister."

"That all sounds quite impressive, although I must admit that I wasn't the best student when our governess was attempting to beat the history of our country into my head. Lydia would probably know all about this League of Armed Neutrality, but all I can say is that you must have been very proud of your father. And did you go to London with him?"

Lucas shook his head, and then took her hand and led her back to the couches. "No. Three weeks after that portrait was completed, my father locked himself in his study and put one of his dueling pistols to his head."

"Lucas!" Nicole put her hand on his arm. "I'm so sorry." She turned to look at the portrait once more. "But…but you all look so happy. Your mother?"

"She remains at Basingstoke, and has completely cut herself off from Society. She never really fully recovered from my father's death. In many ways, neither have I. I shouldn't try to influence you, Nicole, but I wanted you to see that portrait, see my family as it was. It's no excuse for my behavior, but it is a reason."

The food remained on the table, untouched, as Lucas told Nicole what had happened to his father. She remained silent, her hands in his, asking no questions, but only listening. It made telling her somehow easier.

When he was finished, Nicole let go of his hand and used a corner of the cook's apron to wipe at her eyes. "And it was really believed that your father helped plan the assassination? But he wasn't even in Russia when the emperor was killed. He was with you."

"True enough, but communications were discovered, and my father was implicated. He was to come to London to answer to charges brought privately, and probably to be hanged, God only knows. Instead, given the choice in order to keep his family from scandal, he killed himself. Until last year I thought my father a traitor and a coward. I hated him, what he'd done to us."

"What happened last year?"

"I won't bore you by producing the letter I received. Unsigned, of course. According to whoever penned the letter, my father was innocent, named only to protect someone else, but he would surely have been brought to a public trial and condemned. In other words, he didn't die a coward, but in a brave act meant to protect us. I've spent the last year attempting to discover who wrote that letter to me, and why."

Nicole pressed her head against his arm. "I would have gone out of my mind," she said quietly. "How can you stand not knowing?"

She'd given him the opening he needed to tell her what she had to be told. He pressed his chin against the top of her head for a moment, gaining courage, because what he'd already told her had been difficult, but what he'd still left unsaid might drive her away forever.

"You haven't eaten anything," he told her, easing her away from him and getting to his feet. He needed to be up, pacing, doing his best to look her in the eye.

"I'm not hungry anymore," she said, watching him. "Lucas, just say what you feel I need to hear and no more. But, before you begin, thank you for telling me what you have told me. It couldn't have been easy for you. And I promise, I'll never tell a soul."

Her brother thought her a child? No, Nicole was no child. Young in years, yes, but there was an understanding there, a familiarity with pains of the heart, that had aged her beyond her years.

"Thank you for that, but what I'm going to tell you now may change your opinion of me, I'm afraid. When, in just this past week, I was offered the name of the man who had accused my father to protect himself, I grabbed at the opportunity with both hands. Without a doubt in my mind or a single twinge of conscience over what I'd agreed to do. I want you to understand that. I'm not proud of what I did, and I'm most definitely not proud of involving you even marginally. I'm only telling you the truth."

Nicole's eyes widened as she looked up at him. "I don't understand."

He picked up one of the mugs and took a drink, grimacing when he realized he hadn't drunk milk in dog's years, and with good reason. He loathed the taste. He put down the mug and went to the drinks table to pour himself a glass of wine.

"Again, I won't bore you with all of the particulars. Last week I somehow found myself making a rather impassioned speech about the tribulations of many of our countrymen thanks to the war, this damnable weather, the scarcity of food and the high price of grain, and the very real possibility that there could be riots here in London, all over England, if the government didn't step in to help its citizens."

Nicole nodded. "Like those poor soldiers we saw."

"Yes, like those soldiers we saw. Lord Frayne overheard me, realized I could suit his purpose, and offered me the name of the man who accused my father in exchange for my help in a plan of his own. I would perform a service for him, and he'd give me the name in return, once I was successful."

When Nicole said nothing, but just bit her bottom lip between her teeth, her cheeks pale, he hurried on, wanting this part of his story over.

He told her how he'd agreed to be an *agent provocateur*, infiltrating meetings by groups such as the Citizens for Justice she already knew about thanks to the broadsheet her sister had discovered. Inciting them to march, to riot, so that Frayne and his ilk could press for stronger laws meant to keep the populace under the iron hand of the government.

And worse. He'd realized almost too late that Frayne had also planned to use him to eliminate an enemy. By giving Lucas the name of the man who had accused his father, Frayne would be rid of someone who was getting in his way as he moved to not only strengthen the government, but raise himself up at the same time. The man saw himself as another Cromwell, but without that man's supposedly noble intentions.

"What would you have done if Frayne gave you a name, Lucas? It sounds as if he would have expected you to kill the man for him."

"A duel, yes. It would be the obvious solution. I don't share Frayne's appreciation of my oratorical powers, but I will admit that I'm a fairly good shot. I would have had to flee the country after I'd killed my man, but that would have been a small price to pay to avenge my father, to put my mother's mind at rest at last. I was fully prepared for all of that."

Dared he add *until I met you?* No, he couldn't put that weight on her. He'd made his own decisions.

Nicole nodded. "I understand, Lucas. I would have done the same thing. The man had as good as murdered your father, and he deserves to die. What other choice did you have?"

"When am I going to learn that you are a lot of things, Nicole, but you are most definitely not faint of heart?"

"No, I suppose not. I have said more than once that I would much rather have been born a man. But that's neither here nor there. Tell me the rest."

Lucas sat down beside her once more, taking her hands in his. "I went to The Broken Wheel that night fully intending to do Frayne's bidding, to watch the men he'd already planted in with the Citizens for Justice, gain acceptance, and then take charge of future gatherings. A group, by the way, I'm convinced was born out of Frayne's fertile brain in the first place. I used you to deflect attention away from the speech I'd made, the feathers I'd ruffled, as if assuring everyone that I had something—some-one—else to occupy my mind, and my passion for the common man had been a momentary aberration and nothing more. Frayne felt it important that I do my best to appear as harmless as possible while I did his dirty work for him, you understand. So...so I used you as my foil."

"I wasn't unwilling, as you'll recall." She

squeezed his hand. "You don't have to tell me more, for I'm sure I'm right. You couldn't do what Frayne wanted of you, could you?"

"No, I couldn't. Not for my parents, not for my own hopes of revenge. Unfortunately, I didn't consider the consequences when I came to that realization while at The Broken Wheel. Which," he said, glancing at the mantel clock, "leaves us with Lord Frayne and his dangerous ambitions. Come on, we'll talk more in the carriage."

She got to her feet, but then bent down and placed slices of cold beef and cheese on the linen square, folded the thing and handed it to him. "Here, we'll take this with us. It seems my appetite is returning. You had me very frightened, you know, as if you were going to tell me something that would make me hate you."

"You still might, because I'm not done. Oh, and fetching as you may look, you might want to leave the apron behind."

She looked down at herself, and then grinned at him. "Or I could start a new fashion. But no. Charlotte made me promise to be on my very best behavior when introduced to Mrs. Drummond-Burrell."

They made their way back down to the kitchens and out into the mews, where the carriage waited.

Nicole giggled deliciously as she sat back against the squabs and Lucas joined her. "You do know that your groom and coachman believe we were up to no good in there, don't you?"

"And that amuses you?"

"For some reason, yes. I also know that servants gossip, and it would probably be very interesting to listen to them attempt to explain away the tray we left behind us in the kitchens. By the time they're done, you may have dropped a notch or two in their estimation of their employer's romantic prowess."

"Ah, and *that's* what amuses you," Lucas said, understanding her humor now. "Nicole," he went on, turning on the seat to look at her, able only to see the smooth curve of her cheek in the darkness, "I thank you again for not condemning me for what I nearly did, but you still don't know the consequences of my mistake."

"Well, of course I do. Lord Frayne is very angry with you. He also probably fears that you'll try to thwart him, since he was so careless as to tell you his plans, which was either incredibly arrogant or exceedingly stupid of him. So, how are we going to do this? Thwart him, I mean."

"*We,* Nicole?"

"Well, yes, of course. Otherwise, why tell me any of this? You wouldn't accept my offer of help when first I gave it, but now you will. Won't you?"

"Don't you want to ask me *why* I finally told you?"

She reached over to drop one of the window flaps, not that the interior of the carriage grew that much lighter. But it was now light enough for her to see him more clearly, he was sure, for him to see the questioning look on her face.

"Tell me."

"First, I'd like you to tell me what you know about the deaths of your uncle and cousins."

He watched her eyes grow wide. "Why would you want to know that?"

God, this wasn't going to be easy. She hadn't reacted at all the way he'd worried she might when he'd told her about his stupidity. Lord bless her, she probably saw a lot of this as the *adventure* she'd longed for when she came to London. But now her family was involved, no thanks to him, and her reaction might be different.

"Because I involved you, because Frayne is no idiot, and could see that I care for you."

"He saw you making calf-eyes at me, you mean," she said, rolling her own eyes. "I didn't realize you'd been quite so convincing. Go on."

"Nicole, this is serious, deadly serious. There's nothing he can do to me that hasn't already been done. So he's threatened to destroy your family if I dare to cross him, try to stop him or report his intentions to God only knows who—because he's not in this alone, that much is certain. Which means I could end up reporting him to one of his cohorts."

Nicole was silent for some moments, looking at him intently. "You met with Rafe this afternoon. Not to ask for my hand, but to tell him about Lord Frayne's threat."

"Exactly. Your uncle, Nicole. Tell me what you know."

"Rafe didn't tell you?"

"He said the duke and his sons drowned in a storm."

She lowered her eyes, avoiding his gaze. "Yes… that's what happened."

Lucas felt a cold chill run down his spine. "That's strange. You're usually such a credible liar."

She looked at him, her chin raised in defiance. "Rafe is guilty of *nothing*. That's what Lord Frayne is suggesting, isn't he? That Rafe had something to do with my uncle's death?"

"Innuendo is a terrible weapon. Whispers, comments made in certain quarters? If my father's death taught me nothing else, it taught me that. I won't ask you to tell me what happened. It's enough for me to know that questions could be raised, putting Rafe in an uncomfortable position. And there's more."

"Isn't that enough?" Nicole asked, her eyes shining in the near darkness. "How could you let this happen? My family…"

The carriage joined a line of other vehicles inching their way to their destination. Lucas knew he didn't have much more time.

"You remember our evening at Covent Garden. You remember seeing Frayne and your mother…together. That wasn't a coincidence, Nicole. Frayne hadn't given his mistress her congé in order to…romance your mother. He knows her reputation, he knew he could turn her to his own purpose. Frayne isn't a stupid man. He didn't trust me, so he prepared for the possibility I would change my mind, refuse to help him."

Nicole's voice, when she spoke, was very tight, very small. "Tell me everything. What did my mother do? How did she betray us?"

"Frayne told me he has damaging letters from your mother in his possession." He stopped, the realization belatedly hitting him that those letters might be more than the indiscreet language of a woman supposedly in love. "Nicole? You said betray us. Would your mother have been reckless enough to put what happened to your uncle and cousins in a letter to her lover? Whatever that information was?"

Now her tone had gone cold as a stone. "My mother is capable of any idiocy. *Any* idiocy. Is that what you and Rafe think she did?"

"No," Lucas said, slightly distracted. "We assumed they were love letters. Until now. This is worse, much worse."

"You have no idea. What happened to my uncle and cousins had nothing to do with us, *nothing,* but it could be made to look as if—" Nicole grabbed his hand, squeezing it tightly, almost painfully between both of hers. "I'm going to ask you again. What are we going to do?"

"And there's the hell of it, Nicole, because you're right. Much as I want you out of it, Rafe and I have agreed, we need your help. Now more than ever."

"How? Tell me."

"As our first step, we're going to kidnap your mother."

The cloth holding the meat and cheese slid, unnoticed, from her lap to the floor of the carriage. *"What?"*

The carriage had inched forward until Lucas could see that they were now directly in front of the

Drummond-Burrell House. "We don't have much more time, so please listen carefully. Tomorrow, we need Lydia to arrange for someone to pack your mother's possessions, her clothes. We need her maid and her luggage put into my traveling coach, which will be pulled up in the mews behind the mansion."

"You're involving Lydia in this?"

"Yes, as we could hardly involve your sister-in-law, not in her condition. Rafe assured me that Lydia can do this, while you, being naturally more devious and daring—his words, not mine, and meant as a compliment—will take care of your mother. We need *you* to take her out of her town house, take her somewhere using whatever ruse you can think of, and then I will take it from there. She can't remain in London, not another day."

"Where is she going? If Rafe takes her to Ashurst Hall he can't tie her to a bedpost, you know. She'll only find her way back here again. And then she'll tell everyone what you did."

"Rafe had a better answer. He is sending her to Italy. Both coaches will depart for Dover the moment we're ready to move. Your brother will stay here, to watch Frayne, the idea being that the man won't suspect that Rafe knows anything, and you and I will make certain your mother sails tomorrow night as planned. That leaves the way clear for us to take on Frayne. Come on. We have to get out of the carriage now. Your brother and sister are probably already here, waiting for us."

"Does…does Lydia know any of this yet?" she asked him just as the carriage door opened.

"Rafe will have told her by now, yes. Nicole…I'm so sorry. None of this would be happening if I hadn't been so blindly bent on avenging my father."

"Yes," she said, refusing his hand and accepting the assistance of a liveried servant instead. "I know. I sympathize with your motives, Lucas, I truly do. I may have done the same thing. But I'm saying this with all of my heart—if any harm comes to my family, I will never forgive you."

CHAPTER FOURTEEN

NICOLE WATCHED AS HER MOTHER stood in front of a long mirror in the exclusive Bond Street shop, admiring her reflection as she turned this way and that, examining the pink cashmere shawl she'd draped around her, flinging one end up and over her left shoulder. Posing.

Helen Daughtry really was a beautiful creature. Nicole could remember, as a child, sitting cross-legged in the huge bed at Willowbrook, watching the woman brushing her long blond hair, playing with her rouge pots and powders, practicing her smiles and simpers.

Lydia closely resembled their mother in looks; slim, almost fragile, with eyes as blue as a summer sky. Nicole, who knew her father only from the portrait over the fireplace, would wonder why she had been cursed with his coal-dark hair and tendency to plumpness.

Sometimes her mother would allow the twins to play in her jewelry box, and drape them with her shawls as she taught them how to walk, how to pose—how to flirt with a fan and coy looks. They'd giggle as they descended the curving staircase to an adoring audience of servants lined up to pretend they were guests at a grand ball, and there would be sugared tea and small cakes set out in the drawing room.

Nicole adored her mother.

And then Helen would be gone, often without a word, only to return with yet another man who either ignored them or, as they grew into their early teens, pinched them when their mother wasn't looking. When Nicole had bitten one of them she and Lydia had been sent to their uncle the duke for the first time, a move that was repeated so often the servants kept bags packed for the twins at all times.

Rafe had escaped to the war, but Nicole and Lydia remained at the whims of their mercurial mama. Lydia retreated into her books, taking her world with her wherever she traveled. She caused no trouble, and everyone called her a good girl, and then ignored her.

But not Nicole. No one would ever ignore her! She climbed trees, she rode neck-or-nothing, she teased and flirted and played pranks. She chafed at every restriction, dared anything. She would not retreat, not ever. And she'd never let anyone hurt her or forget her.

"The shade becomes you," Nicole assured her mother now, privately thinking the garish shade most closely resembled a cow's distended udder at milking time. "I definitely think you should purchase it."

"It's very dear," Helen Daughtry said, and then shrugged. "Then again, my son the duke is very wealthy. And you're certain Rafael said I was to have whatever my heart desires?"

"Yes, *Maman*. He only hopes this would then make some small amends for the way he has neglected you these past months. We know he has been dreadfully busy, what with Ashurst Hall, and with Charlotte increasing. And Lydia's and my Come-out, of course. But Charlotte impressed on him that his *maman* must always come first."

"Dear creature," Helen said, handing the shawl to the clerk and already investigating a small table loaded down with small, jeweled reticules. "I've told him innumerable times how delighted I am with his choice of bride."

Nicole couldn't help herself. "You have? I don't think I was ever present when you told him that. Only when you were impressing on him that to waste himself on an untitled creature of no importance, when he could have reached to any height in his need for a wife, was beyond unreasonable."

Her mother looked daggers at Nicole. "You're mistaken. I never said anything of the sort. You're a pernicious little beast, aren't you?"

My mother's daughter, Nicole thought, and then quickly tried to banish any such notion. "Forgive me, *Maman*. Do you know, I think the silver reticule would be a good choice. Silver going so well with pink."

"You think so? I always wear gold."

"Yes," Nicole said, making sure her smile looked patently false, as if she was trying to be polite. "I know."

The silver reticule was imperiously held up in the air, to be snatched up by the clerk, who bowed in delight before adding the thing to the growing pile on the counter. Rafe would pay dearly for his deception, but the hours spent roaming Bond Street were giving Lydia time to see to having Helen's belongings and maid packed up and ready for transport.

"You—clerk! We desire refreshments. We'll just sit over here, and you may then show us more of your bolts of material. I'm particularly interested in the French silks, *naturellement*."

"Fatigued, *Maman?*" Nicole asked as her mother held out one side of her skirts and gracefully sank into the small slipper chair that matched the one Nicole was already sitting in, the chairs divided by a low round table displaying intricately designed snuff boxes.

"Truth be told, my shoes pinch," Helen said, picking up one of the small boxes. "Nobody who is anybody takes snuff anymore. Filthy habit. But they are pretty, aren't they?"

Nicole watched, appalled, as her mother deftly slipped the box into her bodice. *"Mother."*

"Oh, close your mouth, Nicole, before a fly makes a home in it. The clerk's off getting us refreshments. Besides, everybody does it. Now, tell me about the marquess. Still keeping him at arm's length, aren't you? I've watched him watching you, and he still looks more hungry than satisfied."

"*Maman,* please, I'd rather we didn't discuss the marquess."

"Yes, yes, you pretend to be so prim and proper. That's all well and good, to a point, but you're not your sister, are you? You're more like me than you could wish, in nature if not in looks, and that rankles you, doesn't it?

"But you listen to me, daughter mine, because I know what you need, I know what keeps you awake at night, the needs that drive you. If he's that hot to tip you, my advice is to let him. I've given this some thought, and from his reputation, I'm confident the man knows that once he's poked you he's as good as married you."

"I said, I don't wish to—"

But the woman went on conversationally, just as if she hadn't heard her daughter's protest. "Besides, virginity is not a virtue, my dear, but only a temporary impediment to delight—at least if the man is at all competent. Oh, yes, as a bargaining chip, the hymen does have its uses, but there're ways and ways to make a man think he's got what's already gone. And you won't regret waving it goodbye. Lord knows I didn't."

Nicole got to her feet, not at all certain she wasn't about to run, screaming, from the shop. Her mother was so damnably *crude.* But worse than that, Nicole knew she was feeling some sort of physical *reaction* to the woman's licentious words. Her traitorous body was ruling her mind, her decency and common sense once more.

"You shouldn't speak to me about such things," she told her, sitting down again once the clerk had deposited a small china teapot and two cups on the table and stepped away.

"Nonsense. Who else to tell you the truth, the way of things, if not your own *maman?*" Helen leaned closer, across the small table. "You're past eighteen, Nicole, you've been wondering long enough. I'm only trying to help, dear." She stood up, calling out to the clerk, "We're through here. Send my purchases and the bill to my son in Grosvenor Square."

Nicole looked to the pile of purchases, and then to the untouched tea. "No! That is, we should take your purchases with us."

"Whatever for? I'll have them by tomorrow in any case."

"But…but aren't you thirsty? You asked for tea."

"I *asked* for refreshment, and the fool brought me tea," Helen corrected, as if instructing a child. "All this frank talk has whet my appetite for wine. We have everything else already in Rafe's carriage. We can do without these last few things."

Nicole looked to the pile of purchases once more, and then decided her mother could simply see Italy without that horrid pink shawl. "All right then. I suppose we could be on our way now. As soon as you put back that snuff box."

Helen rolled her eyes. "Just when I think there's some hope for you," she said, sighing as she complied, and then headed for the door.

Nicole's relief was fairly palpable when they stepped onto the flagway and she saw Lucas standing at the corner, pretending an interest in the display in a shop window. His presence meant that Lydia had completed her task, and his fully loaded coach was already on the road to Dover.

Now it was time to get her mother on her way, as well.

She climbed into the coach after her mother, taking the facing seat, worrying for only a moment that she might become ill riding backward all the way to the Channel.

"You know, darling, this has been quite a delightful morning. Just the two of us."

Nicole felt a sudden twinge of conscience, knowing what her mother would soon learn. How on earth was she going to explain any of it to the woman? Why hadn't she thought of that? "Yes, a most delightful morning."

Helen arranged her skirts so that they wouldn't wrinkle. "Of course, I much prefer Lydia's company—she was always so much the easier child—but I don't care for people to compare us. That dew of youth, you understand. Much better that you have your father's coloring. I think the contrast of light and dark draws gentlemanly attention without also inviting comparison."

Nicole honestly believed she felt something go snap inside her head.

"We're not going back to Grosvenor Square," she bit out, wondering what maggot had gotten into her brain that she'd actually had a moment's charitable thought for this impossible woman. "A coach packed with your belongings, and with your maid also inside, is already on the road. We're taking you to Dover, tossing you on a ship, and you will be on your way to Italy for at least a year, more if you don't behave. Rafe is arranging it all through his bankers. A residence, an allowance, everything you'll need."

Her mother's mouth opened and closed several times, her eyes so wide she began to resemble a fish gasping on a riverbank. "*What* did you just say to me?"

"You heard me. You have been writing letters, and you will not be writing any more of them, or else Rafe will cut off your allowance and you can grow whiskers in Italy for all any of us will care."

"How *dare* you! Stop this coach, you hear me!" Helen moved to fling herself across the coach, to pull on the cord that would alert the coachman.

Nicole reacted immediately, pushing her mother square in the chest, so that she fell back against the velvet squabs. "Sit! And I swear to you, *Maman,* if you don't stay there quietly I will take one of these pistols I see tucked into the pockets next to me and hold it pointed at your head, cocked, until you realize I mean what I say. And then you'll have to pray this coach is well sprung and doesn't jostle me too much."

Lady Helen Daughtry, who had seen her share of successes, and her fair portion of failures, seemed to consider this for a few moments. "You said letters. This has to do with Lord Frayne, doesn't it?"

"Did you write him letters?"

Helen shrugged her slim shoulders. "I suppose we may have corresponded. Little love notes delivered on my breakfast tray along with a single rose," she said, smiling. "He's quite the naughty boy. So naughty he begged me to burn the letters he sent to me. Isn't that romantic?"

"And that's all? Love notes?"

"And this and that. He was a dear friend of your late uncle's, you know. I think I may have mentioned how terrible it was that he and my dearest nephews were killed by—"

"They *drowned*," Nicole interrupted.

Helen smiled. "Yes, if that's what we're to say, then that's what I'll say. They *drowned*. Someone should have told me."

"We did. *Repeatedly.*"

"You did? I don't remember." Then she reached into her reticule and extracted a small silver filigree-laced clear glass flask and removed the top. She saluted Nicole with the flask. "Blue Ruin. Stark Naked. Mother's Ruin. *Gin,* darling, the downfall of the lower classes. However, it is cheap, and plentiful. How else, I ask you, is one supposed to make it through the day? I can only hope Giselle had brains enough to pack a few dozen bottles."

Nicole watched as her mother drank directly from the flask, the woman's throat working as she downed considerably more than a sip of the strong spirits.

"There, that's better," Helen said, recapping the flask. "Italy, you said? They speak some foreign language there, don't they?"

TWO HURRIED STOPS FOR FOOD, three changes of horses—and again as many visits to the taprooms to replenish the contents of the flask—and by nightfall Rafe's coach was standing at the docks in Dover, drawn up beside the one bearing the crest of the Marquess of Basingstoke.

"Oh-ho, so that's how the land lies," Helen Daughtry said as she descended none-too-steadily to the ground. "And where is the good marquess, hmm? Ordering up the Bridal Suite in one of those inns we passed? Well, *good* for you, darling!"

Nicole, who had spent the better part of the day wondering where Lucas was, pretended not to have heard her mother's question.

Instead, she concentrated on savoring the clean, fresh scent of the water as a fairly strong breeze from the Channel cleared the sickening smell of gin from her nose, and marveled at all the ships that seemed to stand fore to aft up and down the docks, all of them waiting for the evening tide.

The hustle and bustle everywhere around them was loud and confusing, but the nearly overpowering din of shouts and screeching sea birds faded away when Lucas stepped out from behind the coach to whisper in her ear, "You haven't murdered her? My congratulations on your fortitude and forbearance, my dear."

"Lucas!" She fought the traitorous, yet almost unbearable, urge to throw herself into his arms and beg him to toss her mother on the nearest ship and then allow her to personally cut the ropes holding that vessel to the dock. "Where have you been?"

"Never more than a whisper ahead of you on Thunder, with your Juliet in tow, making arrangements for food and horses. Your mother's luggage and her maid are both already aboard ship. Whoa!"

He stepped away from her, to grab on to her mother's shoulders, holding the swaying woman in place. "There you go, Lady Daughtry. Fatigued from the journey, are you?"

"Foxed half out of her head is more like it," Nicole said, sighing. "I've spent more pleasant days with the bellyache."

Lady Daughtry smiled rather blearily up at Lucas and then waved her finger in his face. "Even a fool can count to nine, my lord. Have your fun, the both of you. I applaud it. But I *am* her mother, for all she loathes me." Her bottom lip began to tremble, and a single tear ran down her cheek. "With good reason."

"Mother, stop, please."

"See? All I ever wanted was what was best, for all my children. Truly. All…all I ever wanted." She shook her head. "No…that's a lie. All I wanted was what was best for me. Always have. But you marry her, you hear me?"

"That's my intention, ma'am, yes," Lucas said as Nicole turned her back on the both of them. "Time for you to go aboard."

"Nicole? Sweetheart? Aren't you going to say goodbye to your mother?" Helen asked, her tone plaintive, her words slurring badly.

Nicole remained with her back to the woman, hugging herself tightly, her bottom lip firmly bitten between her teeth, the stiff breeze blowing her skirts hard against the backs of her legs.

"Well, no matter," Lady Daughtry said, her words light, her tone closer to heartbroken resignation. "My lord, your arm, if you please."

"It would be my pleasure, madam," Lucas said, adding, "Don't move from that spot, Nicole. I'll return shortly."

Nicole nodded to acknowledge that she'd heard him, and then stayed where she was, knowing she was entirely justified in her action. Her mother was crude, immoral. She'd neglected her children shamelessly all of their lives and embarrassed them when she did deign to acknowledge their existence. Now she was growing older, and increasingly desperate. She was pitiful, and increasingly indiscreet as the age she had so enjoyed was now frowned upon by Society. There was nothing, *nothing,* she admired in the woman.

And then she was running, not away from the docks, but toward the ship. Running, and calling out to her mother, catching up to her just as the woman was about to be assisted up the gangplank.

She put her arms around Helen Daughtry and hugged her fiercely. "Have…have a safe journey, *Maman,*" she said, kissing the woman's cheek.

"Dear girl," Helen said, pressing a kiss on Nicole's cheek in return. "I'll be fine, just fine. I always am. I'll write!"

"Mother," Nicole warned, only half in jest.

Lady Daughtry laughed her silvery laugh. "You're the only one who ever understood me. I'll behave, I promise. I never meant any harm."

"You never do, do you?" Nicole said, blinking back tears. "I love you, Mama."

"Yes, yes," Lady Daughtry said briskly, wiping at her own eyes. "Now go away. A rather fine-looking gentleman boarded just ahead of me. I can't let him see me for the first time with my eyes all red, now can I? Go on...*Maman* is off on a grand adventure!"

CHAPTER FIFTEEN

LUCAS SAID NOTHING AS HE LED Nicole back to the coach and they climbed inside, the coachman already knowing their destination.

Nicole sat tucked into a corner of the coach, her head averted, occasionally sniffling.

His heart ached for her. It couldn't have been easy for her, growing up as the ribald and flamboyant Helen Daughtry's daughter. But a parent is a parent, and children love their parents, even when those parents disappoint them. He'd loved his father, even after he'd believed the man had been a traitor to his country.

He hadn't liked him anymore, but he'd still loved him. Nicole couldn't like the way her mother lived, but she still loved her. At any age, it was what children did.

"She'll be all right," he said at last.

"I know that. She's always all right. I...I was just thinking we'll all probably have to learn Italian, as she's sure to return in a year dragging some new Italian husband with her. She'll be the only one who doesn't understand him, but that won't matter to either of them."

Lucas smiled in the dark coach. *"Amor regge senza legge,"* he said. "Love rules without rules."

"Well, aren't you wonderful," Nicole groused, folding her arms at her waist. "Where are we going? You said you brought Juliet."

"I thought you'd enjoy being out in the air after a day spent cooped up in a coach. Lydia had a few things packed for you, including your riding habit. We won't ride all the way back to London, but we should be able to get in a few runs along the way. We'll take our time, spend two nights on the road. Rafe isn't expecting us back immediately."

She finally turned her head away from the window and the sights of Dover.

"Mama, Rafe and most probably Charlotte— even Lydia now, obviously. Why is everyone conniving to get me into bed with you?" she asked him, and then flinched, as if she'd just realized what she'd said.

"In defense of your sister, she has been told that I have a small estate in Kent, and she believes we're visiting my mother, who has traveled here from Hampshire."

"Rafe *lied* to Lydia?"

"No, that was Charlotte, I believe. Then again, your brother and sister-in-law don't know you've taken me in disgust. They still think we'll marry."

"I haven't taken you in disgust," Nicole said quietly. "I told you, I understand why you did what you did, or at least thought you could do what you ended up not doing."

"But I've also managed to put your family in danger. That I understand."

"Do you? I don't think you can, not without knowing what I know."

Lucas waited for her to go on, but when she didn't, he said, "Rafe has told me what happened the day your uncle and cousins died. I know that this information, in the wrong hands, could allow the argument that he had a part in it, even though he was in Paris at the time. At the least there would be a scandal none of you could ever recover from. At the worst?"

"At the worst, Rafe could be hanged." She turned her head away from him again. "This is all my fault. If I hadn't agreed to your plan without insisting I know *why* you wanted me to help you…"

Lucas realized his teeth were clenched. "You're blaming yourself? Nicole, that's ludicrous."

"I'm often ludicrous," she told him, sighing. "But it's true, can't you see that? If you'd told me about your father, about what Lord Frayne wanted you to do, I could have told you that you'd never be able to do it, no matter what he'd promised you. I saw you with those soldiers. You would never have done anything that could end with harm coming to them or anyone like them. You couldn't."

Lucas thought about Johnny and the others, now safely away from the city, but decided not to tell Nicole what he'd done. It would seem much too self-serving. However, she was right. Somewhere inside himself, he must have known he couldn't be Frayne's *agent provocateur,* not when it came right down to the thing.

But he'd allowed himself to believe gaining information on the man who had betrayed his father and destroyed his mother trumped every other consideration.

"You're right, I should have told you. Saying the words out loud, most especially to you, would have made me realize I was putting my own desires above my conscience. I should have listened when you demanded I tell you. Frankly, merely thinking about telling you is probably what stopped me."

And then, as seemed to be her habit, she surprised him again.

She turned to him in the dimness of the coach, and she smiled. "I'm always right, Lucas. Except when I'm wrong. I was wrong to agree to help you when you wouldn't tell me why you needed my help."

"So why did you?"

"Because I wanted to be with you. I wanted the excitement, the adventure, certain I'd learn your secret sooner rather than later. I could never resist a secret. But, mostly, I wanted to be with you. There, I've said it. We were both of us with our reasons, and we are both at fault. Now my mother is on her way out of the country on her grand adventure, and Rafe is in danger, and it's left to the two of us to make things right since we're the ones who made it all wrong. So I think we probably shouldn't fight."

God, she was amazing, the most amazing woman he'd ever met. "We were fighting?"

She shrugged. "I was. I was hating you for what

I helped you do. You didn't notice? Clearly I'm going to have to learn to be more ferocious. Oh, we're stopping. You didn't tell me where we were going."

"We're at The Sign of the Gate Inn on the Dover toll road, near Canterbury. I stopped here earlier and reserved two bedchambers and a private dining room. Are you hungry?"

"Exceedingly. I couldn't eat a thing all day, not riding backward in the coach. You said two chambers?"

"I thought that was best, yes. But now I'm wondering how we'll explain the absence of your maid or other female companion. Off on an adventure or not, we need to protect your reputation. Clearly I'm not as proficient at intrigue as I'd like to believe."

Nicole gave a dismissive wave of her hand. "Oh, don't worry about that. Remember, thanks to a lifetime of practice, I'm an exceedingly convincing liar."

"Most of the time," he corrected, his heart growing lighter with every moment, which was ridiculous, knowing the problems still ahead of them.

"Yes, you seem to be able to see through my fibs. I'll have to remember that."

"On the other hand, I also seem to enjoy those fibs, very much." The groom opened the door and Lucas offered her his arm. "Shall we have at it?"

"I think so, yes. We need everyone to keep their distance from us, correct? Ask no questions? The way the clerks at the shops all did their best to stay clear of Mama today? I swear to you, Lucas, one of them actually hid beneath a table. Yes, that should do it. I'll be my mother at her most imperious. She's very good at being imperious, you know."

Lucas pretended to flinch. "Thank you for the warning."

"You're welcome. Did you see the innkeeper earlier?"

He shook his head. "No. I didn't wish to leave the horses, not with Thunder trying to take a bite out of the ostler. I sent in a note with a few coins. Oh, in case it matters, we're Mr. and Mrs. Paine. I doubt anyone here will recognize my crest on the coach, so we're safe there."

"Good. I think I'm ready now, Mr. Paine."

Nicole put up the hood of her cloak on the short walk from the coach to the front door to the large, whitewashed stucco structure. She stopped in front of the closed door and raised her right hand above her head, "imperiously" snapping her fingers twice in a way that told him he was to leap forward and open the door for her.

He immediately understood his was the role of the browbeaten husband. The minx.

She brushed past him and into the candlelit foyer of the inn, to where the innkeeper stood behind a counter, turning pages in a journal in front of him.

Before Lucas could say a word, she threw back her hood and he saw a look of such perfect disdain on her beautiful face as she gazed about the simple foyer that he had to cover his mouth with his hand or else grin and give the game away.

"*This* is the inn you chose for a woman who is about to spend a week—a *week*, husband—suffering the company of your incredibly tiresome mother and her yapping dogs? On my *feet*, for the love of all that's decent. They piddle on my *feet*. And all without my maid to attend me? Her spots weren't *that* terrible, that we had to leave her behind in— where on earth did we leave her?"

"Smardon, dear," Lucas said, plucking a name out of his head at random as a buxom woman walked into the foyer, probably alerted by the commotion, and looking at Nicole as if she might have two heads. "We'll gather her up on our way home. I did promise."

"You also promised me your man would see that we had lodgings at a premier inn. Does this look like a *premier* inn to you, husband? I think not. You ripped me away from a lovely house party for *this?* All because your mother believes herself to be dying—*again*."

"I am her only child, dear," Lucas said, enjoying himself mightily.

"Humph! I'm surprised your late father even dared to come near her the once. You!" she commanded, turning her fire on the innkeeper. "How long do you suppose to keep me standing here, sirrah? My chamber, now, and a bath prepared within the half hour, as well as someone to attend me. Your wife here, or one of your daughters, and not just some giggling little snip with more hair than wit. Innkeepers always have a multitude of daughters. Well? My chamber, sirrah! Step to it!"

"Yes, ma'am!" the innkeeper exclaimed, racing out from behind the counter, looking as if he feared Nicole's next command might be *off with his head* if he didn't comply at once.

"Maude? Maude! For the love of God, woman, take this lady to her rooms!" He then quickly retreated behind the counter once more, having saved himself by sacrificing his wife.

"I'll see to your luggage, my dear," Lucas said quietly as he watched Nicole climb the stairs behind the innkeeper's wife, her chin raised so high he was surprised she could see the risers beneath her feet. He stifled the urge to applaud.

"You'd be Mr. Paine then, sir?" the innkeeper inquired nervously once they were gone, taking a large linen square from his leather apron pocket and wiping his damp brow with it.

"For my sins, yes, and more and more my name is also my description. Never mind," he added as the innkeeper frowned, not understanding the attempt at humor.

"Yes, sir. Two bedchambers and a private dining room?"

"Two bedchambers, God, yes. Would *you* sleep with that unless you had to?" Lucas asked the fellow, man-to-man, in part to make up for his weak joke.

"Not lessen I could gag—that is, that's not for me to say, sir."

Lucas approached the counter, still enjoying himself more than he ought, he was sure. He leaned an elbow on the wood and lowered his voice to say conspiratorially, "It's the pretty ones who fool you into thinking they're something they're not. But by then it's too late."

"They're all something you think they're not, sir, when you get straight down to it, that's my way of thinking. Would you be wanting to step into the taproom whilst we fetch your luggage up to your rooms?"

"And that, my fine fellow," Lucas said, standing up straight once more, "sounds like an exemplary idea. But it's worse when she's hungry. Are we too late for a bit of cold dinner in, say, an hour? Is there ham? My wife is very partial to ham. But for God's sakes, man, trim the fat or we'll all hear about it."

"Maude will see to it, yes. Wouldn't want your lady wife seeing no fat, no sir!"

"Fine. I suggest you send a tray up to my wife's room. I'll…I'll just go see to my coachman and our horses."

Lucas didn't know quite how he made it outside the inn and around the corner of the building before he all but collapsed against the wall, laughing until his sides hurt.

No, there'd be no questions asked by anyone at The Sign of the Gate. Everyone would be too busy avoiding Nicole to care *where* she slept.

NICOLE SANK INTO THE HOT WATER up to her chin in the high-sided metal tub after the innkeeper's wife had been kind enough to help her wash her hair and then tie it up on her head. She closed her eyes as she heard the door close behind the woman, whom she'd just dismissed, complaining testily that she didn't like people *hovering* over her as she bathed.

She felt terrible, having behaved so imperiously, but better everyone at the inn avoided her rather than looking at her and *wondering*. Lucas would simply have to tip everyone generously when they left.

He had been wonderful, she thought, smiling as she lifted the large sea sponge and dribbled soapy water over her chest. He'd acted just as browbeaten as any of her mother's husbands or suitors had ever looked when that woman had decided to climb onto her high horse.

It had been rather delicious, pretending, playacting. But, when it came down to it, she'd much rather be herself. Being someone else, something she wasn't, was fatiguing, and almost sad.

The sponge remained where it was as Nicole froze in place, the truth finally revealed to her.

Her mother had spent her entire life playacting, Nicole decided, the sudden realization shocking her. Why hadn't she stumbled onto that fact before now? Why, she didn't even *know* her mother, did she? Was the real Helen Daughtry the pretty, delicious-smelling young mother who had dressed up her daughters and pretended they were going to a ball? Or was she the increasingly desperate woman who fussed over her succession of men as if she loved each of them dearly?

Was she the crude woman who spoke so glibly about taking men into her bed, or an unhappy woman who took men into her bed because that was the only way she knew to be noticed? To feel loved?

Her mother had always relied on her looks, her quite exemplary looks, certain that they were all she had. No wonder she shunned Lydia now, who was so young, and fresh, while her mother relied more and more on the paint pots and artifice.

Married off at sixteen to a man she couldn't love, a man who neglected her, leaving her in the country as he gambled away nearly every penny, and then dying, leaving her to the mercies of his brother the duke, who held the purse strings. Clearly disliked by that new guardian of herself and her children, still shunted off to oblivion on the small, run-down estate of Willowbrook, was it any surprise that she'd done whatever she could to take control of her own life?

That's what Nicole would have done, although not in the way her mother had chosen. Her mother had gone looking, was still looking, for someone who would save her, love her. And Nicole, watching, not understanding, had declared that she would never love, never allow a man to control her.

They were so different, mother and daughter, and yet so alike.

"She's frightened," Nicole said quietly in the empty room, her heart skipping a beat as she knew she was correct in her conclusion, that she finally had the right of it. "She's probably lived her whole life frightened, pretending, never feeling free to be herself, always trying to please, to shock, to do anything to be noticed, to feel *real*." She leaned her head against the high back of the oval tub and sighed. "Oh, Mama, I didn't know, I didn't understand. I'm so sorry."

Nicole didn't know how long she sat in the tub, at last noticing that, even with a fire burning in the grate a few yards away, she was beginning to feel chilled.

She had just begun to stand up in the metal tub and was reaching for a towel when she heard a knock coming from a darkened corner of the room and a previously unnoticed door opened.

She expected the innkeeper's wife.

"Lucas!"

Nicole fell back into the bath with an ignominious splash, submerging completely, the towel she'd grabbed hitting the water as she did. She emerged from the water, only to her shoulders, fighting off the large towel that threatened to envelop her, drag her back under the surface, and then pulled it over her body.

"Nicole? My God, are you all right?"

She spit out a mouthful of water and then scrubbed at her eyes with a corner of the wet towel. "You…*idiot!* What were you trying to do? Drown me?"

She kept squeezing her eyes open and shut, for the soapy water stung at them, but she could definitely hear the humor in Lucas's voice as he said, "If I was, my plan obviously didn't work. I'm sorry. I was certain you'd be out of the tub by now. I saw the innkeeper's wife downstairs as I left the taproom."

"I sent her away," Nicole told him, blowing at a

wet ringlet that had fallen into her face. There was water in her ears, and she shook her head, trying to clear them. She'd never been so wet in her life. "Where are you?" she asked, peering into the darkened corner and not seeing him.

"Behind you," he said, and she gasped, dragging the wet towel more fully over her, thankful now that it was so large, and that the sides of the tub were so high. "Do you know that's the only towel?"

"Do you know I would like nothing more at this moment than to choke you?"

"Well, that's comforting. Another woman might have swooned at a predicament like this, and be in danger of drowning. But not you, Mrs. Paine. You're pluck to the backbone."

His laugh was so joyful and unaffected that she would have turned and flung the towel at him, except that would leave her with nothing but her anger to cover her.

"Are you quite finished?" she asked him. "Nothing else to say? Good. Now go find me a towel. This water is getting colder by the moment." Then her eyes went wide and she sank farther into the tub, the towel covering her up to her chin. "What was that?"

"That, *wife,* was the sound of a knock, most probably heralding the arrival of our dinner. Shall I get the door?"

When she got out of this tub, if she ever got out of this tub, she was definitely going to kill him. "Oh, no, don't bother. Please, allow me to do it," she said, her voice dripping with sarcasm.

"If you insist," he said, and then told her to stay where she was, keeping in mind that there was nothing untoward to be seen in a husband being in his wife's bedchamber while she was naked.

"Don't say naked," she told him, but she said the words very quietly, her mind frantic to find a way out of this ridiculous situation. So far, her only solution seemed to be to shut her eyes, as if that childish reaction would thus make her invisible. Since she knew that wouldn't actually work, she finally opened her eyes and looked behind her, to realize that Lucas was gone.

Her teeth began to chatter. And he'd left her here to freeze to death.

He was back a minute later.

She faced forward once more, and once more closed her eyes.

"I've asked that our dinner be set up in my chamber," Lucas said, walking over to stand beside the tub. "I'm also in possession of more towels."

"And you sound so proud of yourself, don't you? I suppose you think I should thank you now?"

One of the folded towels dropped into the tub.

"Lucas!"

"I've still got two more. But only the two. You might want to consider that before you say anything else."

"Lucas, please," she said, probably bleated. But she was *so* cold.

"I'm going to hold up the towel—it's quite large—turn my head, and you're going to stand up and let me wrap it around you."

"I have a better idea. You can put the towel on that stool where the other one was, leave the room, and then I'll get out of the tub."

He grinned down at her. "I like my solution better. And, before you say anything else, remember, Nicole. I am holding the towels."

"Turn your head *and* close your eyes," she bargained.

"This is probably the first time we've been in total agreement since the moment we met. It almost makes me believe anything is possible. All right. And don't slip."

She waited until he'd fully opened the towel—it was quite large, thank God, and would cover her to her knees and beyond. Then, hesitating only until he'd turned his head and closed his eyes, she stood up and *pushed* herself forward into the towel.

Immediately his arms came around her, completely wrapping her in the thick toweling. He lifted her up and out of the tub as if she weighed no more than a feather, holding on to her so that her toes were a good foot off the ground.

"God, you feel good," he whispered into her ear. And then he kissed her just behind that ear. "But you taste like soap."

Once again, she noticed, her arms were trapped at her sides, not by her sleeves this time, but by the towel. "Put…me…*down*."

"Yes, I suppose I should." He lowered her gently and stepped away from her. "Will you be able to manage now on your own?"

"Manage to dry and dress myself, you mean?" she asked as she retreated from the light of the fire and took refuge on the far side of the bed. "Why would you ask? Can't you?"

He reached up and scratched at one eyebrow, but she could still see his smile. "Touché, sweetheart. I'll be in my chamber when you're ready. There's ham, with all the fat trimmed off it."

"Oh. I rather like the fat, when it's nice and brown, that is." Her stomach growled and she wondered if he'd heard it, and she was still wet, and chilled, especially away from the fire. "I'll…I'll join you shortly."

He bowed most elegantly, probably mockingly, and quit the room, carefully closing the door behind him.

Nicole sprang into action.

She padded barefoot back to the fire, holding the toweling closed with one hand as she struggled to rip the wet ribbon from her hair, which was still dripping cool water down her back.

The innkeeper's wife had wanted to unpack the portmanteau that had been brought to the room, but Nicole had waved her away, sure she couldn't keep up her charade a moment longer without collapsing into giggles.

Which left it now to her to see what Lydia had ordered packed for her.

She undid the leather straps and opened the thing, first pulling out her riding habit, and then a sprigged muslin morning gown that—drat it!—had a long row of buttons running down its back. Well, she couldn't wear that, could she?

Nicole found undergarments and tossed them on the bed, and then dug to the bottom of the portmanteau, unearthing a heavy white cotton night rail and dressing gown and looking at both in horror.

Because neither piece was hers. They belonged to Lydia, and she was certain her sister only wore the things when she was ill, and wished to feel warm and cozy.

In other words, the night rail would button halfway up her throat and drag beyond her wrists and toes. The thing held all the allure of a shroud.

Then again, Nicole was still cold, even after drying herself, and it was either the shroud, or climbing into what seemed to be the only fresh underclothing Renée had deigned to pack, and then asking Lucas to not only button her gown but also unbutton it when it was time for bed....

"The devil with it," she said, diving headfirst into the night rail, its long sleeves with the narrow bands of cotton lace nearly swallowed up her hands, and then quickly covering it with the dressing gown that had, dear Lord, small yellow embroidered roses on the bodice.

Nicole had seen her mother's nightwear, and had chosen her own with care in Bond Street, quickly learning that she enjoyed the feel of silk and satin on her otherwise naked body. Lydia couldn't have packed her yellow ensemble? The one with the Venetian lace at the bodice, cuffs and hem?

Sometimes her sister was such a…such a *sister.*

Grabbing up the last dry towel, Nicole lifted her hair and wrapped the thing around her shoulders, then let her wet hair fall once more, hopefully preventing dampening her dressing gown.

She poked around inside the portmanteau one last time, found a small case with her toothbrush and powder in it, along with her silver-backed tortoise-shell combs. Tears coming to her eyes, she dragged the combs through her hair, pulling angrily at the knots until she felt she looked at least marginally human again.

And then, before her bare feet could turn coward on her, and slipping one of the combs into the pocket of the dressing gown, she crossed the room—avoiding the mirror that would show her how ridiculous she looked—and entered Lucas's chamber without bothering to knock.

CHAPTER SIXTEEN

LUCAS HAD STRIPPED OUT OF HIS jacket—not without effort, as it was well-tailored to his body, and he had to admit to missing his valet, not that he'd confess any such thing to Nicole.

He'd used the bootjack to remove his boots, a desecration of good leather but, again, he was not about to ask Nicole's help after her comment, and then shrugged out of his waistcoat, pulled off his neck cloth and opened the top two buttons of his shirt.

He'd left his dark blue silk banyan where it was in his portmanteau, not wishing to frighten her. It was enough that he'd removed his boots.

He'd just had time to wash his face and hands in the basin before he heard the door between the two bedchambers open. He turned to see Nicole walking into the room, her chin held high, as if daring him to say anything.

So he didn't.

He simply sat down on one of the chairs at the fireplace, and laughed out loud.

"I believe I've seen suits of armor that offered less

protection," he said as she glared at him. "You only had to say *no,* Nicole. I know we're alone, but I wasn't going to force myself on you."

"It's Lydia's," she told him, heading straight for the table that had been set in front of the window. "She's the one saying no to you. I'm the one who hasn't seemed to have yet discovered a way to say no to you. However, if you don't stop grinning at me like that, I believe I could learn."

"My apologies," he said, getting to his feet once more. "Here, let me help you with those covers."

He joined her at the table, doing as he'd said, lifting the pewter lids and exposing mounds of ham and a quarter-round of homemade cheese as well as a dish of butter, a loaf of bread and a small bowl of berries already laced with cream.

She picked up one of the berries and popped it into her mouth, a bit of cream dribbling down her chin.

He fought down the urge to lick it from her skin.

"I think I'll just have the ham for now, and take it back to my room," she told him, using her fingers to put a slice on one of the plates. "I have to dry my hair or else I'll have a wet pillow tonight and a damp tangled mess in the morning. There's just so much of it."

"Stay here," he told her, similarly loading a plate, but adding cheese to his. "I've already rung for someone to remove the tub. Once that's done, you can go back to your own room."

She hadn't bothered with a knife and fork, but just

lifted one of the ham slices and took a healthy bite. God, she was so *elemental.* He felt a knot forming in his gut. She chewed for a few moments and then said, "You're not going to ask me to stay?"

How did he answer that? If he said no, he would be lying. If he said yes, he'd be taking advantage of her. Hell, he'd been taking advantage of her since their first meeting. He was older, more experienced, supposedly wiser.

"Circumstance," he said at last. "Circumstance has put us together tonight. That doesn't mean anything has to happen here, Nicole."

She looked at him for several moments, and then took her plate with her and crossed to the fireplace, to sit herself down on the hearth rug, the plate on the floor in front of her. "I need to dry my hair."

He watched as she sat back on her haunches, tipping her head sharply toward the fire so that her long hair fell all to one side of her head like a curtain of midnight silk. She lifted the towel and squeezed it around her hair several times before letting it drop to the floor and extracting a large, heavy comb from her pocket.

And then, as if he weren't even in the room, she began combing that glorious ebony mane, lifting the hair from her neck, sweeping its thick mass up and out, exposing it to the heat, setting small fires of light to dancing through the shimmering locks.

The knot in Lucas's gut tightened as he watched her take what was a simple, ordinary task and turn it into a portrait worthy of a master's brush.

She looked so entirely virginal in her all-enveloping dressing gown, not even the tips of her toes able to escape its sheer volume of material. And yet, somehow, when she raised her hands to her head, he could clearly see the outline of her full breasts, admire the way the soft cotton molded to her buttocks as she knelt there, more alluring than any siren perched on the rocks to lure ancient mariners to their doom. Or to their destiny.

He was no Odysseus, he had no loyal crew to lash him to the mast so that he could resist the sirens' call. He was merely a man, a man who had dreamed of Nicole each and every night since she'd first smiled up into his face on Bond Street, rendering him nearly speechless.

He knelt beside her, took the comb from her hands. "Let me," he said, barely recognizing his own voice, not even sure what all he was asking of her.

She gave her head another quick flip, and with that one movement, her hair settled in a sleek curtain around her shoulders.

It was still damp, and slightly warm from the fire. His fingertips tingled with sensation as he slowly drew the comb through the thick, dark silk.

Nicole leaned her head back and sighed, nearly purred like a contented kitten. "That feels good," she told him. "Renée *yanks* at my hair, so I usually comb it myself. But I like having someone else do it. I feel…pampered. Maybe I won't have it all cut off."

"Let me guess. I'm now supposed to beg you not to do that, aren't I?" As, Lucas recalled, he'd nearly done once before.

She leaned her head back even farther, so that she could look up into his face. "I wouldn't be opposed to it, no. Even a little groveling wouldn't come amiss. That wasn't a nice thing you did to me, you know. Teasing me with that towel. Not that you *saw* anything."

"I didn't?"

The comb caught in her hair as she turned herself around to face him. "No, you didn't. I was barely on my feet when you opened that door, and then I slipped, and— Lucas, stop *waggling* your eyebrows like that. It's extremely childish of you."

"All right, I admit it. I wasn't looking toward the tub, sadly, and by the time you called out my name, I was only able to turn in time to see the splash. It was a mighty splash, by the way."

She smiled. "It was, wasn't it? The carpet was drenched, and probably will be for a week. I've already thought of it, and you probably have as well, but I think you have to be a very generous guest when we depart tomorrow."

"To make up for the abuse they've taken from my shrewish wife, I agree."

She reached up and took the comb. "Here, wait a moment. I adore how well you're doing, but my hair will never dry this way."

So saying, she went up onto her knees and then scooted over so that when she went back on her haunches once more she kept right on going, lowering her head and shoulders back until she was lying across his knees, her hair splayed out over him and down onto the hearth rug. She shifted slightly, unfolding her legs, the dressing gown slightly bunched up now, so that he could see her bare feet and ankles.

These small glimpses of her were proving more provocative than the quick glimpse he'd had of her as she stood naked in the tub. Someday he might even tell her that, once he was sure she wouldn't murder him for having, yes, peeked.

"Put the towel beneath my hair, please," she told him, once more smiling up at him. "Oh, stop looking at me that way. You don't have to comb anymore. It will dry now on its own, and we can talk. I have something I want to tell you. Something I discovered while I was in my bath."

He continued to play with her hair, lifting it, letting it run through his fingers, watching it lightly float back onto the towel. As it dried it began to take on soft waves, and that intrigued him even more.

Soon, very soon, he would not be able to resist bending down and burying his face in it.

"There was something to discover in your bath? A fish? A toad? I don't believe I heard any croaking. A rather abrupt scream and perhaps a gurgle or two, but no croaking."

"Lucas, stop. I'm attempting to be serious."

He looked down at her, saw the deep purple of her magnificent eyes. "Yes, I see that. I'm sorry." He bent his head, kissed the tip of her nose. "Go on, tell me what you discovered."

"Well," she said, and he noticed that she'd folded her hands together, her fingers intertwined, and she was rubbing her fingers against her skin, as if in an attempt to lend comfort to herself. Or courage.

"Is this about…us?"

"No, at least it shouldn't be. But, yes, I suppose it is somewhat about us. I, um, I realized who I am."

His hand stilled as he was drawing his spread fingers through her hair. "Pardon me?"

She turned onto her side and pushed herself up so that she was looking straight into his eyes. As if needing his entire attention while she said what she had to say, she placed her hands on his shoulders before she spoke. "I'm my mother's daughter, Lucas. I am, just as everyone always says. And that's all right, it really is. But I'm not my mother. I'm *me*. And I think I'm finally happy with me, with who I am. I have no reason to be anyone else."

He reached out his hand, cupped her cheek in his palm. Looked into her eyes as she seemed to search his face for his reaction. He watched the firelight dance across her face, the light sprinkle of freckles that dusted her fair skin.

"I would never want anyone else," he told her quietly, and her eyelids fluttered closed as he touched her lips with his own and they sank, together, to the floor.

He couldn't kiss her long enough, deeply enough. But that was all right, because he was in no hurry.

He took her mouth with his, teaching her with his tongue, teasing her with his teeth, holding her to him, sculpting her every curve with his hands.

He could feel her arousal in the way she moved

against him, as she strove for something she had yet to realize existed outside of her imagination or whatever she'd been told.

And Lord only knew what all her mother had told her.

He wanted her to feel everything, everything there was to feel, every glory their bodies could offer each other. But he needed more than that. She deserved more than that.

She had to understand that the giving, the taking, was more than just an exchange of physical pleasure.

So he lifted her in his arms and carried her to the bed, laying her down gently on the pillows, kissing her one more time before he stepped away into the shadows, disrobed, and then joined her once more beneath the covers.

He kissed her for long minutes: her mouth, her hair, her eyelids. He whispered words that he really didn't understand himself, but that seemed to soothe her as well as inflame her.

He kissed away her clothing, worshipping each new exposed area of skin. Showing her with his mouth, his hands, that she was cherished, that she was desirable, inflaming, irresistible to him.

The base of her throat, where he could feel her heartbeat beneath his lips.

The crook of her elbow, the sweep of her belly, the soft curve behind her knee, the sweet, high arch of her foot.

The night was theirs, and he would use all of it, even as he would love all of her.

She was so pliable beneath him, giving him every access, only saying his name rather breathlessly as he dared each new intimacy, told her without words that she was perfect to him in every way.

When he moved over her, easing her thighs apart, she lifted herself to him and he fused his mouth against her, glorying in the way she cried out his name, first in surprise, then in pleasure.

He suckled her, drawing her into his mouth, finding the tight hard center of her and exploiting it, spreading her wide with his fingers, leaving her defenseless against his flicking tongue.

And still she strove against him, her body taking her places she'd never been, raising her to heights their furtive lovemaking couldn't have prepared her for. Not this freedom, this unleashing of every inhibition, this mad, hot pulsing that at last took her, shook her, centered all of her mind and body on this elemental core that was her womanhood, her right, her ultimate pleasure.

Before it was over, before she could come back to earth, he levered himself between her legs and positioned himself. He said a quick, silent prayer he wouldn't hurt her too badly, and with one swift movement, plunged himself past the final barrier and deep inside her.

He felt her arms go up and around him, her rounded nails digging into his back as she buried her head in his neck.

She was his. She was all his.

Lucas reached down and urged her to raise her

legs, not sure she understood. But a moment later she had wrapped her legs around him, drawing him more deeply inside her.

Her embrace urged him on, the heat of her set him aflame, beyond reason, past any thought other than possessing her, pleasuring her, branding her his own for now, for all time.

He plunged deeper, harder, faster, and she bit him, as she had done that first night, and then began suckling at his neck, taking the taste of him, sealing herself against him as she branded him, left her mark on him.

And then, just as he thought he could stand no more, she seemed to tense in his arms, her head dropping back onto the pillows. "Lucas. *Lucas.* Oh God…"

He felt her body clenching around him, again and again and again, followed by the hot, hard release of his seed deep inside her.

"SHOULD I RING FOR MORE butter?" Lucas asked her as they sat across the small table from each other and he watched her spreading more on the slice of thick, homemade bread.

He was wearing his banyan over his nakedness, which was nearly as delicious as the fact that she was enveloped past her knees in the white shirt he'd discarded earlier, her hair hanging free down her back. The light from the fire had begun to die, and the candles were burning low. Sitting at the small table beside the window, they were together in a cocoon of intimacy that warmed her heart in a way she couldn't understand, but that she would treasure for all of her life.

Nicole looked down at the slice she'd slathered so liberally. "You're insinuating I've used too much?"

"No, not at all. Surely less than a pound."

She made a face at him. "But it's so good. I haven't had butter this fresh since we left Ashurst Hall. There's only one thing missing, you know. Sugar. Have you ever sprinkled sugar on your bread and butter, Lucas? You bite into it, and it is so sweetly crunchy and then smooth and creamy—the butter, you understand. I love the taste, but mostly I think I like the way it feels in my mouth."

He was *looking* at her again. Looking at her the way he'd done when they'd made love. As if she amazed him in some way. As he had amazed her.

"You're a creature of sensation, aren't you?" he asked her, dropping his chin in his hand as he continued to watch her. "The warmth of the sun, the wind blowing in your face, the exhilarating shiver of excitement as you dare a jump, the texture of the food you eat. You enjoy it all, every moment of it. Every moment of life. I envy you that."

"Because you're so ancient and jaded, I suppose," she teased him, taking another bite of the bread. "You know, I don't think I've ever been this hungry. Are you sure you don't want any of the berries?"

He sat back in his chair, waving his hand to indicate that she should take the bowl for herself. "I think I'd rather watch, anyway. Nicole?"

She hesitated, her fingers hovering over the bowl,

as the berries wouldn't taste half so good if she used the spoon. Besides, then she wouldn't be able to lick the cream from her fingers. "Hmm?"

"You're all right?"

"Am I— Oh." She dipped her head, feeling hot color running into her cheeks. Honestly, she'd never blushed in her life, until she'd met him. But he'd been so wonderful, so caring.

After the storm of lovemaking—for that was how she'd always think of it—he had wet a corner of the towel in the washbasin and…and taken care of her. Wiping away the evidence of her first time, speaking nonsense to her as he did so, carefully explaining that there would never again be any pain, he'd not allow any pain.

She hadn't had the heart to tell him that her mother had explained it all to her in embarrassing detail, so that she had known what she was doing, what had been about to happen, and she'd welcomed all of it. Goodness, she hadn't had to come to his room at all, and certainly hadn't been forced to stay.

They'd made love, yes, but that had been *her* decision. Her mother had been right, men only thought it was theirs.

"Yes, Lucas, I'm fine. I, um, I imagine you were quite wonderful, actually."

His eyes darkened. "Well, thank you, but I wasn't asking for a critique of my lovemaking. I suppose I meant, are you all right with the two of us marrying. Because there's no longer even the slightest question that—"

"Don't, Lucas. Please. Don't ruin it all now."

He sat forward, his elbows on the table once more. "Don't *ruin* it? But that's a good choice of word, when you consider that Society, and your family, would not be faulted to think that I have *ruined* you. That's simply the way it is, and you know that as well as I. Nicole, for God's sake—"

She held up her hands to him, begging him to be silent. "Please, Lucas, don't lecture me. Don't take what happened here tonight and twist it into some perfunctory marriage proposal that makes me your obligation. We made love. We both came here tonight expecting what happened to happen. You don't…you don't *owe* me anything. You most definitely don't *owe* me a marriage."

He sat back again, smiling, a reaction that had her hands bunching up into tight fists. "That's quite the word, perfunctory. One might almost think you've rehearsed that entire speech."

She hated when he was right. "I did not!" she shot back at him quickly. Too quickly, drat the man. "Oh, all right, possibly I did. But I mean what I say. I told you and told you, I came to London to have an adventure. I'll grant you, I hadn't expected you…or *this*. But I never thought to come to London to force a man into marriage. That's…that's shabby. Embarrassing, even calculated. I want no part of it."

"I'm your victim now, is that it? I'm the poor, dumb sot dazzled by your beauty, manipulated by your lures, enticed to my own destruction by your provocative ways? Next you'll be telling me you seduced me."

She looked up at the ceiling. "Well…"

His bark of laughter had her jumping to her feet, ready to flee the room. "Don't you do that! I'm being deadly serious. Don't you dare laugh at me!"

He stood up, as well. "I will if what you're saying is laughable."

"My mother—"

"No!" he snapped, pointing his finger at her, all traces of humor gone from his eyes, his voice. "We had that conversation earlier, Nicole, didn't we? You said it yourself. You are *not* your mother, remember? I don't know what she's said to you over the years, what you've witnessed, what you think you know."

Tears stung her eyes, but she blinked them away. "She might say I should be sure you married me, but she married, too. Among the others, she married, too."

"My God," he said, his anger leaving him. "You think…you think that now…that now that I've *had* you, my interest will wane. Don't you? My interest—or yours. Which is it? Are all men shallow, Nicole, or all women? Tell me. I want to know what you're thinking, what she taught you to believe."

Her heart was breaking. She could feel it falling into little pieces. She was so confused. She wanted to believe that he loved her, that what he felt for her went beyond wanting. Wanting what she'd offered. God, what she'd *offered*. What man turned away from such a blatant invitation?

"I'm going to bed now," she told him, suddenly so weary that she felt herself swaying where she stood. "And I'm taking these with me," she said, snatching up the bowl of berries and clutching it to her chest as if it was a shield meant to protect her.

Lucas pinched the bridge of his nose between his fingers. "All right, yes, go to bed. It has been a long day, one way or another. That's probably for the best. For now."

"Thank you," she said quietly. "Lucas, I'm sorry."

"I know you are. I also know you're wrong. But it's not enough that I know it. You have to know it, too. It's after midnight now, so you need some rest. I'll knock on your door at eight and we'll go down to breakfast. You'll probably want to ride out on Juliet."

She nodded, unable to speak for the lump in her throat, and left the room. Once safe in her own chamber, she looked down at the bowl of berries and cream—the stupid bowl of berries and cream—and flung it away from her, so that it crashed against the far wall, spilling everywhere.

"Just like something the horrible Mrs. Paine would do," she muttered, looking at the mess. And then she climbed into bed, pulled the collar of his shirt up against her face so she could keep the heady smell of him close to her... and let the tears fall.

CHAPTER SEVENTEEN

LUCAS WOKE BEFORE DAWN to a message for Mr. Paine. He hesitated for only a second before breaking the deliberately plain wax seal, knowing something important had happened, or else Rafe wouldn't have sent a man all the way to The Sign of the Gate.

He thanked the innkeeper and closed the door, walking over to the pale light just beginning to come in the window as he unfolded the single sheet. He scanned the short message quickly, and then read it again before tossing it into the fire.

He was washed and dressed in less time than his valet would have supposed, the fuller cut of his hacking jacket easing his way. He tied a fresh neck cloth loosely around his neck, not even bothering to check his reflection in the mirror, and stamped his feet into his boots.

Then, running his fingers through blond hair mussed from sleep, he crossed to the door that separated his room from Nicole's.

"Nicole! I'm coming in," he called out as he knocked on the door. "We have to leave now."

He'd expected to find her still in bed, but she was

just tying back her hair in a black grosgrain ribbon, the jacket of her riding habit still hanging open over a snow-white camisole.

Even in the revealing light of the newly dawning day, she didn't immediately attempt to pull the jacket more closely around her, but only finished tying back her hair.

She was so beautiful, so fresh and exciting. He'd always known that. But now, having kissed damn near every inch of her, he knew she was more than a beautiful, desirable woman. She was *his* woman, even if she didn't yet admit to that fact. Even with all that was still ahead of them, he knew himself to be the luckiest man in the world.

"Then I was right," she said, taking a pin from her mouth and picking up her hat. "I heard a horse ride in earlier, and thought I heard someone mention your name when I opened my window and looked down on the courtyard. Well, calling for Mr. Paine. I immediately got up and began to dress. I'm already packed and ready to leave. You might want to comb your hair," she ended, summoning a small smile.

He admired her lack of panic, but this wasn't the time to applaud her. Or to kiss her, which had been his first thought. It hadn't occurred to her that he could travel faster without her, leaving her here to be escorted back to London by the man Rafe had sent.

Strangely, until this moment, that very reasonable solution hadn't occurred to him, either. He immediately put it out of his head.

"Rafe has his coach and fresh teams already in

place along the way. The Dover road will be crowded this close to the ports at this time of the morning. We can make better time leaving our baggage with my coach and getting ourselves to the first stopping point if we ride across country. I don't know how he found out, but the march on Westminster Bridge is scheduled for tonight, and more than fifty miles still separate us from London."

She nodded sharply, quickly securing her shako hat to her curls. "And you have to get back to town in time to stop it," she said, reaching for her gloves. "Go have the horses saddled and I'll be right down. Oh—do you suppose there's a *real* saddle in the stables you could purchase for me? We'll make better time if I'm not forced to ride sidesaddle over unfamiliar ground."

There were a thousand questions he could have asked her after that statement, but he asked none of them. "I'll see what I can do. Five minutes, Nicole. I'm sorry there won't be time for breakfast, but we can eat when we get to Lynsted. That's a good twenty miles, less across country. We'll pace them. Can your Juliet last that long?"

"I've never taken her that far in one go. But she'll manage. She has to."

They didn't have a moment to waste, but surely kissing her just the once couldn't be considered a waste of time. He pulled her close and brought his mouth down hard on hers, glorying in the way she grabbed him and held on, each of them taking strength, resolve, from the other.

"Ready?" he asked her as she broke off the kiss.

She was slightly breathless as she nodded, and then said, "I can't go with you to The Broken Wheel, can I?"

He shook his head. "You shouldn't be riding with me now."

"But you wouldn't have left me here."

"No," he said, holding her gaze with his own, knowing he was answering her question, hoping she understood he was answering more than just that one question. "I would never leave you."

He watched as her eyes went darkly purple, but when she spoke it was to tell him she'd meet him in the stableyard, but first she had something she needed to do.

Five minutes later, as he watched the mare being fitted with the well-worn saddle he'd purchased for three times its cost, the innkeeper came up to him to inquire as to whether his guest had been mistaken of the amount when he'd paid the bill of fare.

Looking at the man's hopeful face, Lucas told him no, he was well aware of the amount he had paid to the man's wife, at which point the innkeeper broke into a wide smile.

"Spent a good night, then, did you, sir? Lord love a woman, no matter how she goes on, who knows how to give a man a happy night."

Lucas knew he had probably invited such frankness with his teasing of the night before, but he couldn't hide his surprise. "I beg your pardon?"

The innkeeper tapped at the side of his own neck,

and smiled. "You have yourself a pleasant trip, sir, and my best wishes for your mother's recovery," he said, and then turned and headed back into the inn, whistling a tuneless melody.

Lucas raised a hand to the side of his throat, remembering the haphazard way he'd tied his neck cloth, but mostly recalling how Nicole had buried her face against him in the heat of her passion, and suckled hard at his neck.

He adjusted the neck cloth higher, then walked over to seek out Rafe's man, to give him final instructions on gathering up the luggage and returning to Grosvenor Square.

With trouble ahead of him, uncertainty his only certainty, he whistled as he walked.

NICOLE EXITED FROM THE REAR of the inn, wishing she might remain in the kitchens a while longer to take in the mouthwatering aroma of baking bread, but she was also anxious to get on her way back to London.

Being alone with Lucas was heady, but it was also confusing, and probably something she shouldn't dwell on very much, or else she'd spend the day thinking both about the night they'd shared and the night they'd never have because of their mad dash back to the metropolis.

"Here—catch!" she called out to Lucas when she saw him with his back turned to her.

He wheeled quickly to look at her, and was just in time to snag the boiled egg she'd launched at him. "Where did you get this?"

"I didn't lay it, if that's what you're asking," she told him, causing the young man in Ashurst livery to snicker into his hand before discreetly returning to the stables. But Nicole had known Felix since he was in short coats, so she wasn't embarrassed…and he hadn't been surprised at her joke.

She'd already peeled both eggs in the kitchens, and eaten hers there, so she watched as Lucas ate his in two large bites as they walked over to the horses.

"Ah, there's my sweet Juliet," she said, retrieving a small carrot from her skirt pocket and feeding it to her, then giving a second one to Thunder. "And how are you two getting along, hmm?"

"I doubt you want to know," Lucas told her. "I'll only say that my pockets will soon be to-let if I have to keep paying for peevish wives, decrepit saddles and the boards Thunder kicked down in order to join Juliet for a late night tête-à-tête in her stall."

Nicole giggled as she walked to the mounting block and allowed a wide-eyed ostler to help her up and into the saddle. She felt a small shock of burning discomfort at her very center, not that she would allow anyone to know that, but then slipped her feet into the stirrups and motioned for the boy to hand up the reins.

Lucas was already astride the stallion, looking at her in some question. "Are you comfortable?" he asked her, and she knew why he was asking.

"I'm perfectly fine, thank you."

"You look magnificent," he told her, words that took any thoughts of discomfort and sent them flying. "No gallops, we have to conserve their strength."

Juliet was already dancing in place, pawing the hard ground of the stable yard. "Good enough. Now tell *her*. Do you know our route?"

"I do. We follow the road for about a mile, and then we set off cross-country. Ready?"

Nicole took a deep breath and nodded. "Ready."

She knew that a fine animal, and Juliet and Thunder were much more than just fine animals, could be pushed into covering close to one hundred miles in a single twenty-four-hour period. That meant that the twenty miles she and Lucas were asking of their mounts was not punishing.

What would be "punishing" was the toll it would take on both horse and rider to travel all the way to London that way. Lucas had barely slept the previous night. She knew that because she hadn't, and she'd heard him prowling the floor in his own room for most of the hours she'd lain awake, listening for him.

Once they were in Rafe's coach, she'd convince Lucas he needed to sleep, to rest himself for what would happen that night.

It would also give her time to plan what she would be doing while he was at The Broken Wheel, attempting to convince an angry crowd of hungry men to listen to him. She already knew that she would not be pacing the floor in Grosvenor Square, twiddling her thumbs or whatever it was everyone would expect her to do.

They left the road just when she thought they would, the wagon and coach traffic on the Dover road as slow and heavy as Lucas had warned, and cut across the fields, their mounts stretching out their legs as they ran through fields not yet planted, soggy from too much rain or holding pitiful crops that looked more sad than anything else.

She pulled Juliet abreast of Thunder as they came to a wider area that ran along the hedgerows. "I suppose I hadn't realized it was this bad," she told him. "Why can't there be more sunny days, like this one?"

"We're lucky to have the few we have, thanks to that damned volcano," he told her, slowing his mount to a walk. "Nicole, what do I say to them? The people aren't fools. They know fine words and promises never filled a belly."

"Then tell them the truth."

"Tell them about the volcano? I doubt they'd be interested."

"No, not the volcano. Tell them there are unscrupulous people who would use their sad plight in order to forward their own ambitions. Men who would goad them into protests that can only lead to the passage of new laws meant to keep them beaten down, put them more firmly under the thumbs of those who seek power."

"In other words, you want me to stand up in front of a roomful of angry, desperate men, many of them armed with pikes and pitchforks, more than eager to wield them, full of false courage courtesy of pots of ale—and tell them they're actually nothing more than a bunch of gullible fools."

He turned to her and smiled. "Will you weep at my funeral?"

"That's not funny," she told him, her stomach clenching. "You don't believe they'll understand the truth?"

"Oh, they'll understand it. But think about this, Nicole. The truth will only make them angrier. God knows it would make me angrier."

"Well, then, they ought to be *angrier* with the right person!"

Lucas looked at her strangely. "Yes…they should be, shouldn't they? I have to think about that. Come on, time to pick up the pace again."

BY TWO O'CLOCK THEY'D ALREADY had two changes of horses at inns they passed, and Nicole had re-thought any notion that she would be able to sleep on the way to London.

It was enough that neither of them had been tossed off the seat as the coachman pushed the hired horses to their limits and beyond.

Atop the roof, a Basingstoke groom blew on the yard of tin again and again as they warned other vehicles and their drivers that they were coming up to pass them, an excitement that had first thrilled Nicole, but now only reminded her that her stomach hadn't been meant for the constant bouncing and swaying of a coach driven neck-or-nothing.

She pressed herself against the side of the coach

and held tight to the strap as they rounded a bend in the road, looking down through the window to see that they were coming within inches of toppling into a ditch, and then turned to look at Lucas, who was sound asleep on the other end of the seat.

He'd braced his long legs against the facing seat, his left arm slipped through the strap to keep him anchored before he'd crossed his arms over his stomach, slipped his hat low over his forehead and was now—how dare he!—softly snoring.

At least he hadn't seen her bring back the luncheon she'd just eaten at the last inn when she'd gone off to tend to her more private needs. The innkeeper's wife had given her a drink that had tasted of peppermint afterward, but even that hadn't helped settle her queasy belly. Her stomach felt hollow, and seemed to be sliding back and forth inside her, and she was even now entertaining the thought that she might never eat mutton again, not even if urged to at gunpoint.

"Lucas? Are you asleep?" She reached over and nudged him none too gently in the ribs. "Lucas? Are you sleeping?"

"Apparently not anymore, no," he told her, levering himself more fully onto the seat as he took off his hat and tossed it on the facing seat. "Is something wrong?"

"Yes, something's wrong," she told him testily. "How can you sleep?"

He rubbed at his face, wiping away any remaining drowsiness, she supposed. "It should be obvious, but very well. First, I close my eyes—"

"Stop that!"

"—although I should have thought to also stop up my ears with cotton," he went on, and then quickly lowered his arms to protect his ribs from another assault. "May I remind you that it was your idea that I sleep?"

"That's when I thought I would be able to sleep, too. But I'm not, and I think it's exceedingly rude of you to sleep when I can't."

"Yes, I see your point. Must I also be hungry when you're hungry? Happy when you're happy? Sad when you're sad?"

"Dead, when I murder you," she told him, laughing in spite of herself. "Never mind, go back to sleep. I'll just sit here and think up some way for you to halt the march on Parliament without being trampled by the marchers, if they haven't already beaten you to flinders and left you behind at The Broken Wheel. Don't you worry about a thing."

"Come here," he said, holding out his arm to her.

"No. I won't be mollified. This is a very serious business you're about to undertake, you know."

"And I promise to go about it very seriously, Rafe and I both."

She looked at him in surprise. "Rafe? He's going with you?"

"I imagine so, yes. This is all happening too fast. Rafe and I both thought we'd have more time. You do know, don't you, that if we succeed in staving off tonight's march, it will only infuriate Frayne the more. We not only have to stop the march, but

Frayne, as well. Right now, tonight, before he can do anything with whatever nonsense your mother mistakenly provided him. He won't be expecting that, as he thinks he holds all the cards."

"Which he does," she reminded him. "Well, the letters."

"Yes, sweetheart, but is he prepared to parcel them out immediately? I've given this some thought, and I don't think so. Once he's played those cards, those letters, he'll have no other moves left, no further way to control me—or believe he can control me, keep me silent as to his plans."

"But Rafe—"

"Yes, I know. Granted, Rafe then would be the subject of gossip, looked on as a possible murderer, but it's a little late in the day for Frayne to bring out anything about my father. He moves on Rafe, on your family, and that leaves me free to go to Liverpool and Sidmouth about what I know of his lordship's plans."

"You'd go straight to the Prime Minister and the Home Secretary?"

"Yes, absolutely. All the while praying they aren't either of them in this up to their necks with Frayne. Now come here. Please."

She held out her hands, keeping her distance. "You're right. It would be easier all the way around for Lord Frayne if he simply killed you."

Lucas raised one eyebrow as he looked at her. "Remind me not to make you my enemy."

"But it's only logical, Lucas. Surely you see that? Either you destroy Lord Frayne, or he destroys you."

"I know, sweetheart. I was foolishly hoping that you didn't."

She slid across the seat, helped by the coachman, who had just entered another sharp curve in the road, and settled herself against Lucas. Which was where she'd wanted to be all day in any case.

Honestly, you'd think the man would know that on his own!

Rubbing her cheek against his coat, she said, "You know, Lord Frayne will never tell you now who it was that betrayed your father. Is it enough for you and your mother to know that he was innocent of the charges that were going to be put to him?"

"I imagine it's going to have to be, yes. There were only ever whispers of suspicion when he died, nothing ever said outright about his supposed assistance in arranging the assassination of the Russian Emperor. I may have noticed a few stares, overheard a few comments, when I first entered Society, but nothing ever came of it and I was…accepted. Society feeds on scandal, needs it like mother's milk, but there are always new scandals to excite, to titillate.

"My father's suicide and whispered shame were all a long time ago. My mother and I are the only ones who were really hurt by what happened. So, yes. As much as I wish the person or persons could be exposed and punished, it's best if I let it go, let the past stay in the past."

Nicole snuggled in closer. "You're a good man, Lucas. A good son. When my mother returns from Italy I'm going to attempt to be a better daughter.

But, knowing me, and, most especially, knowing my mother, I doubt we'll be celebrating some grand birth of kindness and understanding. At least none that lasts above a fortnight."

She looked up at Lucas, to see he was smiling, which was why she'd said what she said.

She felt his arm come around her and his hand cup her breast. Almost absently, as if he was doing it without realizing what he was doing, he began stroking her with his thumb, sending her nipple into a tight bud beneath the fabric of her riding habit.

His next words rid her of the thought that he hadn't realized what he was doing.

"I want to love you. As I've been asleep, how long do you suppose we've been on the road this time?"

She hid her face from him. "I…I don't know. Not long. Not above a quarter hour."

He shifted slightly on the seat, pulling up the closest window shade and hooking it shut. When he turned back to her, she saw the passion in his eyes. "Then we've at least another hour before the next stop to change horses. You say you like adventures." He leaned forward and lifted the other two window shades on that side of the coach. "So, let's *adventure*."

She felt a rather pleasant tightness growing between her thighs, a near itch that had her pressing her legs together, hoping he didn't notice. "You can't possibly mean that we…that we'd…"

"I can't? Why not? You've thought of it."

"I did not!"

He kissed her right on the tip of her nose. "Possibly not first, but you've thought of it now. I can see it in your eyes. God knows I've been thinking about it all day."

He picked her up, moved her sideways onto his lap, and then scooted the both of them across the seat in order to close up the other windows, throwing the coach into almost complete darkness.

Then, with one arm still around her, and with her more than casually aware of his arousal, he began unbuttoning the front of her jacket.

"You…you've been thinking about this all day?"

He was nuzzling her neck now. "Hmm…yes. It would appear, sweetheart, that I'm a bad man. An exceedingly bad man. I've been thinking about this from the moment I watched you mount Juliet. You enjoy riding astride?"

"Lucas!"

Her jacket was entirely unbuttoned now, and he immediately lowered his mouth to her breasts, kissing her through the thin material of her camisole. She could feel the cool wetness of the material that skimmed over her nipples as, first with one, then the other, he drew her nipple into his mouth, sucking at her as he ran his tongue over her, flicking at the tight buds he'd encouraged to bloom for him.

She'd wrapped her arms around his neck, her upper body turned toward him as she offered him full access to her body. She felt a thickness in her throat, the rise of desire that couldn't be denied. Clearly wouldn't be denied.

Then he was kissing her again, and she sighed into his mouth as she felt his hand beneath the hem of her divided skirt. Shifting again, bracing her booted foot against the facing seat, she opened herself to him, aided and abetted his climb up her leg until he'd found her center, pushing aside her fragile silken undergarment as if it proved no barrier at all to his searching fingers.

She would have been more fascinated with the *how* of what he'd planned if she could have focused her attention on anything other than the way he made her feel, the wild excitement that coursed through her entire body.

"Help me," he whispered against her, taking her hand and lowering it to his lap. She felt the buttons of his trousers beneath her fingers. He was asking her cooperation, to aid and abet him in what would come next.

No longer the virgin, no longer to be slowly and carefully introduced to the ultimate delight, he now expected her full participation.

She was more than happy to comply.

Her divided skirt proved more troublesome, and at last Lucas fumbled at the buttons holding it closed at the waist. Beyond maidenly shame, she raised her legs into the air, the better for him to tug both down past her hips, and quickly her skirt and undergarment were consigned to the floor of the coach, leaving her clad in only her opened jacket, her riding boots and hose.

And her silly shako hat still perched saucily on her head.

"Dear God," he said, looking at her in the dim glow of the thin shafts of daylight slicing into the interior of the coach alongside the edges of the shades, his smile more than slightly wicked. "We're insane, the both of us."

And then he reached for her.

It seemed so natural to slide herself over him, straddling him with her knees pressed against the back of the seat, sinking onto him, taking him, taking him so deeply, so fully.

The motion of the coach became part of their own rhythm as Lucas held her sealed to him, kissing her throat as she arched her head backward, glorying in the feeling of power her position gave her, at the same time trusting him to know just how to take them both where they wanted, needed, to go.

There was no pain this time, no silly apprehension of what was surely the most beautiful, glorious union two people could possibly imagine.

But there was hunger. Dear God, how the hunger was growing inside her, consuming her. She moved against him, riding him, taking all he could give her. Faster. Deeper.

The explosion, their mutual explosion, when it came, melded them solidly together as they both tried to trap the overwhelming ecstasy, hold it fast.

They remained as they were for long moments, rocked in place by the movement of the coach, sharing kisses, whispers…and at long last, soft, sweet laughter.

Each turn of the coach's wheels brought them closer to London, to the reality of what awaited them. But for now, for these moments, there was nothing else, no one else. No past, no future. No questions without answers, no arguments about where their lovemaking would take them.

They were simply two people, lost in the moment…and whatever awaited them in London seemed blessedly far away.

CHAPTER EIGHTEEN

LUCAS SLIPPED INTO THE CHAIR across from Rafe even as a servant set down a second wineglass on the table in front of the fire.

"You made good time," Rafe said, saluting him with his own glass. "You also look like hell. I imagine I can lay the responsibility for that at my sister's door."

"Your sister and I are soon going to have words, very serious words," Lucas responded, glancing around him at the fairly empty clubroom. With Brummell all but a nonentity thanks to his falling out with the Prince Regent and his mounting debts, the bow window at White's had lost much of its allure, and its patrons.

"You've been in each other's company rather exclusively for nearly two days. Surely you found time to talk?"

"She still insists on turning me down."

Rafe chuckled softly. "You expected anything else? According to my wife, Nicole has never made a secret of the fact that she intends never to marry. I thought you could convince her differently. Declarations of undying love and devotion have changed many a mind, or so I've heard—I've heard that from my wife, actually."

Lucas froze in place with the wineglass halfway to his mouth. "Sweet Jesus."

"You didn't tell her?"

"I…well, certainly I…" Lucas speared his fingers through his hair, as if that might jog something loose in his brain. "I *think* I have. Yes, yes, of course I did. At some point…"

"Far be it from me to criticize, but if you did, I don't believe the moment could have been very memorable, since you don't seem able to recall it."

Lucas put down the wineglass, its contents untouched, although he'd been longing to get to White's and down at least three glasses, and got to his feet. "I have to go."

"*Now?* Lucas, sit down. I was only teasing with you. Something I shouldn't have done, considering my own not quite stellar history when it comes to how best to court the woman you love."

"But you don't understand. Marry me. I've said— I've said that a dozen times. Demanded it. *Yelled* it, I believe, at least once." He shook his head in bemusement. "Why didn't I tell her I love her? I told *you.*"

"Yes, I think I remember that. A very touching moment. I'll always treasure it, certainly."

Lucas sat down again with a near thump. "This isn't all that amusing, Rafe."

"Oh, but there you'd be very wrong. Especially

if you could be sitting over here as I am, looking at you. I tried to warn you. Nicole is…well, my sister is unique."

"Your sister is a bloody pain in— I have to talk to her. How much time do we have?"

Rafe glanced up at the mantel clock. "My valet tells me they gather at The Broken Wheel at eight, and it has already gone past six. Oh, and in case you've been wondering how I gained the information I did, we can thank Phineas, who was employed as a Bow Street Runner until he decided to throw in his lot with me. He's still learning his way around the intricacies of the Waterfall, but my neck cloths aren't actually embarrassing, are they?"

"Rafe, I've had very little sleep, so the devil with your neck cloths," Lucas warned him. "I need to see Nicole, damn it. So can we get on with this? How many will there be?"

"Sorry. By Phineas's count, there will be considerably more than one hundred marchers. Some of them armed, most not. All of them hell-bent on advancing across Westminster Bridge and nailing up their demands on the very doors of Parliament. If what you believe is correct, and Frayne has already alerted the Guard, I don't see how we'll avoid a massacre."

"So how do you suggest we stop them?"

"Well, I can't seem to conjure up a rosy picture of the two of us dropping in unannounced to tell them they're all a bloody bunch of fools being led by the nose by *agent provocateurs* sent expressly by the government to incite them. Seems a good way to get our throats cut."

"Now you sound like me, when Nicole asked the same question. Her answer was that, if these men are going to be angry, they ought to be angry with the right person."

"That's sensible enough. So how do we do that?"

Lucas leaned forward, his elbows on his knees. "I do have one idea...."

NICOLE LIFTED ONE EYELID as she heard the door to her bedchamber open and saw Lydia entering, her expression questioning and her step perhaps a bit tentative.

"Oh, I didn't realize you were in your bath," she said, already turning toward the door.

"That's all right," Nicole said, lifting her head from the rim of the tub, where she'd been half dozing, half pondering the universe as a whole as well as her place in it. "I'm becoming used to it."

"And what does that mean? No, never mind. I'm sorry I wasn't here when you returned. The Duke of Malvern insisted upon taking me out for some air while the weather was fine. We, um, we visited the Tower, but there wasn't much time to explore it, as I wanted to be back when you returned."

"The duke, is it? So you don't hate him anymore?"

Lydia spread her skirts as she sat down on the striped slipper chair that was her usual seat when she came to Nicole's bedchamber. She was so innately graceful, her movements less studied, more natural, than their mother's. Though very alike in looks, there was something about Lydia, something quietly regal, that set her apart from their mother. No wonder Helen didn't encourage comparison.

"I have never *hated* His Grace," Lydia told her, but without looking her sister full in the face. "He's actually a…a very nice man. I believe he is soon to be betrothed to his third cousin, a Miss Harburton. She's very pretty. Dark-haired, like you. Mama told me yesterday morning, just before you kidnapped her."

Nicole stood up in the tub and reached for the enormous towel that had been warming in front of the fire. "And how does Mama know this?" she asked, not sure she heard a hint of sadness in Lydia's voice, but also unable to ignore the possibility.

"I didn't ask her. That would have signaled to her that I cared one way or another, and she'd already told me the duke was out of the question for someone like me."

Every time Nicole wanted to be in charity with her mother, she heard something like this, and wanted only to throttle the woman. "And did she also tell you what she meant by that? Someone like you?"

"Oh, yes, she certainly did. You know Mama. She doesn't cavil at saying exactly what she thinks. I'm pretty enough, she told me, pointing out that I favor her, but I don't have the…the *bottom* necessary to a duke's lady. Better I find myself a well-placed vicar and stay safe and quiet in the country with all the other country mice."

"Our mother is an ass," Nicole said, patting herself dry as she headed for the folded screen in the corner and the clothing Renée had set out for her before she'd been dismissed. "If you want him, Lydia, go get him."

"But that's just it. I don't want him. But...but I really didn't appreciate Mama telling me I couldn't get him. Is that perverse of me?"

Nicole leaned her head out from behind the screen to grin at her sister. "You're never perverse, or cranky, or stubborn, or even mildly contrary. That's all *my* province. And our mother is still an ass."

"She means well."

"I know," Nicole said, poking her head out once more, hopping on one foot as she struggled with her hose. "I've finally come to terms with that, I think. And about why she is the way she is. But that doesn't mean anyone without maggots in their brainboxes should ever *listen* to her."

Lydia giggled as she tipped her head to one side as if trying to see behind the screen. "What are you doing back there?"

"Nothing," Nicole told her as she tugged the breeches up and over her hips. "So? Are you going to do it?"

"Do what? And be careful, you're soon going to knock over that screen."

"Are you going to convince the Duke of Malvern that his third cousin Miss Halibut is totally unsuitable for him?"

"Harburton. A halibut is a fish. It was reserved

mostly for meals marking the celebration of holy days in the time before William the Conqueror arrived on our shores." She sighed, as if knowing she was rambling about nothing, and then added, "I believe Edward the Confessor was particularly fond of the dish."

Yet again, Nicole stuck her head out from behind the screen. "Do you know something, sister mine? At times, you really frighten me. We're not talking about fish, we're talking about the Duke of Malvern."

"Not if I don't want to, we're not," Lydia said with a definite lift of her chin. "We could talk about what the marquess thought of the night clothes I had packed for you. Do you want to talk about that?"

Nicole finally stepped from behind the screen, still buttoning her homespun shirt. "If we were still children, I would have taken some terrible revenge on you for that. So, no, I don't want to talk about—"

"Nicole! What are you wearing!"

"I think that should be fairly obvious." Nicole looked down at the clothing she'd commandeered from their youngest footman, and then grinned at Lydia. "I think they fit tolerably well, don't you?"

Lydia leaped to her feet. "Oh, no," she said, shaking her head. "I will not allow this."

"You won't allow what? You don't know what I'm going to do, and if I don't tell you, then you won't be able to tell anyone else, will you?"

Her sister's eyes narrowed. "I love you, but there are times I could just *slap* you."

"Lucas needs me. He and Rafe are—"

"Exactly!" her sister interrupted. "Rafe and the marquess. *They* are going to handle this...this problem at The Broken Wheel. They don't need you rushing about looking for some sort of adventure, getting...getting in their way. Grow up, Nicole. Trust others to know what they're doing, without your help. Please!"

Nicole felt her bottom lip begin to tremble and quickly bit it between her teeth so that her sister wouldn't notice. But she couldn't halt the tears that had sprung to her eyes at Lydia's words.

"You don't understand the danger they're going to be in tonight."

"And how is turning up at The Broken Wheel in that outrageous outfit going to aid in ridding them of that danger?"

"You've said that twice now, haven't you? You know about The Broken Wheel?"

Lydia rolled her eyes, clearly in a temper. It was fascinating, for nobody even supposed Lydia *had* a temper.

"Phineas and I have had several talks on the subject, yes. You didn't think I was going to allow you to go off with the marquess—kidnap Mama, for pity's sake—without knowing why. Charlotte told me much of it, but it was Phineas who went to The Broken Wheel last night, and came back with the information about the march on Parliament tonight. Oh! Is that where you think you're going? To Parliament? Because I won't let you do that, either."

"No, not Parliament," Nicole told her at last, motioning for her sister to sit down again. "Lydia, I'm sorry."

"Sorry for what?" she asked as she arranged her skirts so that they wouldn't wrinkle. Even in the midst of a crisis, Lydia was every inch the lady. She couldn't help herself.

"For…for everything. From the day I convinced you to help me get the stable cat down from the roof at Willowbrook when the cat wasn't up there at all but I simply wanted to see what the world looked like from that high, until…well, until right this very minute, I'm sorry."

Lydia was silent for some moments, and then smiled. "The view was pretty, wasn't it? We thought we were on the top of the world. Oh, and now who is knocking at your door? Get behind the screen, for pity's sake, while I see who it is."

Nicole did as she was told—in truth, she was still so shocked at Lydia's unusual behavior she probably would have done anything her sister said—and then stepped out again when she heard the door close. "Who was it?"

"One of the footmen." She held out a folded note before sitting down once more. "This was just delivered. Your name is on it."

Nicole took the note, frowning, as she didn't recognize the handwriting. Besides, she knew so few people in London, unless she considered the hopeful suitors she'd had to deal with the other night, and she really didn't wish to consider any of them.

She broke the seal and opened the page.

Nicole, dearest, dearest Nicole. I'm an idiot. You're the most wonderful and exasperating woman in creation and I love you to desperation and beyond. I should have told you that. Marry me. Please.

The note was signed with a large "L," and beneath it was another line that looked as if it had been scribbled as an afterthought: *I'll grovel later, I promise, down on one knee if that's what you want. In the meantime, behave!*

Wordlessly, Nicole handed the note to her sister and then knelt at her feet. "I can't believe I love him, Lydia. He's maddening, and he laughs at me, and he gets so angry with me and…and he takes me as I am. But it's true—I love him so much. Do you understand now? I can't just stay here and wait for someone to come and tell us what happened. I know that's what I should do, what women are supposed to do, even that it's clearly what Lucas wants me to do. But I can't. I…I just *can't*."

Lydia folded the note and laid it on the table beside her.

"There…there are women, wives, who follow their husbands into battle. Did you know that? There were many wives, or simply women who loved a soldier, who traveled to Brussels last year, daring every hardship. They…they, um, walked the battlefield when the fighting stopped, looking for their men, dead or alive. I've read some accounts of a few of them."

"Sweetheart, don't…"

"They went to war to follow the men they loved.

I stayed at Ashurst Hall and wrote silly letters telling the captain about the weather, and the cook's burned thumb when she mistakenly took hold of a hot pot handle."

"I know," Nicole said, wiping at her tears with the back of her hand. "Rafe wouldn't have let you go in any case. You were seventeen."

Her sister shook her head. "No. What is age when it's measured against the heart? I was a woman in love. I should have gone, dared everything. You would have found some way to manage getting yourself to Brussels if your marquess had been about to go into battle. I know you would have. At least, then, at…at the end, I could have been with him. He died imploring the duke to come tell us. If the captain had to die, he should have died as I held his hand. But I didn't *dare*. I just sat, and waited. I'm…I'm such a *mouse,* just as Mama said."

Nicole laid her cheek against her sister's knee. "The captain understood. He loved you. He wouldn't have wanted to think about you being in any sort of danger."

"Just as the marquess couldn't stand the idea of *you* being in any danger?" Lydia asked as she stroked her sister's hair. "And look at how well you're heeding what he wants."

Nicole raised her head to look up at her twin. "If…if you had it to do again. Would you go?"

The mantel clock slowly struck out the hour of seven before Lydia spoke.

"I'd like to think I would have, yes. So please understand that I know how you feel right now. But getting in the way at The Broken Wheel would do no one any good," she said at last. "We have to believe that Rafe and the marquess will be able to…to defuse the situation. Agreed?"

"But—"

"I said—agreed?"

"Yes, I suppose so."

"And if they can't, if something goes awry at The Broken Wheel, then there really wouldn't be much more they could do on Westminster Bridge except to watch the carnage and attempt to rescue those they could. Correct?"

"Correct," Nicole said, sighing. "So you're saying I shouldn't attempt to go there, either. I understand. I just…I just wanted to *do* something."

Lydia motioned for her sister to move and then stood up, beginning to pace the carpet. "Which, logically, leaves us with Lord Frayne." She stopped, turned to look at her sister. "You have all realized that his lordship will be very angry if Rafe and the marquess manage to put a halt to the march?"

Nicole nodded. "We've already discussed that, yes. By tomorrow, Mama's letters could be God only knows where. And she did write them. She told me as much. Within a few days' time, all of London could know that our uncle and cousins—"

"Then it's simple, isn't it? That's what we have to do. I've given the whole thing a lot of thought since yesterday and, to me, it's the only answer. To Phineas, as well. He's already…taken steps."

Nicole got to her feet, looking questioningly at her sister. "What is what we have to do?"

"Go change out of those ridiculous clothes and put on your most fetching gown. The pink, I think, as it has that outrageously low bodice. I'll go find Phineas."

"To do what?" Nicole's head was spinning. Who was this person standing in front of her, taking command so imperiously? Surely not her sister!

"Why, to go to Lord Frayne's and retrieve Mama's letters, of course. I would have thought that perfectly obvious and immensely reasonable. Phineas certainly did. This is our family under threat, remember? Rafe, and through him, the rest of us. Charlotte's unborn baby, as well. So we remove the ammunition from Lord Frayne's gun. Figuratively, of course. I hadn't planned on tonight, but with the march set for tonight, we've prepared ourselves. Phineas and I, I mean. I can't be a mouse forever, Nicole."

"Lydia, you're a genius. A bloody genius."

Her sister smiled. "Am I? Possibly Mama's right. I did get all the brains."

"I'll ignore that horribly un-sister-like remark, as I mostly want to hug you right now. But how are we going to do this?"

"By using *our* strengths. I've already used my brain. Now it's your turn. You, Nicole, and please believe that I cringe as I say this, will be Mama. In other words, you will *flirt*."

CHAPTER NINETEEN

THEY DIDN'T BOTHER WITH disguises, on any hope
of blending in with the other potential marchers.
They also didn't bother attempting to get past the
burly guards at the door to the cellars behind The
Broken Wheel.

Instead, Lucas and Rafe walked into the tavern
using the front door. They walked up to the small bar
area where a very large man stood resting his elbows
on the scarred wood and told him they would need
two bottles of the man's best delivered to the table
at the very back of the tavern.

The table next to the door that led to the kegs in
the cellars. Phineas had already told them of this
door.

"Don't see yer kind much 'ere. Flash coves like
yer," the barman said, not moving to fetch their
drinks. "Lose yer way, did yer? Mayhap yer'd be best
served findin' yer way back agin to that somewheres
else."

Lucas laid his hand on the wood and then lifted
it away, to show the gold coin he'd left behind. "And
mayhap you'd be wisest to mind your own business.

Bring the bottles yourself. No glasses. That way, you won't be tempted to spit in them first, will you?"

"That's probably how he always washes them," Rafe said quietly as they walked to the back of the tavern, both men aware that every eye was on their progress. "I'd feel more popular walking in here if I'd just cleaned out a cesspit."

"You might have fit in better, as well," Lucas said, taking up the chair closest to the door to the cellars. "Or haven't you noticed the less than charming smell in here?"

"I'm only pleased to see the place so sparsely populated. Although that means most of the regular patrons are probably beneath our feet right now. Ah, and here comes our new friend. Ready?"

"Looking forward to it, actually. It has been some time since I've seen any action. I hadn't realized I missed it."

The burly man approached the table, a sullen look on his ugly face, a bottle in each hand.

Rafe stayed where he was, his chair near to the door to the cellars, but Lucas stood up, as if to stretch.

The barman leaned over the table.

Rafe snaked out his hands and grabbed the man's beefy wrists in an iron grip.

Lucas produced the knife he'd secreted up his sleeve, and pressed it against the man's lower back. He bent his head to the man's ear.

"A single word and the last thing you see will be your left kidney, right there on the table in front of you. We're going downstairs now, my good man. You have the key. Right there in the pocket of your apron. My friend is going to release your right hand and you're going to reach into your apron, remove the key and open the door. Then we're all three of us, being oh-so-chummy, going to go downstairs to inspect your most excellent cellars in hopes of a more superior brew. Agreed? Oh, that's right. Just nod. There's a good fellow."

The exercise went even more smoothly than Lucas could have hoped, and without a single patron in the taproom any the wiser.

With the barman leading the way down the rough wooden stairs, Lucas and Rafe descended to the large, low-ceilinged room Lucas remembered from his prior visit.

There were dozens of casks piled against the walls, and the table that had served as a speaking dais was still in place.

But, as Lucas and Rafe had suspected, neither of the two men Lucas had seen that first night could be seen anywhere.

"He's got a sticker in m'side!" the barman shouted over the general din made by one hundred men all speaking quietly, and every face was immediately turned toward the stairs.

"And now I don't. However, you have become superfluous, haven't you?" Lucas said, removing the blade and then deftly raising his booted foot, planting it against the barman's rump and sending the man tumbling down the last three steps and into a stack of kegs—which immediately loudly tumbled all around him.

"Well, now that you have everyone's attention…" Rafe said, giving their observers a small wave. "Gentleman! Allow me, please, to introduce my friend and myself. I am Captain Rafael Daughtry, having served six years on the Peninsula, and this is Major Lucas Paine, directly from Wellington's staff and our final victory at Waterloo. We come as friends to the men who served with us so valiantly and bravely."

"Come ta ask fer the buttons back off'n our coats now?" someone yelled from the back of the room. "Yer gots everthin' else."

A gray-complexioned man at the front of the room added his bit to the general uproar that followed. "Got yer there! Mayhap yer wants m'other arm whilst yer here? Yer gonna wipe m'arse fer me then?"

"Nobody said this was going to be a stroll in Hyde Park," Rafe said quietly, motioning for Lucas to step forward. "Your turn."

Lucas hadn't served under Wellington without learning a few things about the men who would profess to die for their country or their duke in a heartbeat, and then spend the night after the battle huddled around campfires and cursing both.

"That will be enough!" he shouted imperiously. "We're here to tell you that you've been betrayed, so the next one of you men who speaks out of turn answers to me! Or are you that damn anxious to die in a gutter tonight?"

"Listen to 'em!" one of the assembled men shouted, elbowing his way to the front of the room. "That there's Basingstoke, that is. Saw three horses shot out from unner him, ridin' ahead o' his men.'"

"Well, we'd hoped someone would recognize one of us. You're a bloody damn hero. I had no idea," Rafe said, sidling up beside Lucas. "Three?"

"Two, and one of those stumbled, wasn't shot. But I don't think I'll correct him."

Lucas, knowing he had to take his advantage now or lose it to one of these men who would soon point out that they weren't at war anymore, waved his hands for silence and launched into his prepared arguments.

Convincing angry men that they were being played as dupes wasn't easy, nor was it quick. But by the time the three men sent to the other taverns where, supposedly, other groups of the Citizens for Justice were preparing themselves for the march on Parliament returned to say that there *were* no other groups—well, Lucas had their full attention.

At last, with twenty of the men in tow acting as a forward patrol, and the others agreeing to wait at The Broken Wheel, Lucas and Rafe allowed the man who'd recognized him to lead them all through dark streets and darker alleys, all the way to Westminster Bridge.

They peeked out from one of those dark alleys to see contingents of the King's Guard already amassing at the end of the bridge where it spilled out toward Parliament, waiting for the march that would not come, the riot that would not happen, the excuse for crushing new laws that no longer existed.

It was a silent and sullen—yet grateful—group that made its way back to The Broken Wheel.

The barman, a large once-white strip of bandage wrapped around his abused head that had come in contact with one of the kegs, finally asked the question Lucas and Rafe had been waiting for, hoping for—and ready to suggest themselves if no one else did, thanks to Nicole's very logical reasoning.

"Which one o' them gov'ment bastards wanted us ta die fer him?"

IN THE END, CHARLOTTE went with them, as no amount of argument could dissuade her.

The three women arrived in staid old Belgrave Square shortly before nine, as Phineas had chatted up the Frayne cook the day before, and knew that the man only sat down to supper at six-thirty, and never left the mansion for his evening social rounds until ten, at the earliest.

Charlotte yawned into her gloved hand as the coach stopped in front of the large but rather ugly stone mansion.

"Are we perhaps boring you?" Nicole asked her sister-in-law.

"Hardly. But it is nearly my bedtime. Especially since Rafe's child insists on waking me promptly at two every morning with either his kicks or a case of the hiccups, poor thing. Are we all clear now as to our roles?"

"The hysterical mother-to-be, the voice of calm yet calculating reason and the outrageous flirt who thinks she can cajole with her charms what the other two cannot," Nicole said, and then frowned. "I really have to pretend I'm Mama? I'd rather promised myself I wouldn't do that anymore."

"You can't very well pretend you're the voice of reason, sweetheart," Charlotte said as a groom opened the door and put down the steps, earning a giggle from Lydia.

"And Phineas is certain he can do this?"

"Nicole, stop asking the same questions over and over again," Lydia ordered as they waited for Charlotte to descend to the flagway. "If Phineas says he can do it, he can do it. The man was a Bow Street Runner."

"Which means he was a thief catcher, not a thief."

"He *caught* them, didn't he?" Lydia countered, and Nicole had no answer for that, so she simply made a face and climbed down to the flagway.

They remained at the bottom of the set of marble steps leading up to the portico until a Frayne footman had answered their groom's knock, and then Lydia nudged Nicole in the ribs, signaling that it was time for her to turn on her considerable charm.

Nicole lightly climbed up the few steps, allowing her shawl to slide off her bare shoulders, and then smiled directly into the face of the servant who was more boy than man, and the owner of an Adam's apple of near epic proportions.

"Her Grace the Duchess of Ashurst to see Lord

Frayne at once on a *most* personal matter, and accompanied by her sisters-in-law, Lady Lydia and Lady Nicole Daughtry. My, wasn't that a mouthful all at once for you to remember? Shall I repeat myself?"

The Adam's apple climbed so high she was surprised the boy didn't choke on it, and then bobbed up and down a few times before he could answer her. "No, ma'am, um, miss, um, my lady."

Nicole turned to triumphantly grin down at her sister and sister-in-law. They were almost immediately escorted into the main drawing room by a starchy majordomo who had come bustling into the foyer. The man promised refreshments, and the appearance of Lord Frayne, both within a few moments.

While Charlotte naturally gravitated to the most comfortable-looking couch in the large room, already pulling a lace-edged handkerchief from her reticule, Nicole walked around the room, deciding that she hated it.

"Rather ostentatious and overdone, don't you think? All this gilt?" she asked her sister as she walked over to the fireplace. "And a portrait of himself above the mantel? I think the man is quite fond of himself."

"Nicole, *shh,*" Lydia warned as she took up her own seat on a chair turned at an angle to the matching couches flanking a large, low round table, the top of it supported by a trio of gilt angels with their hands raised above their heads. "Just strike a provocative pose, or whatever it is you think you should do."

"Next she'll be selling me for tuppence on the streets around Covent Garden," Nicole said quietly to Charlotte, who had been attempting to produce some nervous tears, but who now was forced to turn her laugh into a sob as Lord Frayne entered the room.

"Your Grace, what an unexpected pleasure," he said, immediately crossing to Charlotte, who kept the handkerchief to her mouth as she rather distractedly lifted her hand so the man could bow over it. "Both an honor and a most lovely surprise, I must say."

Charlotte mumbled something unintelligible and quickly withdrew her hand.

"Ladies," he continued, bowing to Nicole and Lydia. "Is something amiss?"

"Our mother and her indiscretions sailed for Italy last night, no thanks to you," Lydia told him coldly. "Our brother, poor Charlotte's husband and father of her unborn child, has somehow been left to your mercies, and my sister and I stand to be disgraced and turned out of Society, to either die old maids or be forced to marry considerably beneath our stations. Yes, my lord, you would be correct to say that something is *amiss*."

"And all because of that *stupid* Basingstoke, who never did come up to scratch as we'd hoped. He disappointed you as well, didn't he?" Nicole said as she maintained her pose in front of the fireplace. "Now, really, my lord—*how* can we fix this? Hmm?"

Frayne looked from one to the other, his gaze

landing last on the obviously pregnant and still-weeping-into-her-handkerchief Duchess of Ashurst before he turned to Nicole once again, his gaze more on her bosom than her face.

"I'm sorry. I don't understand. Your brother? And what's this about Basingstoke? I fear you ladies have the advantage of me."

Nicole longed to choke the lying cretin, but Lydia seemed to be prepared for the man's denial.

"Don't bother to attempt to dissemble, my lord. We know all about our mother's letters. We're here to buy them back. Name your price."

Nicole lifted one hand and slowly ran her middle finger along the rather low neckline of her gown before lightly *massaging* the skin at the very center of her chest. She thought she might vomit, but only pouted fearfully at the man before biting her full lower lip between her teeth, showing him that, yes, they had come here prepared to pay any price.

Any price.

Such as the willing virgin daughter with the talented whore for a mother. The man had to be asking himself: *like mother, like daughter?*

Nicole saw it all, all the questions, the considerations, on the man's face, in his sly, beady eyes. How could he have the daughter *and* the letters? How could he take his pleasure, and still keep the Marquess of Basingstoke in his clutches? How could he win, and then win again?

"I…" Frayne cleared his throat and turned away from Nicole, only to glance back at her before

addressing Lydia. "I may have some small understanding of what concerns you. But, er, but it is my
duty, when information of a possible murder—
several murders—comes to my attention." He looked
to Nicole yet a third time, and she tipped her head
ever so slightly, blinked and looked at him in mute
appeal. "You can…you can understand my dilemma."

"I understand that you are a most terrible man,"
Lydia said sternly. "I understand that we are desperate, and I believe that you know that, as well. The
marquess has deserted us, left us to your mercies as
he runs to the country to escape you, and we cannot
tell our brother for fear he will do something drastic.
You are…our only hope."

"Basingstoke is gone?"

Nicole had moved from the fireplace, and was now
standing just behind Lord Frayne, close enough to
figuratively hear the wheels turning inside his head.
"After confessing what he'd done to us, yes. The
man's a coward. He disgusts me. Men should be…
strong."

"And…and he told you *why* I was, that is, why I
am prepared to expose your brother's crime?"

Nicole shrugged her bare shoulders. "He mumbled some nonsense about his dead father and being
asked to do something he couldn't do. As if we could
care about any of that."

"I'm finding this difficult to believe. He told
you what he'd done, and then left you to fend for
yourselves?"

"As we said, a coward, a white-feather man. Rafe would probably call him out, if we were to tell him, and what good would that do his unborn child, I ask you? But it's often left to women to clean up the messes men make. So we put our heads together and thought up our own plan to set things right."

"And by coming here, you thought you could set things right," Frayne said, nodding. "I see."

Nicole bit her bottom lip once more, this time in real concern, but then purred, "Do you, my lord?"

Charlotte's wails grew louder. "I cannot believe I have agreed to this…this *shame!* This most terrible *sacrifice,* my dearest, dearest Nicole! But my child, my poor child!"

Nicole looked to Lydia, not knowing what to do next, say next. Phineas should have been done by now, if everything went according to plan. In a moment Frayne was either going to shoo her sister and Charlotte out and invite her upstairs, or begin dickering over a price, for the love of God!

She stumbled on, saying, "Oh, Charlotte, stifle yourself. I told you his lordship would see reason, didn't I? And you, too, Lydia. Anger and demands mean nothing. Did *Maman* teach you nothing? She certainly taught me what a woman does to survive."

Lydia opened her mouth, obviously to protest, but at that same moment Nicole heard the sound of pebbles striking the front window.

Clearly, Charlotte heard it as well, for she instantly put both hands to her swollen abdomen and shrieked, "The baby! The baby's coming!"

Lord Frayne's face went as white as his cravat. "What did she just say?"

Lydia sprang to her feet, going to Charlotte and helping her up, and the two of them began making their way toward the foyer, Charlotte still moaning and holding her belly. "It's coming! It's coming!"

"Here? It's coming *here?* But—but you're not leaving, surely?"

Nicole rolled her eyes as she brushed past the horrified man, who immediately followed after her like some obedient puppy. Men! They thought they ruled the world. They made plans, they made war and they routinely lorded over women, keeping their wives and daughters stripped of all autonomy just as they did the lower classes.

But really, when you got right down to it, men could be incredibly thick, and more easily swayed by a pretty turn of ankle than a well-oiled gate in a spring breeze. Thank goodness Lucas was the exception—he would have seen through her subterfuge in a heartbeat.

"Of course I'm leaving. We'll have to save this discussion for another time, my lord, unless you wish her to have her lying-in here? We'd need your servants, a doctor called at once, a thick layer of straw spread in the street outside so that carriage wheels won't disturb her in her agony. I understand this may also help to drown out her screams. Oh, and towels, lots and lots of towels. I hear the process can be rather messy."

"No! That is, no, no. When? When will you be

back? I mean, it was obvious what I've just been offered. I'm a reasonable man, a fair man. Marriage would be a consideration if you play your cards right, I've need of an heir at any rate. Besides, after tonight, or very soon, I will be a most powerful man, and you'll be happy you've aligned yourself with me. Just tell me when."

The overweening arrogance of the man! Nicole kept on walking, relieved to see that Lydia and Charlotte were already passing through the doorway and back out onto the street.

She should say something innocuous and simply leave. That was the plan. That was the promise she'd made to Lydia and Charlotte. Lydia had warned her: do not gloat, Nicole, just follow us out the door.

But the man was such an unconscionable beast!

She fluffed out the ends of her gauzy pink shawl and then imperiously flipped one end up and over her shoulder, as she'd seen her mother do in the Bond Street shop, and turned to glare at him.

"When, my lord? With those damning letters now back in our possession while you were so busy leering at what you couldn't have even if you were the last man on earth? I would think the answer would be obvious by now, even to such a block-headed lech as you. *Never.*"

"Smithers," Frayne called out in some rage to his majordomo even as he grabbed Nicole by the elbow and roughly turned her back toward the drawing room. "Smithers! Shut the door!"

LUCAS WAS BEGINNING to have second thoughts.

Not that Frayne didn't deserve to have every last window in his residence broken by the mob of men now appearing by twos and threes from darkened alleys and mews and gathering in front of the mansion. They'd left The Broken Wheel, not as a mob to be easily noticed, but covertly, in those twos and threes, all of them sidling through the darkness, all with the same destination in mind.

And not that Frayne didn't deserve his front door broken down by these same men, his belongings carried off into the night…and with one hundred angry men all working together under explicit orders, as they had done so brilliantly defeating Napoleon during wartime, the mission would be accomplished swiftly, and most thoroughly.

But, given more time to plan, could there have been a better way to retrieve Helen Daughtry's letters tonight other than to ride into the mansion on the backs of these angry men, to find those letters and take them away?

Still, Frayne had wanted a riot, so they'd give him a riot. They'd bring the weight of hunger and grinding poverty and righteous frustration straight to his doorstep. Not an uprising against a city, a government, but an attack on one man, an assault that would be, yes, unfortunate for this victim of housebreakers, but not enough to give Frayne the new laws he wanted.

That had been the plan.

But now Lucas wondered if he had exposed these men to a new danger even while protecting them from the certain tragedy that would have been their march on Parliament.

"Rafe," he said as they entered the square, coming out from a narrow carriage lane that led back to the stables behind one of the mansions. "Perhaps we could have found a way to do this without them."

But Rafe wasn't listening. He'd stopped in his tracks, and was now staring at Frayne's mansion. "Charlie?" he said, clearly disbelieving the sight his eyes presented to him. And then he was running. *"Charlie!"*

Lucas ran with him, his heart hoping he'd see Nicole once he got abreast of the Ashurst coach. He could already see Lydia's blond hair glinting in the light from the flambeaux on either side of Frayne's front door.

But while his heart hoped, his mind was already certain that if Nicole was indeed anywhere in the vicinity, it would not be on the safe side of Frayne's door.

"What did she do?" Lucas demanded of Lydia, who was looking rather white-faced as he grabbed both her arms. "Tell me! What harebrained idiocy is she up to now!"

"No…no…it was me. It was my idea. It was all my idea, all my fault. I didn't want to be a mouse anymore. Oh, thank God you're here.…"

"Yes, yes, we're here. Don't try to defend her, Lydia," Lucas warned her. "I don't know what's going on here, but don't try to tell me Nicole wasn't a happy participant. Damn her!"

Rafe, holding his wife's hand, joined them on the

flagway. "She's inside. With Frayne. He's only had her for a moment, we got here just as he took her."

"But what in bloody blazes was she— No, never mind. I'll shake it out of her once we've got her back." He turned to face the men from The Broken Wheel, the men carrying clubs and pitchforks, their pockets sagging from the cobblestones they'd pried out of the streets on their way to the Square.

Already four men were waiting for the command to employ the uprooted lamppost they'd commandeered to break down the door.

Belgrave Square was deserted except for the assembled men and the Ashurst coach. Thank God the residents were mostly a staid and older sort, and not prone to stepping outside their doors until the round of parties at ten—besides, if they heard any uproar, the residents were more likely to lock their doors and hide than offer to help their neighbor.

Still, Lucas knew they all had to be quick about whatever they planned to do. It wouldn't do to have their faces seen.

"To me, men! *To me!*" he called out, and then raised his hand high, dropped it and ran toward the portico.

The door opened before he could get to it, a tall, older man in the black garb of a majordomo stepping back, his hand still on the door latch. "He dragged the young woman into the drawing room, my lord," he said, pointing toward a pair of closed doors. "Just spare the staff, if you'd please. We have no part in this."

Lucas stepped into the foyer, holding up his hand

to keep his small army behind him. "Then I suggest you gather your staff and retire to the cellars—with my thanks."

"Yes, my lord Basingstoke, at once. And we never saw you here this evening, my lord? Nor the ladies."

Lucas grinned, although he was fairly sure the result was more of a grimace. "Good man. Come see me tomorrow. There won't be much left to do here by then except to sweep up the pieces at any rate, in case you and your staff are interested in taking up new positions."

The majordomo bowed deeply, as if inviting in the Prince Regent himself rather than a pair of well-dressed housebreakers and a horde of angry, weapon-carrying men of the streets, and then hustled his footmen to the back of the house.

"Five minutes and you're all ghosts—gone, never here. Understood? Any longer and you risk discovery by the Watch. Take what you want, break what you want, it's no nevermind to me." Lucas pointed behind him, to the doors to the drawing room. "But this room is mine."

The men in the front of the ragtag ranks saluted smartly before half of them started off through the lower floors and the rest climbed the stairs.

"Where is she?" Rafe asked, at last able to enter past the lessening crush of bodies at the door.

"In there. Hunt down those letters or wait outside with your wife. He's mine."

"No need for a search. Charlie told me what they were up to. A diversion, while my man Phineas

climbed through a window and found the letters in
Frayne's study, among other things. I've got them,
so that's one worry gone. Just don't kill the bastard.
I don't want my sister living with a fugitive in
France."

All of this, the seeing, the learning, the breaking in,
the quick conversations with Frayne's majordomo
and Rafe—all of it had taken moments, yet felt like
years.

Years during which Frayne had Nicole locked up
with him in his drawing room. The man had to know
his home was under assault, had to know that
Nicole's rescue was at hand, that all his grand plans
were, if not completely foiled, at least badly dented.

Did that make him defeated, or more dangerous
than ever? Lucas knew he was soon to find out.

CHAPTER TWENTY

NICOLE SAT ON THE COUCH Charlotte had so recently occupied, rubbing her abused arm where Frayne had grabbed her and watching him pace the carpet.

They could both hear running footsteps above their heads, triumphant shouts, the sounds of breaking glass and the thumps of heavy objects hitting the floor.

"What's happening? What's happening? Where's the Watch? They should be here! My house...my possessions. My God, it's a revolution! I told them. I *told* them it would come to this!"

"If I might correct you on that, my lord," Nicole said, her confidence growing by the moment. "You *planned* for it to come to this. Although probably not so close to home, hmm? Somebody else's house and possessions, somebody else's life given over to the mercies of the mob. Not yours—never yours. Lucas is brilliant, isn't he?"

"Shut up!" Frayne wheeled around and advanced across the room toward her, his eyes wild with panic and anger, his hands drawn up into white-knuckled fists. "Shut up, shut up, *shut up!*"

Nicole was impulsive. Headstrong. Always looking for adventure. But she wasn't stupid. She stood up quickly and ran around to put the couch between herself and this enraged man just as the double doors burst open, slamming back against the walls as Lucas stalked into the room.

"Lucas, I can explain…" she began, and then prudently shut her mouth, realizing that he had barely looked at her.

She looked past him, into the foyer, and could see men running to and fro like confined hounds suddenly left off their leashes, carrying silver plates clutched to their chests, holding silver candelabras high in the air, the candles still lit. One of the men halted in front of the doorway, grinned toothlessly as he raised one of Frayne's curly brimmed beavers that he had clapped to his filthy, matted hair, and tipped it to her in greeting before moving on.

"*You,*" Frayne said, whirling to confront Lucas. "You did this. You'll *hang* for this!"

"Why are you so upset? You wanted a riot tonight, Frayne, and you've got one. Just not on Westminster Bridge. Nicole, go to your brother. Now."

She loved him so desperately—but was the man insane? He really thought she'd leave *now?* Especially since she felt she'd at last had the perfect answer to everything, to all of their problems.

"No, Lucas, I'm staying. I want to hear how his lordship expects you to hang, when he is the one who was inciting insurrection. Phineas was sent to retrieve Mama's letters, certainly, but we told him to also take any correspondence he might have discovered that would tie Frayne to the Citizens for Justice. You and Rafe can take it all to lords Liverpool and Sidmouth, who probably won't be happy to hear that his lordship planned their downfall as well, and that will be that. Isn't it the perfect solution? I think it's perfect."

She had her fingers crossed as she said those words, but the stricken look that overtook Frayne told her that there had been evidence in the man's study to be found. Like, perhaps, stacks and stacks of the sort of broadsheet Lydia had found in her maid's apron pocket.

And having Phineas look for and retrieve the broadsheets or anything else had been all Nicole's idea. Ha, and her sister thought *she* had gotten all the brains!

The chandelier above their heads began to shake and the sound of something heavy being dragged across the floor had them all looking up for a moment, just long enough for Frayne—who had to know his luck had just firmly run out—to cannon into Lucas, knocking him to the carpet.

"Lucas!" Nicole exclaimed, racing out from behind the couch as the two men rolled about on the floor, each trying to punch the other, their bodies too close together for punches to be effective.

But Lucas was both the younger and the stronger man, and within moments the outcome of the fight was evident. Nicole put down the porcelain statuette she'd armed herself with, hoping to conk Frayne on the head with it, and sighed in relief. After all, it would be better if Lucas rescued himself, men being so *fragile* about things like that.

Frayne was picked up by the back of his jacket collar and tossed into the nearest chair, where he sat, winded, attempting to straighten his neck cloth.

"You'll never know now, Basingstoke. You'll never know who accused your father."

"I can live with that, knowing you and your dreams of power are finished," Lucas told him as he held out his hand to Nicole, so that she joined him as they faced Frayne.

The *thump-thump-thump* of that same something heavy being dragged down the marble stairs caused them to look toward the foyer in time to see an immense painted armoire being maneuvered toward the street.

"We're not greedy, sir, so that'll do it. M'wife'll be that pleased. Never had nuthin' near so fine as this. The kiddies can sleep in it, it's so big. Others woulda picked the carcass clean ter the walls, but we're fair men," the man who had recognized Lucas said as he appeared in the doorway to salute him, and then bow to Nicole. "Ma'am. And m'friend Hughie says ter tell yer all that the Citizens fer Justice finally got theirselves some tonight, and ter thank yer. That Hughie, he's a fair treat."

"My armoire!" Frayne ran past Lucas and out into the street, just in time to see what was clearly a prized possession being carried off into an alley by six strong men.

He turned and looked up at his house, his mansion. Other than those fronting the drawing room, every pane of every window in the structure had been shattered.

"My windows! My windows are all gone!"

As if Mother Nature wished to sanction the efforts of the housebreakers, it began to rain.

Lucas, with Nicole on his arm, stopped next to Frayne and said, "One complaint, one whispered word, and Liverpool and Sidmouth both get an earful, and the honest men you planned to sacrifice to your ambition come back here, this time carrying torches. Better damp furnishings than charred, yes? Understood? Tonight never happened, Frayne. *None of it* ever happened."

Then he laid his hand over Nicole's as hers rested on his arm. "Your brother's coach awaits us. Shall we?"

"Yes, I suppose we shall," Nicole answered, lifting her chin. "Good evening to you, Lord Frayne. And as I suspect you'll be rusticating for the remainder of the Season, goodbye. Or as my mother would say in a most atrocious accent, *au revoir.*"

"You always need the last word, don't you?" Lucas said just before he handed her up into the coach, where Charlotte and Lydia awaited her.

She ascended the two steps and then turned, looked back at him from the doorway. "But I'm not going to get that tonight, am I? You're mad as fire, aren't you?"

"You felt it necessary to ask?"

"No, I suppose not." She sat back against the velvet squabs, squeezed in next to the clearly relieved Lydia and Charlotte, watching as Lucas took up his seat beside Rafe. She then sat silently with her hands folded in her lap and her gaze centered on her fingers, all the way back to… She looked up as the coach stopped sooner than she'd expected.

All the way to Lucas's residence in Park Lane?

Her eyes shifted to her brother, who was sitting there, looking quite unconcerned and very possibly amused as Lucas opened the door and jumped down to the flagway, then wordlessly raised his arms to her.

"Rafe? Charlotte? *Lydia?* You're all just going to sit there and make me go with him? Do you have any idea how *angry* he is with me?"

Her sister looked to Rafe. "She's right. And it *was* mostly my idea. Well, except for that last part, when she didn't leave with us the way she was supposed to. Perhaps we should—"

Rafe leaned forward on the seat to say to Lucas, "We breakfast at ten. Have a good night."

Nicole gave up and allowed herself to be lifted down from the coach.

A SINGLE LOOK WAS ENOUGH to have his butler quickly glaring at the two footmen, so that they put their heads down, pretending they hadn't noticed that their employer had just entered the foyer dragging a beautiful and slightly damp young woman by the hand and heading straight for the stairs.

Lucas didn't stop until he'd slammed open the

doors to his bedchamber and then kicked them shut behind him.

"Well, aren't you imposing when you're out to get your own way?" she taunted him, walking over to stand at the foot of his large bed. "This is where you want me, isn't it?"

"What I want is to put you over my knee and spank you, as your father should have done when you were even more of a child."

"Which father, Lucas? I've had three. Now say whatever it is you want to say, and have done with it."

"Thank you, I will. What in bloody damn hell did you think you were doing? All of you!" he exploded, having held in his anger to the point where it seemed entirely possible the top of his head might simply blow off. "Of all the stupid, muddle-headed, asinine—"

"I'm fine, thank you. How was your evening?" Nicole answered, returning glare for glare.

Not that he cared. Not right at this moment.

"A pregnant woman? How can a pregnant woman have so little sense? Just charging into a man's house, and a man like Frayne, no less? Without telling anyone? Without a thought, either, I'm sure. And your sister? Such idiocy from you I can understand. But her?"

"Now you just wait one minute, Lucas Paine," Nicole said, wagging a finger in his direction, and then seemed to reconsider the gesture, so that she quickly dropped her hand to her side. "All right, yes. It was my idea. All of it. I dragged them both there against their will. And all to save you and Rafe. I'm still glad we saved Rafe, but I'm not that in charity with you right now. And what are we doing in your rooms if it's not to toss me into this bed? In anger, Lucas?"

Yes, the top of his skull was definitely to go flying up to the ceiling. In hopes of keeping it in place, he lifted his hands to his head as he turned away from her and walked across the large room.

Once there was some distance between them, he turned to confront her once more.

"All right, all right. You didn't drag them against their will. They might even have helped you with whatever damned plan you thought you had."

"Our damned plan worked, Lucas," she told him, her chin lifted in defiance. "You can thank us at any time. Once you're done with being a stupid *man* about the fact that women can actually help themselves, that is."

He rubbed at his mouth until all the profanities eager to be set loose had been pushed back down his throat. But his hold on his temper was still tenuous.

"You…you…you call being locked in Frayne's drawing room helping yourself?"

"We hadn't quite planned on that happening, no," she said quietly, taking off her shawl and making a business out of folding it again and again. "We were merely there as a diversion, to make sure his lordship didn't wander into his study while Phineas was searching it for Mama's letters."

"A diversion. It took three of you for a diversion?"

She nodded, her eyes wide and innocent, although

he was certain she knew she was standing in very deep water, and sinking fast. "Lydia would argue with him, Charlotte would weep about her unborn child having no father if Rafe went to the gallows and…well, I was simply supposed to stand there."

"In that gown," Lucas said, raking his eyes over the pink confection that had nearly driven him mad only a few days earlier. The gown he'd slipped down from her shoulders as he… No, he wouldn't think about that right now. He wanted to be angry, he needed to be angry. "And is that what you did? You simply stood there?"

"I…I may have flirted with the man. Just a little bit." She held up her hand, her thumb and index finger just an inch apart, as an example of what a *little bit* might be. "Phineas believed he needed a quarter hour to do all we'd asked him to do. To, um, to pass the time, Lydia said we should all do what we're good at, and I'm good at— Oh, stop looking at me that way!"

He didn't know where it had gone, but suddenly Lucas realized he wasn't angry anymore. He might wake in a cold sweat some nights, reliving the horror he'd felt when he'd realized that Nicole was with Frayne on the other side of a locked door, but he was no longer angry.

He reached up and began undoing his neck cloth. "Yes, sweetheart, you are very good at flirting. One could almost say exceptional."

"Almost?" she asked, a smile playing around her mouth as she watched him. "Surely better than almost."

He pulled the long white cloth down and away

from his neck. He wadded it into a ball, tossing it in the general direction of the bed, and began shrugging out of his jacket.

"Perhaps. Or it may be the gown. Although I do think I like you even better without it."

"Is that so?"

Never taking her eyes from his, she bent both her arms behind her back, to work at the line of covered buttons. The action pushed her full breasts tight against her bodice.

His jacket dropped, unheeded, to the floor, and he began his own assault on the buttons of his waistcoat.

"Did you receive my note?"

She sighed and moved her hands forward once more; the gown now easily slipped down her body to pool at her feet, leaving her bare to her waist. "I did, yes. Lydia thought it was very sweet."

His waistcoat was gone now, the buttons of his shirt open, the tails pulled free of his formfitting breeches as he began walking toward her.

"I'm really not interested in your sister's reaction to what I wrote."

Nicole reached up to tug the pink satin ribbon from her hair and then ran her fingers through the curls that tumbled free, down past her shoulders. She stepped away from her gown and began untying the strings of her petticoat. "I particularly liked two parts of it."

He felt sure he knew what she would say next, but only asked her to please elaborate.

"Well…" The petticoat fell to the floor. He could

see the dark nest of her curls through the thin lawn of her pantaloons, and nearly lost track of the conversation. "I particularly liked when you called yourself an idiot. And then there's that business of groveling at my feet? That was rather enjoyable. Aren't you going to take off your breeches?"

He was closer now, close enough to touch her, but he didn't. He liked the way the tension caused by not touching her held his body taut, intensified his already strong desire. "Can't. Can't get them past the boots, and there's no bootjack. Sorry."

Nicole rolled her eyes and sighed. "There's always a penance. I don't know why, but there always is. All right, I'll help you get them off."

Now he did step closer, putting his hands on her waist as she backed up provocatively, until the bed allowed her to back up no farther. "No, I don't think so. I don't think there's time, do you?"

She wet her lips. "In that case, I suppose…I suppose we'll simply have to work around them. Do you have any suggestions?"

"I think so, yes. But first, touch your breasts for me, Nicole. I want you to feel how your nipples tighten when I look at you."

She didn't respond immediately and he was afraid he'd moved too fast for her, had frightened her. But then he realized that nothing frightened Nicole, not his marvelous, exasperating, free and passionate Nicole.

"Sweet God," he breathed as she cupped the undersides of her breasts, and then used her thumbs in a mimic of the way he had touched her. "Yes, that's it. Love yourself, even as I love you. Don't stop," he said as he pulled on the ties holding her pantaloons in place and pushed the material down before lifting her onto the edge of the mattress.

She seemed to understand what he wanted now, and when he spread her legs and lightly pushed on her midriff she let herself gracefully fall back against the satin coverlet, her dark hair splayed all around her.

She blossomed under his intimate touch, raised herself to his stroking fingers, matched his stroke against her core in the way that she touched her breasts.

The night air between them fairly crackled with the sparks they set off in each other as he undid his buttons and stepped close against her, fitting himself to her moist heat.

His hands at her waist, he pulled her toward him, onto him, felt himself surrounded by her, joined with her. Where he belonged. Where she belonged.

The exhilaration, the relief, the sheer joy of having survived a battle, having not only survived but won; he remembered how that all felt. But this was so much more. This was the woman he loved, the woman who loved him enough to give him everything, to risk everything.

She'd stand beside him in all things, except for those times he'd find himself running to catch up with her. They'd be sweet, profane, tender and passionate. They'd laugh, they'd fight, they'd cry and they'd rejoice.

Together.

And, like now, for these few utterly incredible moments, they'd touch heaven together...and beyond.

NICOLE WOKE SLOWLY, tempted to smile even as she was only half-awake, and then stretched her body as if she were a kitten rousing from a nap in the sunshine.

"Ooh," she breathed, realizing that her muscles were protesting slightly as she moved, and that there was a not unpleasant heaviness between her thighs.

"Something wrong?"

She snuggled more closely against the man who had served as her pillow for the night, or what had been left of the night after hours and hours of loving that had introduced her to delights she was sure most women could never imagine, poor things.

"No, nothing's wrong," she told him. "However, if I ever volunteer to help you off with your boots again, remind me that I'd really rather not."

"You were supposed to let go once my heel was free, not give another pull. You should have seen the look on your face, sweetheart."

Remembering the way she had somehow found herself all but flying backward across the room to land on her rump with a thump, Lucas's boot still in her hands—and the way he had laughed at her as she struggled to regain her breath—she only answered him by delivering a small punch to his midsection.

"Nicole?"

"Hmm?" she murmured, having kept her hand against his bare midsection, deciding whether she wanted to leave it there or go exploring. North? Or south? Both held such intriguing possibilities.

"I love you."

Her hand stilled and she looked up into his face. "Well, I should certainly hope so. But say it again."

His smile had her heart doing a small flip in her chest. "To desperation, and beyond. I love you."

"That's what you said in your note. Why did you send that to me?"

He held on to her as he pushed himself higher against the pillows. "Rafe pointed out that I'd told him that I love you, but I probably would have been wiser to tell *you*. There was no time to come to you before we left for The Broken Wheel, but I knew I had to tell you."

"You and my brother must have some interesting conversations. Did he also tell you to promise to grovel?"

"No, that was my idea," he said, curling one of her dark locks around his finger. "Feel free to ignore it."

"I'll consider it. But I won't burn the note, if that's what you were going to ask next. I think our children will enjoy it. Especially our daughters."

"Daughters," he breathed as if she'd said something alarming. "We'll have to watch them very closely. After all, I'd have to kill the man who dared with one of them what I've dared with you."

Then he shifted on the bed. "Ah, wait a moment. You said daughters."

She'd begun her small march north, her fingers walking up his chest. "I did, yes. So did you."

"And yet I still have not heard you say you love me, or that you'll marry me."

"We're very alike, Lucas. I didn't tell you, no. But I did tell Lydia. Does that count?"

"And next you'll write me a letter? Is that how it works? If so, please remember to begin it with *Lucas, I am an idiot.*"

Nicole laughed as she began running the sensitive pads of her fingers over his nipple, feeling it tighten in response. What he did to her, she could do to him. It was deliciously mind-boggling.

"I love you, Lucas. I wouldn't be here if I didn't love you. All my life I've looked for where I belong…and now I know. I belong with you. So, yes, I'll marry you. But more than marry you, I will always love you."

He squeezed her arm as he bent to kiss her hair. "Thank you, Nicole."

She looked up at him. "Thank you?"

"Yes. I know how difficult that was for you. How difficult I've been for you. I will never leave you. I will always love you."

She blinked back sudden tears. "Even when I drive you to desperation, and beyond?"

"Even then. And now, sad to say, we need to get dressed and to Grosvenor Square. Your family is waiting for us."

"Not yet," she said, lowering her head so that she could run her tongue around his hardened nipple.

Then she flicked her tongue lightly across the tip before settling her mouth more fully against him. When she felt him tense, she decided that, while north was delicious, south had probably just made a bid for her attention.

She slid her hand down his belly.

"All right," Lucas breathed, shifting his hips as she captured him. "Maybe not just yet…"

EPILOGUE

FOUR DAYS AFTER LUCAS AND RAFE had led the men from The Broken Wheel to Belgrave Square, and three days after Lord Frayne unexpectedly departed London for his estate in Lincolnshire, Lucas joined Rafe in his study to read the letters Helen Daughtry had written to the man.

"Poor Mama," Rafe said as he tossed the letters into the fire, nudging them with the poker until they'd all turned to ash. "She's never really gotten the straight of anything in her life. No wonder Frayne thought he held all the cards. I'd think I was guilty, to read her interpretation of what actually occurred."

"What else do you have sitting on your desk? More of the Citizens for Justice broadsheets?"

"Those," Rafe said as he returned to sit behind his desk, "and a few personal scribblings you might find interesting. Frayne had already written his speech to Parliament, decrying the Citizens for Justice as thugs and hooligans and demanding stricter laws to save us from revolution."

Lucas leaned forward on his chair and held out his hand. "Let me see that."

But when he had the pages in his hand his smile faded, and a chill ran down his spine. Not at seeing the words, but the hand of the man who had penned them.

"Lucas? Is something wrong?"

"You could say that, yes. I recognize this handwriting. It's very distinctive."

He looked across the desk at his friend, his mind whirling, trying to understand.

"You know I received a letter about a year ago. About my father."

Rafe nodded. "Informing you that your father was innocent, that someone else had thrown suspicion on him in order to further his own career."

"Yes. After my father's successes on the continent, his name was being put forward for Prime Minister when Pitt stepped away, which he did in favor of Addington only a short time after my father... In any case, it wasn't to be."

"And you're going to tell me that Frayne wrote that letter?"

"That's exactly what I'm going to tell you, yes," Lucas said, getting to his feet. He thought better on his feet. "But why?"

"With an ambitious man like Frayne, who could possibly know? He casts a lot of nets, just in case he might someday have to reel one in. As he did you, promising you the name of the man who betrayed your father in exchange for your help with his grandiose scheme."

"I've privately thought Frayne wanted somebody dead, and saw me as the instrument." He put down the pages and looked at his friend. "Now? Now I think he was either the one who damned my father, hoping to replace Pitt himself, or that he knows nothing about my father, or who betrayed him."

"And you'll probably never know. Frayne's lost all credibility in Parliament thanks to what happened at his house, his political career is over, but he won't be punished for what he may have done to your family. Can you live with that, my friend?"

Lucas walked to the window that looked out over the small garden behind the Grosvenor Square mansion.

Lydia and Nicole were sitting on a white wrought-iron bench that was half in shade, half in sun.

Lydia, wearing her bonnet, sat in the shade, her nose buried in a book.

Beside her, and with her bonnet resting in her lap, Nicole had her head flung back so that the sun hit her full in the face, probably able to feel a whole new batch of freckles blooming on her delectable, touchable skin. She had slipped out of her shoes in order to wiggle her bare toes in the soft green grass.

Lucas felt his heart swell with love. He adored her. His mother would adore her. The children they would have together would adore her, and bring his mother back from her sorrow at long last.

The past was gone, unchangeable and irre-claimable. But the future was bright.

"Yes, Rafe," he said, knowing he believed every word. "I can live with that...."

* * * * *

AUTHOR NOTE

Tambora's violent eruption in 1815 served to send a cloud of volcanic ash into the atmosphere and more than halfway around the globe, temporarily changing the climate in parts of North America, England and Europe. In fact, the weather became so cold and wet, the sun was seen so seldom, that 1816 came to be known as The Year without a Summer.

The shortage of food, and the general miserable living situation of the masses did indeed lead to marches and near riots in the streets toward the end of 1816, the anger of the citizens helped along by *agent provocateurs* most probably hired by lords Liverpool and Sidmouth. As a result, a Reform Bill proposed by the Whigs in Parliament was easily defeated, and it would be another sixteen years before any notion of reform laws was entertained again.

Oh, and just as an aside I found intriguing—it has been written that gangs of housebreakers did invade the homes of London's upper classes from time to time. Huge mobs working with almost admirable efficiency, these housebreakers were said to have been able to strip an entire mansion to the walls in less than five minutes, and then disappear into the alleys and byways of London.

On sale 6th February 2010

A NOTORIOUS WOMAN
by Amanda McCabe

Venice belongs to the mysteries of night, to darkness and deep waters

And so does Julietta Bassano. The beautiful perfumer hides her secrets from the light of day, selling rosewater to elegant ladies rather than taking her rightful place in society.

Enter Marc Antonio Velazquez – a fierce sea warrior determined to claim her! Seduced by his powerful masculinity, Julietta begins to let down her defences.

But in the city of masks plots spiral and form around Marc and Julietta – plots that will endanger their lives, and their growing love…

The only woman he wanted – and the one he couldn't have...

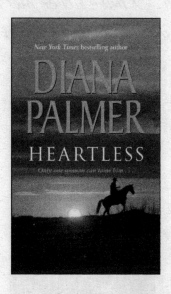

When a moment of unbridled passion results in a kiss, wealthy ranch owner Jason realises that he's falling for Gracie. But Gracie harbours a shameful secret that makes her deeply afraid to love. Stung by her rejection, Jason leaves, ready to put the past – and the one woman he can't have – behind him.

But when danger threatens, Jason will have her heart forever!

Available 5th February 2010

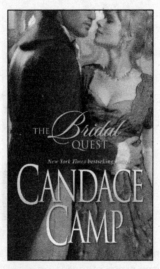

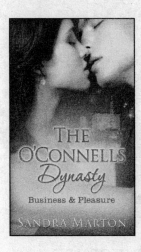
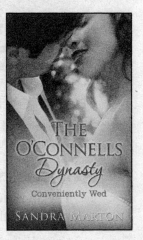

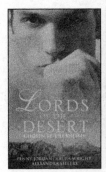

millsandboon.co.uk Community

Join Us!

The Community is the perfect place to meet and chat to kindred spirits who love books and reading as much as you do, but it's also the place to:

- **Get the inside scoop from authors about their latest books**
- **Learn how to write a romance book with advice from our editors**
- **Help us to continue publishing the best in women's fiction**
- **Share your thoughts on the books we publish**
- **Befriend other users**

Forums: Interact with each other as well as authors, editors and a whole host of other users worldwide.

Blogs: Every registered community member has their own blog to tell the world what they're up to and what's on their mind.

Book Challenge: We're aiming to read 5,000 books and have joined forces with The Reading Agency in our inaugural Book Challenge.

Profile Page: Showcase yourself and keep a record of your recent community activity.

Social Networking: We've added buttons at the end of every post to share via digg, Facebook, Google, Yahoo, technorati and de.licio.us.

www.millsandboon.co.uk